Death By Misadventure

By
Thomas Kearnes

www.DarkInkBooks.com

www.AMInkPublishing.com

Contents

For my father, Bob Kearnes (1944-2009),
who taught me that stories are necessary.

Help Wanted

No one can go out after sunset. Don't freak, Phillip says. I'm surprised no one told you. His fingers graze the small of my back. I'm the new girl, he's the manager. Graveyard shift. He's tall enough for me to nestle my head against the shaving rash on his throat. I won't do this, of course. He has quite a beer gut, but I'm not sure that explains anything.

At another Busy Burger, in Houston, twenty miles down the highway, a crew member smoked a cigarette. It was well past nightfall. He stood beside the store. No one inside saw a thing. Some fucker walked up and smashed his face with a wrench. He almost died, Phillip says. This fucker, I wonder why he bolted, but I don't ask. I would've gazed upon that spattered blood, made it my fetish. Does Phillip know the word's definition? What's his fetish? Would he tell me, just us two in the storeroom, at some lonesome hour? I'm married. When a guy has no chance with you, though, not even the single you, it's harmless to imagine how the scene might unspool.

Anyway, no smoke breaks till sunrise. That's seven hours from now.

Phillip is wearing a headset. In an instant, he stops talking to me and starts taking a drive-thru order. Would you like one of our all-time favorite sandwiches? No one calls them burgers. Goon and Gump, the cooks, stare out over the grill like gargoyles atop a roof. Melanie dumps a heap of frozen fries into the boiling grease. I'm at the register.

Rosemary, she's leaning against the drive-thru window. She's been here every night this week, same as me. She's not friendly. She shoves the bagged burgers and fries into the idling cars. She never smiles. Phillip doesn't say a word. Everyone else on graveyard jokes and fucks around, but Rosemary stands like her date never showed. She has a face like an ongoing argument: her nose disagrees with her chin, her lips find fault with her eyelids. Her feelings announce themselves like neon blinking in a storefront window.

This is my fourth night here. When I'm not working, I lie in bed. I won't go home.

It's another half-hour till eleven, but the drunken hick wants the breakfast platter. He spits when he speaks. If I wipe my face, I'll embarrass him. His belt is undone, a tin buckle shaped like Texas flops above his crotch. I tell him it's not time for breakfast. Would he like one of our all-time favorite sandwiches? He looks at me like I stink. Slowly, he backs up. A skinny girl in hot pants and scuffed cowboy boots joins him. He bitches about our breakfast policy. The girl tries to console him. She wraps a bony arm around his shoulders. He shoves it away. He looks at me. Everyone else is busy or, at least, they seem so. Even Rosemary makes sullen small talk with the customer pulled up to her window.

You bitches. He slurs his words. You think you deserve fifteen bucks an hour? Bullshit! He's so wound up, the skinny girl has to restrain him before he tips over. She apologizes for him. I'm sure she's had practice.

By now, Phillip has returned to the front counter. He asks if he can help. The skinny girl politely says no. The hick lets her steer him toward the glass double doors. After a few awkward steps, he stops and bends over, arms braced against his knees. He vomits. First a little, then a lot.

Phillip doesn't dally. He orders me to fetch the mop and bucket. They're in the back. He makes sure I see how sorry he is, making me clean puke. As I walk through the kitchen, he zips toward the drive-thru. Rosemary is gone. No one knows where she went.

The mop and bucket greet me in the storeroom. Whoever mopped last left the bucket filled with dirty water. I'm not mad. I'm hardly even here. Rosemary clears her throat. I'd missed her in the storeroom's far corner, standing in the shadows. She holds a box of napkins, five paper-wrapped packages in all. She looks at me like I'm the only person she's seen in ages.

She asks me why I took this job.

You look too smart, she says. Goon thinks you went to college. She doesn't ask if it's true.

I hit a rough patch. That's how I phrase it.

She steps toward me, napkins held before her like pretty flowers. I'll teach you to trip the alarm, she says. You can smoke. Just don't get greedy.

She isn't done with me, I suspect. I tell her I have to go. I thank her for the tip. I promise that she can show me later how to trip the alarm.

After I'm done mopping, I roll the bucket towards the storeroom. I use the mop, sunk in the nasty water, to steer. While I cleaned the floor, Melanie looked at me like she needed to talk. Her eyes darted back and forth, guilty. She hasn't spoken to me once tonight. While I dump the filthy water in the back, she approaches me. She's almost an albino. She even has colorless lashes. Only her bright blue eyes ruin the effect.

She tells me to watch myself around Rosemary. Just because she can get away with certain things doesn't mean we can. The pop and sizzle of the grease beckons from the front. Phillip probably dumped more fries in Melanie's absence. Be nice to her, she says. She's so tentative. She reminds me of Berlin.

I *am* nice to her.

No, she says, be nicer than your usual nice.

She stares at me like she's set forth a code, simple to crack. Behind me at the drive-thru window, Phillip and Rosemary are talking low. Their voices, though, are harsh and urgent. Rosemary is almost a foot shorter than him. Head tilted back, she wags her finger. Phillip holds up his hands, maybe in surrender. They don't notice me. Finally, Melanie jabs my side. When I face her, she vigorously shakes her head. She looks desperate.

I don't like her. That's my final decision. It's a relief to pass judgment on a new acquaintance—you can finally stop thinking about her.

Starting back, I see Goon staring at the grill, but it doesn't *register*. I can tell—his eyes are milky and wide, useless. Gump gazes at the ceiling. I look up. There's nothing there.

To the right of the drive-thru, a bank of four black-and-white monitors flips among the various angles captured by the security cameras. We can see anyone approach at least thirty seconds before the double doors at the side of the building swing open. After the barflies depart, usually by three, there isn't much to do. We stare at the monitors and wait for signs of life.

It's slow, so Melanie gets the axe. She says goodbye, but no one responds. This isn't the sort of workplace where you'd take that personally. I always make sure to say hi at the start of my shift. Especially when I don't want to.

Goon and Gump man the grill. They're either shy or retarded or stoned.

Phillip emerges from the back. He doesn't even wait till he's outside to light his cigarette. He apologizes. He sounds sincere. It's not his fault the manager can break whatever rule he chooses. Kind of like Rosemary, if Melanie's right. I catch her eye and bunch my brows in confusion. The double doors whisper shut behind Phillip. Rosemary simply lifts her head and glares at the monitors. Phillip appears on the lower right screen. He smokes in front of an overstuffed Dumpster.

Rosemary sighs. That fucking douche, she says, has no spine and no guts. She glances at me over her shoulder. She's not talking to herself. You'll see, she promises.

I ask why he didn't use the back door. Surely, he knows how to trip the alarm.

Because he's a thoughtless tool, she says. She pauses, her features unreadable. I could show you something fucked up, she says, something *obscene*. She smiles, her eyes don't. She's wearing the headset now. She abruptly spins back to her station. Would you like one of our all-time favorite sandwiches?

* * *

I used to have a job I liked. Some days, I loved it. I proofread copy for an ad agency. I'd been

with the boys for six years. Two or three wanted me naked. Bennett enjoyed teasing me about the lovesick Ivy-Leaguers who lusted after me. My husband liked that I was desired. Half the reason he married me was to disappoint those adoring men.

Our home had one bedroom too many. There was a vast backyard that the junior-high kid next door clipped. Complete satisfaction with ourselves and our lives seemed ordained. I've never believed in guilt, certainly not over the comforts one has earned. When Bennett said he loved me, I said the same. Sometimes, I even said it first.

I knew letting Berlin hole up in our rear cottage was a mistake. I think Bennett knew it, too, but the guilt I eluded without effort had besieged him like a summer cold.

She was ten years younger than us. She should've been in college. She should've been scamming cocktails off horny frat boys. Instead, she rented a stream of Blu-rays from the Redbox outside the corner store. Bennett let her smoke indoors. He bought her groceries.

I couldn't bring myself to hate her with abandon. Instead, I let it fester. It kept me company.

Whenever I tried to make conversation, she talked around me. Once, a few days after she nested, I asked about her weekend, her last weekend before coming here. She kept focused on the flat-screen, told me she'd stepped quietly into her friend's upstairs bedroom. She knew her friend smoked joints halfway then forgot about them. A party simmered below. Some beefy dude in a Texans jersey was fucking her friend on the daybed. Across from me, Berlin laughed softly. She was watching a sitcom with a sassy housekeeper. The beefy dude hadn't bothered to undress. Her friend was unconscious, limp body jutting back and forth with the man's thrusts. He was raping her? I asked the question with an edge in my tone. I wanted to be sure Berlin noted my contempt. She never said yes, Berlin replied. In his defense, she added, she never said no, either. Berlin watched the two fuck. Soft grunts from her friend, breathy gasps from the Texans fan. I decided to join them, she told me. She whipped off her t-shirt, her small, forgettable breasts just a foot from the beefy dude's flushed face. He ignored her. After a while, Berlin screamed. *She's passed out! She might as well be dead! What about me?* Right then, a sharp shudder signaled the beefy man was through. Finally, he noticed my husband's sister, her woebegone tits. For fuck's sake, he cried, cover up! Dumb fuckin' slut...

She looked at me, finally. The sassy housekeeper kept right on sassing. I think she wanted my insight. Instead, I made an excuse. Instead, I left the cottage.

Bennett and I fought over his sister. We were screaming every night. All the while, Berlin chain-smoked and gaped at television. She wasn't *alive*, I insisted. Not like us.

I can't toss her to the wolves. That's how he phrased it.

That's *exactly* what she wants you to think!

I admired how she manipulated my husband while draped upon the couch. She'd pinpointed our weakness. *His* weakness, at least. I'd given up evicting her.

When I found her sprawled nude in the backyard, throat crudely slashed, I couldn't elude the resentment. She got to check out when she fucking chose while I had nothing but the promise of another damn day. My life before Berlin was perfection. My life after perfection was Berlin.

The cottage reeked of smoke. I had to hire professionals. There was no need for a funeral.

Bennett moved into the cottage. He swore it wasn't meant as a rejection. He just needed to feel closer to her. I could've fought. I could've tried. Instead, I packed my bags and checked into a cheap motel. I could've afforded a nice one, but I believed shitty maid service and basic cable would keep me focused. Anything to eradicate Berlin's ghost, more ambitious than her living self, from my belfry.

I worried the boys at the agency might pity me. I could handle locker-room flirtations, but *never* closeout-bin compassion. I wanted a job that paid little and promised less. Busy Burger was on the same block as my motel. *Help Wanted*, the sign read. Reviewing my application, they asked when I could start. No interview. My nametag reminded me why I needed one.

* * *

Rosemary instructs me to cover drive-thru for a moment. She disappears into the back, still wearing the headset. Only Goon and Gump remain.

A jeep pulls up beside the window. I've no idea if their food is ready. I ease out from their sightline. I'm terrible at this job. It hardly matters that I'm terrible. The driver punches his horn. It's loud. It interrupts my soothing inner soliloquy, the one reminding me no one expects miracles from a burger-joint bitch. A dine-in customer enters, some rail-thin club kid with electric blue spiked hair and piercings wherever piercings are possible. His pupils are so wide that I fear falling into them. The kid's card is declined. I glance at the monitors, wondering if Phillip is still smoking outside. I need him to void the sale.

What I see instead appears on all four screens. The camera is angled on the Dumpster, again overstuffed. No Phillip. Something horrible is about to happen, and I'll watch because horrible events need witnesses. On the monitors, a figure dressed in the Busy Burger uniform, bright yellow blouse and khaki slacks, hauls garbage to the Dumpster. She's barely tall enough to tip the bag over the rim. As she turns to leave, the camera catches her face.

It's Rosemary.

I watch her mosey through the parking lot. The flesh-and-blood Rosemary, however, stands at the drive-thru, having returned. Positioned below the monitors, she watches this recording of herself.

A beefy Mexican tackles her. I gasp. I can't recall from which side of the frame he lunged. Rosemary tries to fight. The monitors offer no sound, so I'm spared her cries for help. Minus volume, she appears to be having a seizure, and the

Mexican is trying to restrain her. Her feet kick wildly, her fists beat his back. The Mexican surely has a name, but I doubt he told her.

He's raping her. No one's stopping him. I wait for someone to save her. I'm still waiting when Phillip barges through the double doors. He's not shocked, like me. Instead, he's furious.

Goddammit, he cries, how many more times can you watch that shit?

The best and worst thing about Berlin's rape anecdote was this: it only horrified me to the extent my imagination permitted. I could pretend it was some plainly simulated violation from a Lifetime weepie. I could pretend it was more devastating than a snuff film. I've never seen a snuff film, but the boys at the agency swear they exist. What was happening to Rosemary on the security video was utterly real and impossible to deny. I can't help wondering how Berlin might've reacted had she stumbled upon this horror. Whenever I try to visualize the story she told while watching a bad sitcom, I can't settle on a face for her friend. After all, I never met the girl. Whenever the events replay inside my head, my imagination simply refuses to focus on her face. From now on, though, I'm certain it will be Rosemary I imagine passed out and penetrated.

She might as well be dead! What about me?

Even as Phillip bellows, she maintains her poise. I thought, she says, the new girl should be fully aware of workplace dangers. She's proud of herself. Back on the monitor, the Mexican has left. She rolls on her back in the parking lot, side to side, like she's warming up for yoga.

Phillip unleashes a string of vulgarities. He orders Rosemary into the manager's office. I passed by the room my first night, expecting a swank and spacious haven. Instead, it's scarcely deeper than a file cabinet. They don't notice me trailing discreetly. The door slams behind them. Phillip shouts and grunts, Rosemary won't respond. At least, I can't hear her. He asks if she'd like to help find another damn cashier, assuming the security footage has driven me to desertion. Four in two months, he reminds her. If you're trying to sabotage this store, forget it. I'll risk a lawsuit first, he swears. Still, Rosemary says nothing.

I finally hear a woman's voice, but it's at the front counter. Passing through the kitchen, I discover Goon embracing Gump. The latter may have been crying. It's hard to tell with his face buried in Goon's shoulder.

The woman at the counter needs a large decaf. I tell her it will be five minutes. She glares at me like I'm dumb. The other girl always had my coffee ready to go, she says. I apologize. Give it another month, and I'll be apologizing *before* I disappoint a customer. The other girl, she asks, what happened to her? I shrug. Probably the same thing that'll happen to me, I tell her. The woman shakes her head and orders food.

The shift's final few hours pass in tense silence, interrupted only by customers and their bleary-eyed demands. Finally, the morning cashier blusters through the doors with only a minute to spare. She's so damn happy, I want to pollute her mind.

When I clock out, boxes slam against a storeroom wall, startling me. I step into the doorway, peer into the darkness. The voice I hear congratulated me on joining the Busy Burger team just last week. I'll never forget how his forced bonhomie brought me close to tears.

Phillip insists I keep the lights off. I ask if he wants anything. Too damn much, he says. I ask if he *needs* anything.

Never could answer that one, he says. I leave him, his self-loathing better company than I could offer.

The morning crew says goodbye to me, despite having said hello moments earlier. Gump and Goon are gone. A black girl with cornrows and a toned, tan college kid replace them.

The sun came up about an hour before my shift ended. Pinks and lavenders fade to a baby blue. It's breezy, and I can't light my cigarette. I quit six years ago, but I can't imagine this version of myself minus a nod to the world of vice.

I pass the Dumpster behind the store. No one calls Busy Burger a *restaurant*. This is where the horror happened. I stand where she lay during the attack. I'm so lost in my new, awful mash-up, made-up memory forever joining Berlin and Rosemary, that I miss the Monte Carlo behind me, crunching gravel beneath its wheels.

Rosemary honks her horn. The speakers crackle with a boy-band standard from two decades ago. I would've never pegged her as a Backstreet Boys fan.

What to say to her? I've never been raped. After thirty-one years on the planet, it's likely I'm friends with at least a few from that evil club. I can't be sure. No one tells me their secrets. My friendships are seldom complicated. We talk about bullshit. When I see a meme on Facebook about the value of *true* friendships, I share it on my wall. It seems like something those with actual friends might appreciate. I like the Facebook version of myself almost as much as I liked my actual self before Berlin arrived with her sob story. I haven't ventured online since leaving Bennett. Too many questions, too much pity—even thoughtless wishes and prayers require cursory replies. I suspect I'd lack the energy to phone in the expected gratitude.

It's much easier to just fucking disappear.

I don't run from Rosemary, I walk. My motel is just a few parking lots away. She keeps pace with me, car rolling so slowly, I'm surprised it doesn't stall.

Do you want breakfast? She stops.

I'm too tired. I just wanna sleep.

We'll go to the other Busy Burger, she says. The one that doesn't suck.

She reaches over to unlock the passenger door. I haven't moved toward her. She trusts that I'll say yes. I want her confidence, but only if it comes packaged and postage paid.

This Busy Burger, on the south side of town, feels so different. The décor is the same: orange, green and pink, glowing neon in the windows. The crew wears the same tragic slacks and bright yellow polo shirts. The heaviness that almost breaks me each night is absent. Folks enjoy their food, and the crew enjoys making it. I bet they don't even care their wages condemn them to a life eked out from one paycheck to the next.

I wish I could transfer. Rosemary laughs long and loud after muttering the wish. Maybe she was joking. I can't match the merry glint in her eyes. She's been violated in the most awful way, and everything else is bullshit. How did this happen to her? I must lift the veil and meet its gaze, whatever it may be, however repulsive. Does that desire make me a vulture?

This breakfast needs booze, she declares. She takes us home. Her home.

I expect screaming children and a surly husband, but Rosemary lives alone. That's the secret to a happy life, she says. Keep the overhead low. She keeps her vodka in the freezer. Perhaps it banters, too saucy for visitors to enjoy, with the carton of Rocky Road and the half-empty jar of salsa. The label reads MILD.

As we drink, I do most of the talking. I tell her about my life before Busy Burger: Bennett, the agency, Berlin's suicide. I can feel her coolly appraising me, like a jeweler inspecting a family stone. A couple of times, I imagine bursting into tears. I'm nowhere near that point, but I suspect most would weep a moment or two. It's simple etiquette. She murmurs encouragement. If you need to cry, she says, cry. She reaches for my hand and lightly squeezes it.

You're still here, sister-child.

I swallow air, feel my face flush. I can't meet her gaze. W-we still haven't... I don't know how to finish. We still haven't talked about... I try again, fake a casual tone. I mean, I don't know if you *want* to still talk about...

Rosemary takes my other hand, now clasping both. It all started, she says, when lazy-ass Pedro didn't dump the trash into the Dumpster.

It was after dark, I say.

The trash had to go somewhere.

Someone could've escorted you. Isn't that store policy?

Yeah, but no one did.

So, she goes on, the fucker caught me with my guard down. She releases my hands, rests her chin atop joined fingers. I don't know which was worse: waiting for someone to rescue me or waiting for that fat bastard to finish fucking me. You can't imagine, she says, how slowly time crawls with wetback cock shoved inside you, and your only hope is a hodgepodge of pussies.

Why didn't Phillip help? He's a big guy.

She smiles. Her lips and jaw tighten so quickly, I fear she'll scream. Phillip couldn't risk a second crew member, she says. He called the police. He did what the manual recommended. My co-workers said there was nothing they could do.

I can't picture it. My imagination can't conjure cowardice that extreme. Even Berlin had the courage to act on her horrid selfishness. I don't admire the dead girl. I never did. It's become obvious, however, my coworkers disgust me more.

She tells me to finish my drink. I down it in one gulp. It burns in my chest. She tells me if she could relive that night, she wouldn't change a moment.

I wait for the punchline: no, she's serious.

She sips her vodka. How many people, she asks, can truly say they've survived the worst?

Worst what?

Worst anything. You think if Melanie got jumped, there'd be anything left but white hair?

She's right. I think about Berlin, submerged in a wash of fantasy and celluloid. She didn't leave a note. I try not to guess her motives. It's easier to hate a woman when you don't know the many ways she disappoints herself.

You, girl, you're like me.

My eyes narrow. My mouth twists.

You can survive whatever life brings. I could tell on your first night. Again, she has my hands clasped between hers. She leans back. She has a beautiful smile, full of hope. I'm baffled all this warmth welcomes *me*. I don't deserve it, but I don't refuse it.

You're doing it right now, she promises.

What?

Surviving. I know what the word means, of course. I haven't a clue, though, what it means to *her*. The rest of our conversation is comprised of hushed confessions and the urge to weep. I keep myself composed, however, because I'm not sure how she'll react. Like Rosemary, a lot of women promise sympathy.

A half-hour later, Rosemary drops me at my motel. I offer her my cheek. Her lip gloss is sticky. She says she'll see me tomorrow night. It's a varsity game, she says, we'll get slammed for sure. I thank her for breakfast. I wave as she leaves. I don't stop until I lose sight of the car.

I'll never see her again. She saw something deep inside me. If I return for my next shift, she'll no doubt see it again. One day, *I* might see it. And I won't ever look away. I have no doubt this quality, whatever its name and wherever it resides, is stunning to behold. I mourn it while shivering outside the motel. I mourn it like my husband mourns his sister.

She might as well be dead! What about me?

The boys at the agency would scamper over hot coals to get me back. As for home, as for Bennett, I find myself at a loss. My husband needs to finish grieving. I will not watch that. He'll wonder why I don't. Berlin tried to seduce a rapist, I might tell him. She couldn't even wait until he was done defiling her friend.

She wouldn't have survived in our cottage, no matter what my husband and I did. She wouldn't survive in a convent. She wouldn't survive in a classroom or a coatroom or a carousel. She wouldn't survive on a fucking cloud.

I will. Any misfortune, any nightfall. I'm doing it right now.

Actual Miles

It was the cheapest motel on the beltway. Dakota knew it was a crapshoot how large a dent his mother had made into the amount owed on his sole credit card. He'd nearly shit himself when the tired old man behind the front desk told him the room's cost. Couldn't Barclay suck him off in a Walmart parking lot? Was the bathhouse on Fannin Street really that gauche?

"Just you tonight, young man?" The old man coughed.

"Tried to make Louisiana, but I'm too exhausted to even think."

"Sign here. I'll get your keycard. Ten bucks if you lose it."

The plan was simple, the plan to avoid paying for both himself and Barclay, his guest. He'd call Barclay from the room and disclose its number. Barclay would slip past the front desk, casual but quick. Most importantly, he'd conceal the pipe, crystal meth, lubricant and other trappings of a dope fuck inside his cargo shorts' numerous deep pockets.

Dakota tried not to think about Finn crumpled on the floor, dead before he could remove the needle from his arm. It was all he thought about, however, and only the speed neutralized those thoughts, made them nebulous and innocuous, like Dakota's love of puppies.

The room was surprisingly spacious. He felt small perched on the edge of the bed. The mattress was hard as brick, the bedspread a vertigo-inducing plaid. He turned on the television but found himself too high to follow the intricacies of the "Friends" rerun. He drew the drapes. The possible view didn't interest him. A battered air conditioner exhaled a current cold enough to rival the December air outside. Tweaked and ambivalent, he considered not answering when Barclay knocked.

They smoked the dope. They undressed. They smoked more. They fell onto the bed. There was nothing memorable in this scenario. Dakota didn't find Barclay dull but became distracted by the possibility of more men. When he visited the toilet, Dakota whipped out his smartphone and fired up Grindr, the app with which he brokered his sexual encounters.

Grindr tracked the location of all the gay men in the user's immediate vicinity. Not all of them were looking for sex, but most were horny, albeit selectively horny. A grid of profile pics spooled down the smartphone's screen, the user's finger determining how quickly the faces (and occasional torsos) flickered past. If the user tapped a certain profile pic, the picture expanded to fill the screen, the guy's headline tucked into the lower left corner. Below blurbs like "Top Looking for Now" and "Lick My Ass," you found how far that guy resided from you. Control-freak users could track a trick's trek, the mileage dwindling as he neared your doorstep.

"See anything promising?" Barclay peered over at the smartphone's screen.

"The usual faggots and flakes."

"I can't compete, you know."

"Compete? What do you—"

"That app." Barclay smiled ruefully. "It sucks you in."

"I'll be done soon." Neither man believed him.

Barclay fired up a porn download, his laptop feeding into the room's television. When Dakota activated his "white men only" filter, men over two hours away appeared on the screen. He looked at Finn's profile pic twice before realizing it was him. He'd been dead six months. According to Grindr, he lurked 120 miles away. Dakota dropped the smartphone.

"You all right, stud?" Barclay didn't look up.

There was no way Dakota could talk about Finn. He didn't discuss his ex-lover with anyone. At least, he didn't with anyone who saw him naked. He picked up the smartphone and refreshed the screen. Tucked among the grid of profile pics, still, was Finn. Dakota again tapped his profile pic. He'd come closer. Only 105 miles now separated Dakota from the embodiment of his darkest secret.

He'd been a pretty young man, Finn. Not handsome or beautiful, but pretty. His face arranged itself in a way that pleased but did not excite. Dakota always envisioned him as the callow prince from one of Disney's old-school animated epics—by story's end, he'd prove his newfound maturity by foiling whatever evil plot threatened the kingdom. If Dakota persisted with this fanciful metaphor, however, it left him to fill the role of winsome maiden, forever anxious at the sidelines.

Dakota had approached Finn, on a balmy June evening two years ago, offering his future prince a cosmopolitan. The drink had been intended for Dakota's then-boyfriend, Grover. But from the moment he'd spied Finn's earnest wholesomeness, Dakota had found thoughts of Grover increasingly rare.

The general consensus on Dakota was clear—too fickle for marriage. He was handsome, he was witty, he was fun— and, before you knew it, he was gone. His fellow queers mocked of what, he firmly believed, were painful upheavals, these un-couplings all demanding private and pious reflection. Often, he'd been forced—he didn't enjoy breaking hearts!— to choose between loves old and new.

He wouldn't have admitted this to another man, but he yearned for a lover to command his eye uninterrupted. Constant hunger for new flesh exhausted him. He'd vowed to make whatever compromises necessary to become, along with whichever partner, an old and tiresome queer couple who ignited envy among younger men.

Barclay narrowed his eyes in quiet alarm and asked if Dakota was all right. Beside him, a porn download played on his laptop, the same image simultaneously airing on the plasma television. The nude models' moans, from both computer and TV, merged and spawned an uneasy stereo effect. Barclay offered Dakota the pipe, assured him the bowl wasn't yet empty

In some dim, neglected recess of his mind, he knew Finn's seemingly impossible return from the grave would require a sober strategy. That dim and neglected recess, however, forgot to raise its hand and be called. Dakota sucked on the stem, birthing one immense white bank of smoke after another.

"Feel better?" Barclay seemed mollified.

Dakota nodded, the urge to confess exacerbated by the speed. Another dim, neglected recess of his mind, fortunately, insisted on discretion. He explained, in as casual a tone as possible, that a deceased lover had just surfaced on Grindr.

"Someone's gotta be fucking with you, dude." Barclay betrayed no sign of fear or wonder, and Dakota felt foolish assuming this was anything more sinister than a prank.

"Half the profile pics on that app are fake," Barclay continued. Someone obviously had hijacked a photo of Finn from somewhere in cyberspace and created a bogus account. Barclay sneered, and it touched Dakota to see his trick express disdain on his behalf. "That's one sick fuck." He grinned. "Looks like you've made an enemy."

Dakota returned his grin as if the news delighted him. He waited for Barclay to turn away. He told Dakota he needed a shower. There was enough room for both, he added. After the dope, after the sex, Barclay was still trying to charm him. When did men who *try* become ripe for ridicule?

The bathroom door shut, and Dakota's smile went flat. It was unnerving, his first moments alone following a trick. What to feel with no one watching, anticipating? It embarrassed him to sit only in his briefs. He scanned the room and located his clothes, scattered in a moment of long-expired lust. As if underwater, his movements were clumsy and slow. He almost didn't notice the app make the *thunk* that announced a new message.

His insatiable need to acquire more men fueled his thumbs, tapping this screen and that. He needed distraction from not-Finn's ghoulish online return. Instead, a message from not-Finn greeted him: *Be careful. Looks like you've made an enemy.*

Dakota sprung off the bed, gasping. Someone was in the room! Someone was listening! He checked behind the drapes: an uninspired panorama of the parking lot. They were on the second floor; no chance of anyone peeking from outside. Barclay had left his smartphone on the bed. Eyes wide, Dakota was aware and awake and alive, blindly hoping someone hid under the bed. No one. He was alone, an evil world using his smartphone for access.

He refreshed the screen and scrolled back to Finn's profile pic. The information bar informed him that Finn was now less than 90 miles away. If traveling by car, only an hour and a half. He was traveling, however, too fast for Houston highways. Finn would arrive in less than half an hour at this steadily accelerating rate. Dakota's heart pounded as he sat helpless, in his briefs, on the ugly bedspread.

Barclay said something from behind the bathroom door, but the running shower muffled him. Dakota gingerly tried the knob and found that his trick had locked him out.

He needed Barclay to assure him this was a hoax, don't be scared, this was a hoax, you're not *really* a bad person.

Dakota fumbled with his clothes, scanned the room for anything forgotten. Barclay remained oblivious in the shower.

He'd be pissed. Dakota couldn't help that. He was headed for the safest haven he knew, desperate for explanations or maybe a reprieve. He slipped out of the door, the shower falling silent. Dakota had made another enemy.

Speeding north on Highway 249, out of Houston, out of the sleaze and into the suburbs, Dakota dreaded the next *thunk*. Finn might write anything: an accusation, a threat, a spasm of grief. He never fiddled with his smartphone while driving, so he hadn't refreshed the procession of profile pics since Finn's message. How long had he been driving? Ten minutes, fifteen? He was too wired, and terrified, to do the math: *if my dead ex-lover travels x miles every minute, then what time will he arrive at...?*

He hadn't visited Grover in two months. They'd see one another on Twitter or Facebook or Snapchat or Instagram, and they'd banter like two men with full desire for, but no faith in, the other. He lived in a far corner of the county, an outlet mall dominating the neighborhood. He rented a garage apartment from a divorcee who demanded payment in cash and strictly forbid overnight guests; tonight, however, she was away at a revival. Dakota relied on his ex-lover, mild and pragmatic, to put his quixotic notions in necessary perspective. Shortly after he'd dumped Grover— but not soon enough!—he'd realized that Grover had banished him from his life forever. What's done is done, he reminded himself, but the tenor of integrity he strived for had long since departed.

After Dakota's wild story, Grover signed into his own Grindr account. His theory, he said, was that he should be able to see Finn's profile pic, too, among the others.

"I didn't know you used Grindr." Dakota's pang of disillusionment surprised him.

"More accurately, it uses me."

"I wanna see your profile."

Grover, a whole head taller than Dakota, hoisted his smartphone above his head, beyond his guest's reach. He arched an eyebrow, a small and measured gesture. "You're being harassed by a cyber-ghost. Seeing my sad little selfie won't help." After Dakota relented, Grover's thumbs danced upon the smartphone's screen. His puzzlement wilted into worry. Dakota had hoped a boost of his ex-lover's sensibility would silence his fear. His voice thick and uneven, he asked Grover what he saw.

"Finn's profile pic isn't on my grid," he said. "I've refreshed it five goddamn times."

He asked to see Dakota's smartphone, deploying his thumbs once more. Moments later, he shook his head, defeated, and returned the phone. "My only guess would be that someone's hacking your phone from a remote location," he said. "It's like a puppet onstage with the puppeteer high above. Easy to forget he's there."

"But what happens when he gets here? He's moving so *fast.*"

Grover reclined on his sofa, a monstrosity of cushions and fabric culled from discarded sofas. In his royal blue dressing gown and silk pajamas, his unexpected elegance ignited within Dakota a lukewarm and confusing desire. After a split, Dakota wished his ex-lovers to oblige him and lose their looks and charm and kindness. Romantic history was a tenacious temptress.

"We'll both wait on him," Grover said. "Traveling that fast, he'll be here soon enough."

"But he's *dead.*"

"It's just a hacker, Cody." Grover hadn't called him that since their breakup. A silence followed the slip: a sad understanding passed between the two men.

Grover cleared his throat. "On the off, off chance an actual physical being shows up, just ask him what he wants."

What Finn *wanted?* He'd lied to Finn the day of his suicide, even after promising the hysterical man, during their final phone conversation, that it would be done. *If you ever fucking loved me,* Finn had sobbed, *make sure they get that envelope. If you ever fucking loved me.* If there were an afterlife, he must've been furious, that fury at last manifesting itself in cyberspace.

Six months before, he'd offered Finn, his would-be prince, a cosmopolitan meant for another man. It was a gesture, empty and soon forgotten—unless successful. Dakota refused to hold himself responsible for what followed. *He was handsome, he was witty, he was fun...*

Tears threatened to descend. Grover had never seen him cry. To Dakota, that was sacrosanct, like watching a trick sleep for a few moments before beating the sunrise out the door. He refreshed the screen of his smartphone. Dakota and Grover had been talking for a bit. Who knew how much closer Finn had come? He'd been silent since spooking Dakota in the motel.

His dead ex-lover, he learned, neared the 60-mile mark. He was 62 miles away, to be exact, and Dakota knew as the distance dwindled, he would need to be exact. Finn's parents had moved into a smaller home after his death. He tried to recall their address. Finn's mother had reached out to him a few days after the funeral. Hadn't she told him?

Dakota viewed suicide not as the ultimate white flag but, instead, a failure of the imagination. When he'd broken the news to Finn, over the phone but at least not via text, he'd already envisioned himself with a new man. Indeed, an assortment of potential lovers had presented itself. Finn, on the other hand, had seemed, at least to Dakota, incapable of pondering any future that insisted on his absence. The heartbreaker hadn't any idea how to bestow upon Finn this clarity of vision, this optimism. People with no imagination can't imagine what it's like to have one, and people with an imagination can't imagine having none.

"You know how relationships are," he'd assure his ex, finally answering his cell on the tenth ring. "You'll be shitting on my good name before your one-week anniversary."

Finn had never pretended that his solace provided a moment's comfort. "We had a one-week anniversary." He'd groan. "One month, two months, six months!"

Dakota had returned home that evening, the evening of his lover's death, Finn's frantic final phone call looping endlessly inside his head. His warm body offered both evidence and rebuke to Dakota's attempt at devotion.

Heroin. He'd plucked the syringe from Finn's lifeless arm but had no idea what to do with it. He'd finally placed it, gently, on the glass coffee table next to Finn's body. Upon the table, he'd found an envelope addressed *Mom and Dad*. This was the message Finn had desperately wanted him to safeguard. He'd scanned the room, hoping Finn had allotted some last words to *him*. He'd lifted the sofa, wondering if beneath lurked a note festering with pathos.

Dakota's expected assortment of potential lovers had failed to arrive. No one, it seemed, was eager to date a man whose last lover chose death over an evening clubbing or afternoon shopping. Unconscious of whether it was payback, he hadn't kept his word. Finn's parents had blamed him for their son's death. He'd skipped the funeral. He'd never opened the envelope, though, loathe to know what Finn had written, knowing he'd never speak, in this world, again.

Creased and rumpled from months of hiding, the envelope remained in his back pocket. One day, he still promised himself, he'd grant his ex-lover's dying request. Dakota, unfortunately, broke promises, to others and himself, like a stuntman breaks bones.

Finn's parents still believed their son overdosed by accident. In fact, his friends and co-workers believed that as well. In the beginning, Dakota's primary motive for silence had been to spare himself whatever painful message he carried in his back pocket. The shame of never coming forward, however, and the outcry likely ignited by the written revelation, muzzled him. He'd simply tripped over a lie, unavoidable as a weed, and hoped it might thrive—he'd shown it tenderness, vigilance and care.

Finn's family sported an oddly-spelled last name. Since his parents kept their landline in service, all Dakota needed was a quick stroll through the White Pages to get the address. Grover had promised he would call every hour to assure Dakota's safety. Dakota drove to the south end of the city. Not a short drive, at least thirty minutes. When he refreshed Grindr, Finn was at 39 miles and counting.

It was a modest, fearful neighborhood. Every bungalow boasted burglar bars. Mildewed furniture and standing ashtrays embarrassed the porches. Finn's parents lived between a green old-model Cadillac rusting in a dirt driveway and a tool shed with flaking white paint, the door chained shut. Dakota's mother rescued him from the fallout of his shopping sprees. He'd known Finn came from a "working class" background.

Dakota opened the screen door and knocked.

No answer. No lights. Of course, it was almost two in the morning. They were obviously sleeping. He knocked louder. He called their names. Neighborhood dogs howled. Among the neighboring houses, a handful of windows blazed with new light.

They weren't home. It hadn't occurred to him that they might've had a life outside Dakota's ham-fisted bid for redemption. His tremor worsened, more from terror than a pipe. His brow was damp. He fondled his back pocket, the tattered envelope inside. What the fuck was he doing? Knowing the truth wouldn't benefit a soul. All pains, in his mind, were on level pegging.

An old woman in curlers and untied pink robe called out to him. Finn's parents had gone to California. At least a month, maybe two. They'd be back before Easter, though. Did Dakota want to leave a message, drop off anything? He apologized, said it wasn't important. I'll try another time, he said. Anytime after Easter, the woman in curlers repeated.

Back in his car, Dakota refreshed his screen. Finn had only twenty-eight miles to go. He didn't know what to do. He couldn't return to Grover; a dim and neglected recess of his mind was convinced that "Finn," whatever version of him was now in play, might wish Grover harm. He needed somewhere indoors but with a crowd, a mass of people to camouflage him. Finn couldn't hurt what he couldn't find.

Finn's parents would never learn the truth about their son. If he couldn't tell them now, why tell them at all? Finn would reach him long before their return, and wasn't his desperation to confess compelled solely by his fear of that reunion? If he'd finally admitted to himself that he would never show them Finn's message, he should probably dispose

27

of it. Quickly, before his curiosity overcame him. Quickly, before his guilt bested his fear…

He ripped open the envelope.

Written in black laundry pen, all capital letters, centered on the page: HE DID TO ME WHAT WINTER DOES TO A BUDDING ROSE. His heartbeat dared his gasping breaths to keep up. His hands were damp. Every muscle in his body tensed as if there were a roll call. He held the note in his hand, motionless, until finally that part of his body detached itself.

I don't understand, Dakota thought.

And then: *I don't* need *to understand. I don't* want *to understand.*

It felt good to stop thinking. It felt good to blindly *accept.*

By the time Dakota reached Montrose, Finn was at spell out miles. He hadn't intended to return here; this gay club was rowdier than its high-toned competitors, cheaper drinks but fewer hot bods. In winking red neon, above the wide main entrance, a sign greeted all: The Desperado Den. During their time together, Finn had always nagged Dakota to return to the place where a rerouted cosmopolitan had ignited passion.

After buying a beer, Dakota drank in the roughneck ambience. Being Tuesday, well drinks and mixed potions were half off. A drag revue on the club's main dance floor was just concluding, garrulous queens blowing kisses and scooping up dollar bills. Men held drinks in one hand and smartphones in the other. A handful scanned Grindr's turnstile grid of men. He checked his own phone: nine miles. He could now count the miles using only his fingers.

He found a table on the lanai, a corner table, hardly enough room for chairs thanks to the bountiful plastic plants. Having no one share the view sparked a pain almost physical.

These men can't help me, he thought. *It was stupid to hide. Let him find me. I've saved him a seat.* Without looking at the screen, he powered off his smartphone. Nine miles, three miles, six miles: every journey invariably took you home.

A trim and dapper man, a waiter, stepped through the crowd, balancing a tray. A single drink caught a ride.

The waiter stopped at his table. A cosmopolitan—what else?

"I didn't order this," Dakota said mildly.

"Compliments of the gentleman at the bar."

"The one by the entrance or the one in back?"

"In the back, sir."

Dakota thanked him. He savored his cocktail's alkaline jolt. Not thinking, he rose from his table and crossed the lanai back into the club. He'd neglected to call Grover. It had been well over two hours, nearing a third. Dakota hated to disappoint, but he did it so well.

As promised, a man waited at the back bar. He reminded Dakota of a callow prince from an animated epic. After saving the kingdom, he'd come back for his fair maiden. When their eyes met, the man lifted his own cosmopolitan in toast. Dakota joined him. He was handsome, he was witty, he was fun. Let me show you, the man said, what winter does to a budding rose.

Prom King and the Geek

Bishop Medical resembles a big beige cereal box. Sunlight hits the building at a slant. The main entrance, its row of moving glass doors, buzzes in shadow. Would-be patients rush inside on two feet, but the discharged creep out in wheelchairs. Some won't survive. That's the nature of a hospital: no one can guarantee escape. I'm reasonably sure, myself, entering, I will be lucky. Bishop Medical will not claim me today.

I drove two hundred miles to see him. Two hundred miles to watch him wither. Two hundred miles to bid him good night. Stomach cancer. Terminal.

He's not dead yet.

There is time. There is this afternoon. There is the matter dangling from the tiny canister on my keychain. There is the box cutter snug and secure in my pocket.

He told me his room number when I called from the interstate. I look really different, he warned. I kept tabs on his Facebook page. It's how I knew he was in the hospital. We aren't friends, but he agreed to a visit. I was halfway to Dallas before I called. I was stunned to learn that he must have, at some point, unblocked me.

I approach the help desk. Caden Quaid, I tell the lady. I tell her I'm visiting. I'm an old friend.

It's been a while since I've stepped inside a hospital. Dell didn't need a hospital. When the ambulance ferried him away, the driver didn't engage his siren. No need for flashing lights. It was too late for Dell O'Dowd.

Getting that apartment in Houston suddenly seemed deeply naïve.

The oblivious old woman behind the desk gives me the information I already possess. I never have problems accessing the forbidden. I appear meek and pleasant. Strangers often strike up conversations. No one considers me a threat. No one bothers to speculate the damage I might do.

I don't expect Caden to be alone. In almost all the Facebook photos of his quickly dwindling frame, his best friend poses beside him. Ken is balls-out queer, one of those middle-aged gym rats so common in gay circles: the two-day scruff, biceps showcased beneath short sleeves, shirttail tucked to leave no doubt his waist is trim. I'd let Ken fuck me on one condition: photographic evidence for Caden. I'd savor his reaction to me pissing on his favorite hydrant.

The elevator deposits me on the fifth floor. Going up, an old man, scabs covering his bald head, attempted conversation. When I made no reply, the chunky woman behind me volunteered. I wasn't being cruel, simply too focused on the box cutter tucked in my jeans. My timing has to be precise. Walking the fifth floor, browsing room numbers until I spy 534, I rehearse in my mind the moment I'll press the blade against Caden's throat.

"Knock, knock."

My Converses squeak as I enter the room. It's bigger than I expected, private: the walls and linoleum floor are each the same soothing gray. The stiff cream-colored curtain is drawn back, but the sun nears the opposite horizon. Caden must enjoy the dawn each day. At rehab, he was always up before sunrise, crossing the courtyard while I had my nightcap cigarette.

"I knew you'd come." There's a slight tremor to his voice, but it brims still with mischief. "I told Ken—I said, Don't worry, Avery will absolutely be here."

"And on time, too." I smile.

The clock's minute hand stands a few ticks shy of twelve.

Caden laughs. The sound dies in his throat. "Actually, a little early."

He's a neglected prune, the last in the box. Were we not acquainted, I'd peg his age at sixty, maybe even sixty-five. In truth, he hovers well within his mid-forties. His face, once round and plump, has collapsed. Sunken cheeks and eyes, his hair now gray and perilously thin. Stringy tendons articulate themselves down his neck. I make a point of landscaping that throat. He was once overweight—not much, and the extra pounds perched agreeably atop his hips. Now he might top out at 130 pounds, that sparse mass stretched over his six-foot frame. His arms and legs shed all their meat—they're sticks, twigs, the brittle kindling used to nurse a new flame.

He's not dead yet.

The box cutter, still in pocket, presses against my thigh. I carried my keys loose while searching for his room. It's an old habit. I like the dull jingle. But I don't want him to make note of the tiny canister dangling from the keyring. At rehab, I once mentioned it's where I kept my tweak. It was a precaution, jamming my keys into my other pocket just before I entered his room.

Ken glares at me. I respect his frank disapproval. I'll soon confirm his worst suspicions.

"When did you finally get clean?"

"Caden says you're in recovery yourself."

"And gratefully so. How long, Avery?"

He's a tenacious muscle mutt. During that exchange, Caden has eased himself from bed into his wheelchair. An IV pole stands at the ready, but no tube connects the hanging bag of solution to his arm. Will he soon be released? No one wants to die in a hospital, though that's often the point. Had I waited just one day more, I might've missed him. Caden groans as he settles into the chair.

Ken rests his elbows atop the bed's metal rail, arms folded. He can foil my little plan, insist I conduct my visit under his eye. Caden is in no position to protest—assuming he would.

"About eight months," I make sure Ken knows it means nothing to me. "Give or take."

"You don't know your sober date?"

"Careful there, Caden. You can't be king without a throne." I cross the room. He smiles and weakly raises an open hand. I reach for his shoulder, but my hand retreats to my side. I'll need to do more than touch him, soon, but not this moment. "What does it matter if I stayed clean last summer?" I counter. "I stayed clean today."

Caden's friend grunts. "He said you were a pragmatist."

I laugh. "Caden doesn't know that word."

Stricken, Ken's eyes pop.

Caden bats my hip, laughing himself. "Still a snob, aren't you, asswipe?"

"Still a philistine, huh, Prom King?"

Back at rehab, Dell and I liked to peer over the balcony as Caden sauntered across the courtyard. So confident, so satisfied with himself. His steps fell upon the grass like kisses, he blessed with a smile all who passed. He's scrumptious, I muttered. I wanna suck his dick, Dell replied. It always came down to sex for him, that dear man. I smirked. All hail the Prom King, I proclaimed. The birds sang of love. The mosquitoes hunted flesh.

Caden and I laugh. I push his wheelchair toward the doorway. Visitors and nurses skitter up and down the hall. Over the loudspeaker, a doctor named Killingsworth receives marching orders: Trauma Room Three, STAT.

"I'm gonna jump in the shower after this show ends," Ken declares. Glancing over my shoulder, I catch him reclining upon Caden's unmade bed. The intimacy of this transition both sickens and stirs me. "Back in thirty?"

Caden gives the affirmative. Thirty minutes, I think. Should be enough time. I imagine the click as the box cutter's blade snaps into place. The hall teems with fated life. It will soon be Thanksgiving. I know this because turkeys and pilgrims cut from construction paper loiter upon the corridor walls. I'm waiting for Caden to resume the conversation.

His wheels on his chair smack upon the sticky linoleum, sounding like a hungry child's lips. My Converses squeak. We exist, Caden Quaid and I. Our tired, mundane noises fill this tired, mundane world. It doesn't register with me that I've slipped my keys from my pocket, not till I hear their jangle. That tiny metal canister complicates the melody.

"I wanted to wait until..." His breath leaves him. He hasn't craned his neck to look back. His bony shoulders hitch as he inhales. "Ken doesn't need to hear this."

"It's just us now, Caden. Prom King and the Geek."

"I'm serious, Avery."

We've lost velocity. I'm looking for an empty room. A room-number placard denied cut-out Turkey Day tokens. An agreeable male nurse passes us, scrubs a bit too snug, haircut a bit too precise. This time, Caden does turn his head. At least until it snaps back, accompanied by a wince.

I smirk. "He's far too young for us. For *you*." I don't break stride. I don't turn to linger on the twitch of his ass as he hurries past. Dell has been gone eight months. I've toured a few bedrooms since his broken heart ceased its beat, but these trysts soothe nothing, solve nothing. I fuck men for the same reason dogs bark—and have just as little to show for it.

The box cutter lies in wait. I've never before threatened a man's life.

"I meant to call you. After you…after *we* lost Dell. I meant to, I swear." He gasps. I'm not sure how to interpret this candor. "I unblocked your number. I don't know what stopped me." He turns back, twists his face toward mine. His hazel eyes have lost none of their salesman shimmer. "Why didn't you call me…?"

Because I imagined every explanation you might offer, and each only nursed my rage. It did not abate. I did not acquit you. I say none of these things.

"You blocked me after our last fight," I remind him. "Right before his overdose. I had to message Ken on fucking Facebook."

"You never tried me."

"You wouldn't have liked what I said."

Caden chuckles. I can't see his expression, but hear the weak, low sound. "I would've listened. I needed to talk, too…"

Room 517! No Thanksgiving kitsch! No placard stamped with a patient's name! Waning afternoon sun fills the room. I swivel Caden's chair a neat ninety degrees. So excited to spring my trap! I lost all hope of an afterlife after turning five, but I can't help—almost forty years later—indulging juvenile fantasies of Dell. He might spy me from the heavens, overjoyed to know vengeance may travel slowly, but it does make the station. I nudge the door shut with my foot.

"If you wanted somewhere private…" He takes a breath, loses it before it can fill his lungs. He takes another. "There's a solarium on the first floor."

"I dare you to define that word." I've stopped pretending we're friends, and so has my voice.

He turns back. Fear pulses across his gaze. "What do you want, Avery?" I wish he'd *yield* to me: hands held aloft to protect his face, a quaking voice, maybe even a startled cry. I must proceed. No doubt Ken counts the minutes.

He's not dead yet.

I maneuver myself before him. I've rehearsed this moment for months. I've never liked speaking in a formal setting. It requires charisma and poise. Dell enjoyed an abundance of both. When he confessed his heart to Caden, he didn't stammer once. I know because I listened, unseen, from the doorway. One day, a man might speak to me so plainly. Dell might have been that man, had heartbreak not hobbled his spirit. I left the doorway before they finished.

"I don't feel good, Avery. I need to—"

"You remember Dell had a sister, don't you?"

I drop to my knees before his chair, my hands folded atop his knobby knees. I shudder to imagine his bare legs. "Imagine calling Eden to say her baby brother has died. Imagine telling her he *wanted* to die."

Caden flinches. He hiccups for air. I watch him struggle. I should've started filming the moment I shut the door. "Avery, I'm sorry. I knew how you felt about Dell. I knew—"

"You *knew* how he felt about *you*."

Beads of sweat flee his forehead.

"And you erased him. From your phone, from Facebook. You erased *me* when I asked why."

His tone sharpens. "I let you keep tabs on me. I'm sure you kept Dell informed."

"I told him you were terminal."

Caden grunts. His eyes brim with tears. I need him to reclaim his composure before I start recording. If Eden pities him, I'll have no one to indulge my forest-blaze rage. It will devour me, like Caden's cancer devours him. "That's why he overdosed…" His face clenches with indignation. "Why did you fucking tell him that, Avery?"

Dell and I spent our first month in rehab, before his arrival, constructing a universe made for two. Brick by brick, confidence by confidence, the bond refusing to sever no matter how brazenly Dell later consumed Caden's each step across the courtyard. We knew each other over three years, and I never lied to him, not once.

"You and your fucking rehab romance," he spits.

I've explained enough. Ken awaits our return. I whip out my iPhone. I will record him confessing his guilt to Eden. His refusal to love Dell cast him into an abyss so deep, he might never—even in death—reach its stone-strewn bottom. No one else will see it. At least his sister will know I loved him enough to obtain his killer's confession.

"Fuck you, Avery." He swivels his chair toward the door. "I'll wheel myself back."

I stride across the room. My keys and the canister jangle still. Somehow, as I advance toward him, the box cutter finds itself in my grip. I make note of the emerging blade's click. I force the blade against Caden's withered throat. He doesn't scream or call for help. I'm not sure how to interpret this toneless moment—the threat of violence shouldn't seem so banal.

"This won't bring Dell back."

"I'm more deeply aware of this than you can fathom."

"I'm so goddamn sorry. I don't—"

"Ready to party, Prom King?"

With my thumb, I flip open the lid of my keyring canister. I instruct him to wheel himself into the bathroom. I follow, box cutter blade wavering at the stretch of shoulder left bare by his gown.

The mirror, a dour rectangle bolted above a gleaming sink, is positioned too high to reflect the seated Caden. But I find myself, trapped inside smudged glass, all too visible. I've filled out since rehab. I think of myself as slender, but my belly flattens only with effort. I'm shorter than the men I pursue, taller than the ones I dismiss. My eyeglasses came cheap, the dark frames defiantly thick and graceless. With my coal-black eyes, cheekbones set at too high a slant and pointed jaw, I am no one's idea of handsome. I used to fret about keeping a lover. I made him laugh, Dell liked to tell me. I found this reassuring, sometimes.

I dump the canister's contents on the counter. Three clear shards, all of modest size—enough for a thick, healthy line once crushed and scraped for snorting. I, however, don't plan to partake.

"You crazy son of a bitch..." His jaw hangs open, he looks at me like he *knows* me. It's an expression I've never seen. For a passing moment, guilt blips on my radar. I congratulate myself: there it is, proof that grief and rage have not eroded my humanity in full.

I return the box cutter to his throat. A single drop of blood hugs its lethal edge. I could hurt him. I could end both his suffering, and mine, with a clean cut.

He looks ashen. "There are tumors in my stomach, Avery." His voice breaks, he brushes his knuckles against his eyes. I hadn't expected him to cry. The Prom King has no reason to weep. "Snorting that shit might kill me."

I crush the shards beneath my bathhouse membership card. "You're terminal, Caden." The card scrapes the counter as a dazzling white line of speed takes shape. "You have a choice: you can die or you can die happy."

"What the fuck will this prove?"

I crouch down, my head level with his. I whisper, like a lullaby for a child already asleep, "If you tattle, I'll demand the doctor test your piss. What would Ken think?" I rise to my feet. "Now finish your dessert like a good faggot. We have to start filming soon."

"Not here, man. Take me to the solarium."

Again with the wheels smacking the sticky corridor floor. Again with the abstractionist pilgrims convened around the placards outside each patient's room. Everyone fleet of foot, so many places to reach, so little time to reach them. There's no plausible way to keep the box cutter at his neck. An orderly or nurse might glimpse the weapon. Getting him spun was my only way to assure his cooperation. It tickles me, though, my lover's killer must endure an unwanted high—and all the urges no doubt ignited in its wake.

Caden pants as I push. He twists and fidgets. He complains of cramps. He's afraid he might die. I hiss one warning after another: can the theatrics. We have less than twenty minutes, and the solarium is five floors below.

He refused to confess in Room 517. He's convinced I'll slash his throat once we're done. Caden assures me the outdoor deck adjoining the solarium boasts privacy and adequate light. Patients, visitors and staff, however, will be within shouting distance. I suppose I could've forced the issue—after all, I have the box cutter. Parading down the hall, knowing he is the Prom King, and this is my coup...well, why not enjoy every one of the thirty minutes afforded me?

As we travel, a trim Latina nurse approaches. Pausing, she tilts slightly forward, her face brightening. I stop pushing. Whether Caden is clever enough to signal her, or anyone we encounter, I'll soon know. She places her hand, tender and graceful, on his shoulder. He won't meet her gaze. He clutches his armrests to tame his tremors. I do not wish him to know kindness.

"Hey there, handsome. Heard you discharge tomorrow."

His torso spasms, head jerking in response. They are now face to face. Still, he does not reply. She rises to full height, perhaps eager to address me. I bend forward and kiss Caden's temple. Whispering, but loud enough to assure she hears, I promise him a few minutes in the cool breeze while we watch the sun surrender to the horizon. He grunts.

He's not dead yet.

"Will you stay with him?" she asks.

"For however long he needs me."

Caden's breathing has grown labored but he finds the fortitude to dazzle her, that same smile beneath which my Dell capsized. She waves and continues down the corridor.

I roll him the opposite direction. One more turn, another corridor and we'll reach the elevators.

"I used to hate hearing I was handsome."

I refuse to engage. The tweak has made him chatty. He requires a witness. Unless another man watches as you bare your soul, it hardly seems worth the toil. The wheels shriek in protest as we take the corner.

"I was other things, too. Besides handsome."

Perhaps fortune will smile upon me, and our car will carry others, strangers. Surely, Caden won't insist they rubber-stamp his humanity as he hopes I might. I punch the down button, and we wait. He won't stop squirming. He moans as if pained.

"Suck it up, Prom King."

"Please, I need…I need to find a bathroom."

"No, sir. The elevator will be here any second."

He chuckles, but it's a bitter sound. "Don't worry, we'll make your fucking movie."

After the ding, the elevator doors slide open. To my delight, we're at no loss for companions. A black, overweight orderly stands at the front of the car, facing the corner. A frazzled woman in her thirties wearing too much eye shadow holds two grade-school girls, one by each hand. The girls' rude stares trouble no one. Finally, an older woman wrapped in an ankle-length corduroy coat stands beside me. I feel her gaze. She wishes to speak. The doors slide shut. She has mere moments to overcome her trepidation.

"Is it cancer?" Her smile flickers. "I'm about to see my husband. Should be done with the chemo by now."

Caden moans. I press a firm hand upon his shoulder.

"My husband's been sick over a year." This answer surprises me, too. I stretch my back, shoulders rotating with affected fatigue. "Whatever time we have left, I want to spend it together."

Her lips part, but she does not speak. Caden's head and shoulders jitter. Why claim Caden as my own? Perhaps it's humiliation. Perhaps it's to force-feed him the toxic tableau of a life spent sharing one bed. He was so unwilling to grant that wish to Dell but now has no choice—he must indulge my perversion of it.

Clutching his abdomen, Caden moans, a deep and primal eruption, then doubles over. This time, everyone reacts: the orderly, the frazzled woman, those impudent girls. Even in sickness, the Prom King has no trouble drawing a crowd.

"Stop the elevator," he pleads. "I need to—" I shush him, crouch down to whisper whatever threat seems plausible. Before I begin, however, he butts his head against mine. "Now, Avery!" My ears ring, and it takes a few moments to remember that I'm a kidnapper, but my hostage refuses to obey.

The older woman reaches for the panel of lighted number beside the sliding doors. She promises Caden that "we" would find him a bathroom. *No!* That simple directive blots out all other thoughts. I'm running out of time. Desperate, I reach out to grab her hand, but the *ding* distracts her. She refrains and, like the rest of us, waits.

The doors slide open. We're on the third floor.

Caden calls out for someone to hold the door. An elderly couple shuffles forward, perplexed, perhaps sensing a discord clumsily tamed for their benefit. They step aside, the husband extending his delicate, spotted hand over the groove into which one of the sliding doors retreated.

We have to go, Caden and I. Delays, delays, delays. Surely less than fifteen minutes now. Still, I've yet to give his wheelchair that bon-voyage push, the force needed to turn the wheels. It's those wheels that Caden, himself, vainly tries to turn, but I clutch the handgrips with brute force. We can't leave this elevator without a plan.

"Sir, your partner's in great pain, it seems." The older woman must have problems with the word *husband.* "Do you need some help?"

The elderly man outside the passenger car flops his open hand against the sliding door each time it tries to emerge. Ignoring the older woman, I push Caden into the lobby. There are six elevators surrounding us. The third floor looks just like the fifth. Even the brazen aroma of antiseptic has been replicated to perfection. Two parallel corridors sandwich the bank of elevators.

Caden whines and curses. "It doesn't matter which way. Just keep going till we find…" He gasps, head thrown back with such force, he lifts from his seat for a moment. "An empty room." He stabs his pointed finger at the left corridor. "Find me an empty room."

Nurses, visitors, they risk leery glances at our two-man revue.

"Fine, Caden. But let's make the potty pitstop a quick one."

We're already in motion.

"You'll get your fucking video, Geek."

Down the corridor, football helmets cut from construction paper festoon the placards bearing patients' names. I wonder who decided the themes for each floor. Helmets seem a mite bland compared to the rosy-cheeked pilgrims two floors above.

Caden's breath turns shallow and harsh, as if he were in labor. The sheen of perspiration coating his face reflects the corridor lights. His hair is drenched. Eyelids clenched shut, he trusts me to find an untaken toilet.

More visitors, more nurses. Orderlies. Even a few doctors. We've passed at least twenty rooms, both sides of the corridor considered. The corridor, itself, opens not far ahead. A nurses' station, probably. If even one indulges her curiosity, filming might be (again) delayed, or worse. Ken won't hesitate to unleash the hounds if I fail to return Caden unharmed. I will not disappoint Dell, however, no matter how formidable the forces against me. I never did our three years together, and his death brings no respite.

"Avery, turn left! Right here! Room 323!"

I instruct him to deep-six the high decibels. If no one looked before, they damn sure might look now. Once we've entered the empty room, I hope, we'll fortunately be forgotten.

Caden sobs, insisting the pain intensifies with each breath. The bathroom door catches against the wheelchair's footrest. I strain my shoulder jerking back the chair, allowing the door to swing wide and admit him. He rolls to a stop beside the toilet, and I dare entertain relief. He's too weak, he cries, to lift himself from the chair to the commode. Hurry, he begs. My belly is about to explode! Just then, a wretched odor fills the bathroom. Caden's bowels, it seems, believe Room 323 needs a fragrance both fecal and fierce. I'm holding his skeletal form upright, by its armpits. I try shifting him to the toilet, but his wheelchair stymies my every move. I refuse to panic. I knew Caden was sick before I hit the road, and sick people have volatile relationships with toilets. Just ten more seconds, and I'll recover my wits—just ten seconds!

Caden Quaid doesn't have ten seconds to spare.

His unplanned bowel movement announces itself with a fanfare loud, wet and lingering. Fortunately, Caden wears gray Nike athletic shorts beneath his papery gown, but the good news stops there. He neglected to slip on briefs beneath those shorts. The runny fecal follies stream down his bony legs and pool upon the linoleum. Moments later, a smattering of foul-smelling chunks, too unformed and moist to bear the label of *turd*, form dainty little heaps upon that same linoleum. The stench is so pervasive, so intense, I wouldn't blame anyone who might doubt one man alone could spawn such epic nasty.

It's humiliating and no shilling of shame could meet the expense. I still hold Caden upright, my hands cupped beneath his armpits. I look him dead in the eyes. I don't offer compassion. Did he show any compassion to my sweet Dell? How will the Prom King handle shitting himself while tweaked and trapped with a man ready to mock his misfortune? If filming must wait, only a distraction this delectable will satisfy. Caden simply stares ahead, blankly, through me, as if this bathroom were measured in acres, not inches.

"No one's calling you handsome now."

"I'm fine with that. Actually, I prefer they call me Caden."

I'm stumped at his refusal to trot no matter which carrot I dangle before him. Whatever abdominal pain he was suffering seems vanquished, but he's no doubt still tweaking. I may have trouble keeping his bitch mouth shut.

He's not dead yet.

"You can put me down, Avery." I drop him abruptly, but his balance does not deny him. "I need a shower. You're not rolling me down the hall while I simmer in my own shit."

I can't argue with his logic. Reeking of turds would draw first the noses, then the nosiness of all who crossed our path. Still, at most, ten minutes remain before Caden's chair reverts back into a pumpkin. I instruct him to hurry. He asks me to excuse myself to the main room. Forget it, I reply. The bathroom door locks from the inside, and fuck him for thinking I haven't noticed. Irritated, he slips off his paper gown and steps into the shower. He hasn't the strength to stand for the entire ordeal, but a wide-topped stool awaits in the stall. I watch as the spray wets his desiccated form. I'm thankful Dell never has to witness his dream lover's decay. He wouldn't allow himself the perspective necessary to enjoy it.

"That tweak you forced up my nose was bunk, by the way." The bathroom is so small and the spray so weak, Caden's voice carries. I'm in no mood for banter so let the remark sink beneath the silence. "Bet you saved the good shit for yourself, huh?" Tweak makes Caden bitchy. He doesn't bother to look my way. "I bet you're spun right now. This very fucking moment."

For the record, I've been sober since Dell's suicide. Eight months—I was telling that pissant Ken the truth. I know tweaking will spur illusory multi-hour conversations with him. Such seductive fantasies, and most would forgive me if I succumbed—but there are boys quite alive who need me more. I work overnights for a gay hotline in Houston. I field everything from coming-out trauma to suicide threats. I stay sober. Indeed, after I record Caden's confession, I must make haste down the interstate, Dallas receding in my rearview. The hotline expects me at midnight.

"Fine," I say, my voice toneless. "I did a couple of bumps in the parking lot. Vindicated?"

Caden shuts off the water. "I'm not judging you. I should, but I won't." He dons his paper gown, perhaps not noticing the dried shit spattered along its hem, then drops into his wheelchair. Its creaks and rattles bemoan the blunt impact of his bones. Clearly, he's exhausted.

"Forget the solarium," he says. "Let's get this fucker over with right here and now."

"What convinced you I won't slash your throat?"

"All those assholes we traumatized in the elevator— they're my witnesses, Geek."

Besides, he adds, his Nike shorts are ruined so he's totally nude beneath his paper gown. While we're outside at the solarium, there might be a gust of wind. If not that, the gowns themselves are more than a little transparent, particularly under harsh fluorescents, hard to avoid at Bishop Medical. Please, he says, I've played along with this. I could've stopped this farce at any time.

Caden has a point. But I have a box cutter, and he's high on crystal meth.

"The solarium seems a reachable goal. We still have time. But we have to scoot."

As we return to the elevators, the squeaks and smacks of the wheelchair form a sort of tune, one played on crude instruments. Caden takes deliberate breaths, his chest and head rippling, adding a kinesthetic component to the wheels' meager music. He hadn't bothered to articulate his disappointment, in expression or with words, when I insisted our adventure end with the solarium. Slumped upon his throne, he muttered capitulation, ready for me to push.

At the elevators, the waiting nurses and suited gentlemen pay us no mind. We lumber into the open car. When the doors open to the ground floor, I allow myself to sample the ripe satisfaction promised me the moment Caden's confession ends. I must discipline myself. He silently lifts a leaden hand, pointing this way or that. We're approaching the lobby. Those sliding glass doors shift left to right, right to left. A half-hour earlier, they admitted me—with my box cutter and bit of crystal. I should recall the scratched twang that calls out from what I only now recognize as the help desk. When I glance her way, though, nothing stirs my memory.

"Yoohoo! Over here, handsome." She laughs. "You didn't come flirt with me today."

Caden smiles, lifts an open hand with more vigor than I would expect, signaling me to stop. We're down to mere minutes, and my only advantage beyond Ken's deadline is that the gym rat has no idea where we are. Our potty break, however, resulted in witnesses, as Caden took pains to mention. As he flirts with the help desk hussy, I speculate whether further booby traps await.

A harried husband barges his way to the help desk. His wife was brought here. Reba Blakely? I wheel Caden away, grateful for the distraction. Moments later, he announces our arrival.

I expect a solarium to be more heavily beset by plant life. Instead, palm leaves and intimidating ferns line three of the walls, rubber-cushioned sofas and chairs positioned before them. It feels like the waiting room at a clinic in a bedroom community, one where several doctors split the steep rent. The only things missing are back issues of *People* and *US Weekly*. Caden slaps my chest with the back of his hand. There, he mutters, that door takes us outside.

Despite the aggressive greenery obscuring the glass walls, I glimpse enough of the sky for my skin to prickle: such maroons and deep oranges appear only at dusk. I extend my arm to push open the hydraulic door, allowing Caden the latitude to wheel himself outside.

"Gentlemen, the observation deck closes at sunset."

Caden pauses upon the threshold. We turn our heads to greet the latest in a ceaseless series of roadblocks. She's a stout woman, her middle years soon ending. Too much foundation showcases instead of conceals her jowls. A badge offering her name and mugshot rests above her left breast.

"Please, ma'am." I smile and furrow my brow to simulate sincerity. "It's the first time in weeks my husband's felt well enough to leave his room." Caden places a loose hand atop mine, and I stutter. I don't want a partner in crime, I want justice for Dell. "After the sun sets—we'll come back, I swear."

The stout woman fingers a strand of pearls not there. "Your *husband*, is that right?"

Caden smiles, and it occurs to me, like a bulb's dying flash: he has an agenda, too, and maybe I've been foolish. Still, Dell is counting on me. Caden thanks our hostess and urges me, in an affable tone the tweak seemed to silence, to wheel him outside.

The deck is comprised of shapeless slabs of burgundy stone, bits of sprouting grass, twigs and acorns shed by the massive oaks, their drooping lank limbs. A squat brick wall, hardly high enough to meet the knee, lines the perimeter. The air has chilled. Errant gusts flirt beneath Caden's gown, its hem ballooning one moment, dropping the next. You see, he snipes, fucking wind. He insists I wheel him to one of several patio tables stationed in front of the solarium's windowed wall. You can sit across from me, he adds.

"You don't have to pretend we're married anymore," I snap. He keeps forgetting who has the box cutter. Across from him, I tap and slide until my iPhone is ready to record.

"Give me another rundown. I'm not confessing more than once."

It's simple, I remind him. Tell my lover's sister your name, how you met Dell, how you learned of his love and how you dismissed it. I glance over my shoulder. That molten orange orb will kiss the horizon in mere moments. If only we'd found an empty room sooner, if only Caden respected the dynamic I forged between us. I double-check the viewfinder. I tell him we're recording.

"Hello, Eden. I'm Caden Quaid. I'm forty-four years old and live in Dallas. I met your brother three years ago at a rehab in Houston." He pauses, gulps air. "As I'm sure you know, Avery was there, too. He's making this little motion picture. You deserve to know what happened to your brother. So do you, Avery."

My shoulders tense. I worry Caden may have fallen from the frame. But we're running out of light and Ken must surely be worried by now. Still, why address me? More disconcerting, I detect no remorse or shame. He speaks like a suburban dad as he delivers punishment to his toddler. He whips through our history as a threesome: Dell, Caden and

Avery—the Three Faggoteers. This may interest Eden, but I'm waiting to hear his misdeeds after we left, after Dell and me found a shitty apartment in a shitty neighborhood, and he returned to Dallas. What precisely did he say to Dell that night over the phone, inducing such anguish I could listen no more?

"We were on the phone. I told him I had cancer. He started crying. He said he loved me too much to lose me. I didn't return your brother's feelings. He knew that. He didn't care."

Dell O'Dowd needed *me*. Dell O'Dowd loved *me*. Dell O'Dowd chose *me*.

"He volunteered to drop everything and move to Dallas. He said he'd nurse me through, no matter how long it took." His eyes dim, and he appears unnerved. "I asked about Avery. What would he think if your brother left him in the dust? All that bastard could manage was some lame-ass promise that Avery would find a way." His breathing becomes labored once more, but it's the anger, nothing else. A vitality besieges him. The Prom King never wastes the spotlight. "I told him I was about to hang up. He and I? We were strangers now. Any man who would shit on some dude so devoted to him had bigger problems than dope. We never spoke again."

I'm looking elsewhere. I'm looking anywhere. Over my shoulder, I glimpse the last of the sun slip behind the horizon. It's good he's nearing the end. Eden needs to see his face. Wait, why is it quiet? Just crickets and white noise from the nearby interstate. I must've zoned out. I can't remember what Caden last said. My eyes dart to my iPhone, wrist resting on the table. No way Caden remains in the frame.

Caden snatches the device from my hand and slams it on the table. His eyes burn with a fury that's my due, not his. He holds my gaze. His breath slows. That stout woman who believes we're married must wonder why we broke our promise.

"Fuck his sister. I'm talking to you. The day I heard Dell died, I had one thought: what will Avery do with his freedom?" He gasps for air. The adrenaline must be wearing off. Dell will be so disappointed in me. "Loyalty should be earned, Avery. You see what Ken and I have? You deserve that, too." He must need what little stamina remains, after our half-hour adventure, to deliver this pep talk. "I'd be happy to cash in my chips, but I stay alive. My best friend needs me."

I can accept failure. I can accept defeat. I'm the Geek. Our tribe rarely ascends the winners' podium. I leave Caden as he hunches over the tabletop, too desperate for oxygen to notice that I'm almost to the solarium door. He calls my name. He whines that he's too weak to roll himself back to his room. The Prom King needs me.

"I hope your death is both painful and pitiful." I don't wait for his reaction.

The stout woman asks what happened to my husband. She needs to close and lock that door, it's security protocol. I don't break my stride. She's too much of a creampuff to accost me. Back in the corridor, I pause. Which way to the lobby? I must go to work. I'm welcome there.

Except, I dart off in the opposite direction, deeper into the hospital. Except, I find the elevators. Except, I wait patiently, my head bereft of thoughts, as I ascend five stories. Except, I hustle down the corridor until I see Caden's name and that perky pilgrim. The door to Room 534 stands ajar.

That night, after Caden hung up on Dell, he flopped onto the bed we shared and sobbed. Did he need to talk? He didn't tell me, not then, that Caden had discarded him. Instead, his small, timid voice insisted he didn't deserve me. Life is chaos, I told him. Be thankful someone wants to hold your hand while the world burns. I don't deserve you, he repeated. Later, dozing, he slung his arm over me. One day, I was certain, he'd open his eyes and truly *see* me for the first time.

Someone, presumably Ken, is taking a shower. It seems he isn't as vigilant as I feared. I slip into the bathroom. I close the door, wince as the lock clicks after giving it a twist. He's nude, of course. Rather impressive rear end. He hasn't noticed me. No one bothers to speculate the damage I might do. The box cutter finds its way into my grip. The blade emerges with a quick nudge from my thumb.

I'm standing close enough to touch him. Instead, I slash his bare back.

I stay alive. My best friend needs me.

He gasps and whips around, stumbling, to find me brandishing my box cutter. He was right about me. He demands to know what I did with Caden. I answer by slashing his face, the gash running from ear to chin. I've prepared for bloodshed. Please, he begs, Caden needs me. I nod. At last, we agree on something.

He struggles, at first, but won't scream. He begs me to stop, but I cannot. He's not dead yet.

Whatever You Can Spare

I never stand outside the store for long. At least, it never seems long after the first kind stranger presses a five or a wad of singles into my hand. The sky is fat with rainclouds. So far, though, no rain. I pray for enough time. It is the least the Lord owes me.

Tyson flicks his gaze, and I catch his eyes in the rearview mirror—the same pale, unsettling green I see every day while brushing my teeth. Whenever my grandson takes me to the store, I try to imagine Leon looking back at me, needing his mother, but I could never kid myself. It's Tyson, my only grandbaby, and he needs things.

"Did you remember the sign?" Tyson asks Adele. She rides beside him.

"Jesus, you expect me to take care of everything?"

"That was your sole responsibility."

Adele leans over the seat, the bump in her belly hard and proud below her small breasts, and rummages through the clothes and fast-food wrappers heaped beside me. "Mema, where'd you put the damn sign?"

"Honey, it's in the trunk," I say, my voice trembling. It wouldn't do any good if they flew off the handle and turned around. It hasn't been nearly long enough. "That's what you asked me to do, wasn't it?"

"No, I told you to—"

"Baby," Tyson cut in, "what does it matter?"

Adele sinks back into her seat. "She got the old, pathetic part down, don't she?" She lights a cigarette and blows out a quivering cloud.

Actually, neither of them asked me to put the sign back there. On purpose, I left it in the hall. My stunt won me a string of profanities from Adele and silent disappointment from my grandson, his neck tense and stringy. I needed an excuse to check the iron one last time. I always forget whether I've left it on. I also checked to make sure neither had moved my bulging tortoise-skin suitcase from inside the car's trunk. I can't afford any mistakes. That house is my universe—Tyson, Adele and me.

"Don't talk that way to Mema," Tyson says. "You show her respect."

"I'll show her respect when we get the damn money."

Tyson shoots Adele a warning glare. The store, it was her idea when she came to live with us. She thought I was asleep. Baby, she whispered, we just need enough for gas. I promise she won't mind. You know she loves you. She'll make money real quick. Listening, I felt the true measurement of old age: helplessness.

It's our exit. My withered hand clenches the armrest as we enter the feeder road. The large, impervious Wal-Mart squats behind a sprawling parking lot. People hurry and stop, conceding to those faster. Sunlight glints off the cars puttering through the lot. I glance into the sky, and notice the clouds darkening. I pray to the Almighty that the rain wait just a little while. I need more time. We crawl through the lot.

The vendor hawking homemade crosses is gone today, Adele announces. Better yet, no police cruisers lurking at the far corners of the lot. "You'll get thirty bucks in no time, Mema," she says, her voice airy like cotton candy.

Tyson drives solemnly toward the handicap spaces. Dark curly hair from his mullet tumbles down his neck. He worries that he and Adele might attract attention, parked in a space meant for cripples but never leaving the car.

"We'll keep an eye on you, Mema," he told me the first time I asked the world for its pocket change and compassion. Tears falling down my face and Adele refusing me a tissue because I'd make more money unkempt, Tyson assured me that Adele would never make money as fast. "If she could, I'd force her ass out in a second," he said. I pretended to believe him.

I rush from the backseat when Tyson parks. Of course, he has the keys, but I brought a spare that I keep underneath the Kleenex box in my room. I unlock the trunk as silently as I can. When Adele hops out, hand over her belly as if a cantaloupe swelled beneath her blouse, I say feebly that she shouldn't trouble herself, a girl in her condition. I'd get the sign myself.

"You wouldn't have to if you'd listened to me the first time," she says.

"Honey, this is so hard on me. I just want—"

She rolls her eyes and slaps the hood. "You didn't live eighty years by being a big baby."

"Adele," Tyson calls. "What have I told you about respect."

"I have to pee," she answers.

"Be quick about it." Tyson lights an unfiltered cigarette. Leon couldn't get enough of those, said it was like fireworks tumbling down his throat. Sometimes late at night, while Tyson and Adele sleep, I sneak one myself. "I don't want Mema out too long in this damp cold."

"Hello? Pregnant woman here!'

He shakes his head, turning his back on her. He smiles, and I see my late husband's smile and Leon's smile and the smiles of all the boys yet to be born. I smile back and promise I'll do my best. He embraces me and apologizes for this happening. He truly believes he has no choice. "We're not budgeted for a second tank of gas," he says. "Adele thinks the car runs on magic beans."

His compassionate reverie stops cold. "Mema, what are you doing? Don't let anyone see that here!" His voice is harsh and scratchy, urging me to hide it. "Adele's coming back."

I peek at the large-lettered word—it's the closest thing to gospel in our house. It reads HOMELESS. My face falls. Tyson awkwardly glances about the lot, eyes so bleary that he surely can't see much. Carefully, he takes the sign from me.

"Don't do the whole dog-and-pony show, Mema. Not today."

"Your father would be so proud of you," I say.

Tyson tosses the HOMELESS sign in the backseat. I think about my suitcase snug in the trunk, my whole life condensed down to a single bag. I didn't like all this tomfoolery, but every family has secrets, secrets in every house, festering in every room. I have another secret: last night I tucked almost two hundred dollars inside my brassier before packing it. I learned early that Tyson and Adele didn't pay close attention to how much I made each time I begged.

A minivan passes the entrance, revealing Adele in its wake. She sips a large Coke and tosses back her two-toned kinky hair as if the whole world's watching. She's too many weeks along to wear shorts that tight, and those flip-flops don't give her any arch support. In the beginning, I encouraged her to act more appropriately, like a young lady, but it became clear that the house on 1249 Windfall Avenue, my house, belongs to me in name only. I'm always close but forever ignored. Adele treats it like her home and treats me like a sideshow attraction that knows how to iron and wash clothes. She insists on plug-in air fresheners in every outlet. The home I shared fifty-seven years with my late husband smells like the mall.

"They serving soda pop in the ladies' room?" Tyson sneers. Adele shoots her bad finger high and proud. I look forward to my job—I suppose you could call begging a job—starting if it means escaping Tyson and Adele's latest spat.

Over the months, I learned things. First, stand in front of the entrance, not the exit. Most shoppers leave the store as broke as any beggar. Never count on church groups, they're full of misers. They might offer you a meal or a night at a shelter but never cash. Also, don't beg at night. Most importantly, be sweet and fragile like snow; no one gives to jackasses. Finally, I learned no encounter will thrill and shame you as fiercely as the first.

* * *

I was terrified but not about getting caught. Even before Tyson assured me it wouldn't happen, I knew no one complains about little old ladies asking for change. They'd pity me, they'd protect me—here, ma'am, take everything I have. We hadn't made a sign yet, that came later. I'd simply walk up with my hand out. It sounds so simple, no wonder it's a crime.

Foolishly, we first went begging at night. It was sticky and still, a typical July evening. I wore a paisley blouse and slacks. Again, we didn't know any better.

After I left Tyson and Adele in the car, I wandered along the storefront, avoiding the smokers inside a verandah at the Gardening department, afraid they knew. I can't recall my own encounters with beggars in the city. To me, those dirty and desperate people seem vaguely menacing, reminders that God may forsake anyone at any time. I understand why most, including myself, avoid them. Having no idea how to approach, I inched toward somebody but backed away the moment he noticed.

I heard Tyson's voice in my head: *You gotta do this, Mema, or Adele's cell phone gets shut off.* Finally, I saw a stout middle-aged woman with large breasts and a pained expression. Her oversized T-shirt read, *This Lady Don't Need Luck.* I thought a miserable person would be more giving than a happy one. During these months, I've been proven right more often than not. The woman, though, lurched forward as if I was a copperhead hidden in tall grass. Unable to comprehend her disgust (*I had a home, a car, a family—I was just like her!*), I dumbly kept after her into the parking lot.

I didn't see the SUV until the driver blared his horn. I staggered, crudely dancing, not recognizing the sound or whether it was meant for me. The vehicle whipped around, followed by others, their drivers impatient, honking like I was a stray dog. I called out for Tyson, I even called out for Adele—no one came. I stopped drifting when an olive green Honda pulled up beside me.

"You poor woman, do you know where you are?"

He was a nice-looking man, a *clean* man, a type of man that Leon will never become. His pinstriped suit was the color of blueberries, and his tie was a rich, deep red. He didn't seem to be wearing his clothes so much as they wore him.

"Are you here with someone?" he asked.

"Please, sir," I said. "Whatever you can spare."

He frowned a bit and his eyes grew soft. "Do you have a home?"

My mouth open, I twisted my neck and pretended to look at the asphalt. I hadn't thought that far ahead. Tyson never said there'd be questions.

"Here, ma'am," he said, some bills folded crisply between two fingers. In the movies, it's the way men offer strippers money. "There's a cheap motel less than a mile down the road. Just be sure to lock the door."

I can't recall what went through my mind after the man spoke. Desperation is a tongue easy to learn. As I fanned the bills in my hand, two twenties and a five, my breath caught and I felt Grace had dropped upon me from the sky followed by the welcome numbness I always associate with eating too much chocolate. I kept staring at the money.

"Ma'am? Do you need a ride?"

I was startled but didn't look up. Whatever it was we did, I thought it was over. I don't think I remembered to thank him. With just one donation, I was more than halfway toward covering Adele's debt. I still wonder if that clean man in the blueberry suit remembers me.

* * *

I'm doing well enough. Hopefully, Adele hasn't figured out I'm not being vigilant like those other times when I knew the faster I reached the total, the sooner I'd be home. A little girl with long, loose pigtails and a red floppy hat offers me a cherry sucker. Embarrassed, her mother jams a few dollars into my hand. Two Army enlistees ask what I'll do for fifty bucks then zip inside before I blush. Another child, a boy, stops his parents, their cart full of fertilizer, and asks them why I look sad. I manage to get through.

The older man tearing off his tan overcoat, however, has something more extravagant in mind for me. "My beautiful siren," he says, whipping the overcoat around my shoulders like a cape, "I will not let you stand in this horrible weather and beg like a dog." His name is Ferdinand and his skin is a deep bronze, darker in his face's folds. Starchy gray hairs sprout from his temples like weeds. He speaks like I'm a dishwasher being showcased on a game show. He's what my late sister would call a fancy man, a confirmed bachelor.

"Sir, you're too kind. I can't take this."

He pulls the lapels together, wrapping me tight. Over his shoulder, I spy Tyson and Adele kissing deep while parked in the handicap slot. I remember when watching young people kiss made me smile.

Ferdinand slaps his meaty hands against my cheeks. "Madame, I will cook you a meal. I have several bedrooms to your liking. When I come to this country, they tell me this time of year is for family. Madame, I will be your family."

I'm trying to step back from his embrace, but he is strong and determined. Other customers might be watching. Should I call for help? I can't afford to make a scene. If I don't return with Tyson and Adele to the house, it'll ruin everything. Finally, I yank myself free and he halts, stunned at my ingratitude. I've made things worse.

"Sir, thank you so much for the coat. You're very kind, but I can't go with you."

Instead of arguing like I expected, his eyebrows jump and he abruptly flits into the lot. I turn to see what spooked him and nearly collide with a potbellied man wearing a Wal-Mart smock and nametag. He's barely thirty, but his hair and mustache are trimmed with such precision, I wonder how proudly he told his wife (his kind always has a wife) about making management.

"Ma'am, unless you need medical assistance, I need you to come with me." His hand is raised, cupped. Will he grab my arm if I resist? I follow, risking one last glance at the car before we enter the store. They're still kissing. Every time, Tyson promises to watch over me. Every time, when I look at their car, I hope I'll find those green eyes that have watched me grow old, watched from one man's face, then another and finally another.

He hustles me through the front, along the line of storefronts most Wal-Marts host: nail salon, hairdresser, optometrist and more. When we pass the bank, I notice a homemade poster with shaky lettering stuck above a large cardboard box. The sign reads, *Help Our Employees Who Can't Afford Thanksgiving.* That makes no sense to me. If you have a job, you can afford food. That's why people work, after all. If Tyson could break his bad luck, we'd be eating better than Hamburger Helper every night.

"Sir," I ask, "why not just pay your people enough so they can eat?"

He whips open a narrow door. "Please, ma'am, I have other responsibilities waiting."

A tight staircase lifts from the floor.

His office could be anyone's office. Even the personal touches tell me nothing. Ferdinand's coat carries his whole history, it seems, embedded in the wool. The photo of the homely woman and sole-eyed son on his desk could be anyone's wife and child. I pull the coat around me. There's no heat. I don't see windows, either. No wonder I always feel sad after shopping here.

He insists I call him Jimmy. He never tells me his last name or official title. No one's calling the police, he assures me, switching to that damn patronizing tone everyone uses when you reach your expiration date. They're concerned about me. Employees remember me, they have me on videotape. A few of the customers threatened to call some agency. I'm panicking like a trapeze acrobat reaching out to find no waiting bar. I wonder once again whether I left the iron on.

"You didn't drive here, did you, Missus…?"

"Call me Mema. I love the sound of that name."

Jimmy chuckles and I feel sick. "Do you have any identification?"

"No... I don't drive anymore so who knows where it is? Maybe I left it—"

"At home? You live close to here?"

I blink, my eyelids sticking. I'm not used to rooms without windows. It tickles me that, despite my slip, this manager is so concerned about my welfare but his workers are starving and surrounded by food. I clear my throat. Do they know about Tyson? Are he and Adele on tape acting like horny ferrets while dignity slips from my bones?

"Sir," I say, bracing myself to stand. Jimmy rushes to assist me but I won't have it. "I'm afraid there's been a mistake. You know, my own family has passed on."

"Even your children?"

"All part of God's plan, I suppose."

"What about those other times we've seen you?"

"Young man, I can't answer why this person or that person saw one thing or another." As I inch toward the door, Jimmy makes no move to stop me. "I hope you don't make a habit of hassling little old ladies..."

Jimmy's eyes snap wide and he gulps. "Not at all, ma'am. Should I help you out?"

"You should give your workers some sandwiches. Thank you for your concern."

"Ma'am!" he cries, rushing toward me, his fist jammed in his pocket, rummaging. He offers me a hundred dollar bill, wadded up in his open hand. I must truly seem out to pasture for such generosity. If you pretend you're helpless long enough, you forget that it's an act, and even when you try to explain yourself, prove your worth, it doesn't matter. People would rather throw a couple of bucks at you and be done with it. If no one needs help, the whole world falls out of balance. Victims are essential. Without them, there'd be no heroes.

I take the cash and smile, call him Jimmy. I wish him a happy Thanksgiving. He reaches above my head and pops open the door. It sticks to the frame; there's a soft crack. "Ma'am," he says. I don't bother to look back. "Please don't return to this Wal-Mart. Next time, we will call the authorities." I hesitate on the steps. All he sees are my slumped shoulders, ruined shoes and the wispy home perm Adele insisted she'd been doing since junior high.

In a brisk wind, I hustle across the lot to the car. Tyson shoves off Adele and wipes his hand across his mouth.

"Where the hell have you been, Gladys?" she snaps, maneuvering a breast back into her brassiere. It's so rare I hear my Christian name, I've begun to think of Gladys as a wholly different woman, one who would never do what I've done.

"Sweetheart, I've told you. Call me Mema."

"We have to get home, Mema," Tyson said. "I bowl tonight. Gotta get my shoes."

I gingerly open the back door and slide in. The HOMELESS sign glares up at me. We back out and leave the lot. I should thank Tyson for letting me leave the sign, Adele snarls. He takes care of your scrawny ass, she says. She whips around and bends over the seat, staring blankly at me like I have something she needs and I'm stupid for not knowing it.

"Babe," Tyson says, "we'll handle it at home."

I ask how long we've been gone. Tyson says maybe an hour, but Adele thinks it's been longer. I gaze into the sky. It never did manage to rain. God is gracious, God is good. Cruising down the interstate, Tyson and Adele squabble about which flavor of Hamburger Helper we'll eat. I'm expected to cook, of course, and I'm not invited to bowl. Adele mutters that if I have any ideas, I should spit them out. I sigh, rest my head against the window and tell her to surprise me.

Adele notices the smoke after our first left into the neighborhood. We're still four blocks from Windfall Lane. Alarmed, Tyson wonders whether it's a house fire. Adele isn't worried, there's not enough smoke. The rising clouds thicken, however, the closer we come to home.

"Holy shit, baby, I think it's our street!" Adele screams for him to hurry.

"Mema, stay back there! Don't get out of the car!" We're still moving.

"Don't worry about me. I'm fine."

My elation bubbles like champagne as we speed down Windfall, and my dear grandson and his tramp fiancée confront total disaster. The house at 1249 Windfall, the house in which I've spent over sixty years of my life, is burning.

I *knew* I'd left the iron on. I left it on and face-down atop a pile of newspapers.

* * *

It seems so long ago, but Tyson was already in high school when Leon burned his wife to death inside their home. He waited till Tyson was away. I wonder if my grandson has ever accorded that fact its true weight. He called me from the back of that honky-tonk where he met the woman he later killed. He'd caught her after she lost her balance dancing on a pool table. He said he needed me to take his boy. Tyson needs you now, Mama, he said. Of course, I promised I'd do whatever I could for as long as I could. It was easier to say yes back then because my husband hadn't departed. Just don't get overwhelmed, he said. You promise me, Mama? You promise you'll look after yourself? I heard sirens in the background. I told him to stop with the nonsense. Leon knows my family is my universe.

* * *

Tyson jumps the curve and bolts from the car. One crew is already fighting the fire, water spraying while the men shout instructions to each other. Tyson tries to pull one aside but they shrug him off as casually as they might their own kids. My grandson pushes his palms against his temples, teeth gritted. It's like he's watching the moments before a terrible wreck, the doomed vehicles charging toward one another. He's forgotten about Adele and me.

"Why is our house burning, Mema?" Adele whimpers. "This isn't supposed to happen."

She's left the car but remains on the curb, absently rubbing her belly and gazing dumbstruck at all she believed was hers turning black and crisp. I'm surprised she isn't crying. I'm standing only a few feet beside her and while she keeps addressing me, she won't look at me; the fire's allure is too powerful. She babbles and jerks her head from side to side. She keeps saying my name, but I can't follow what she means.

I know something that might help.

I slip off my tan overcoat from the fancy man and wrap it around Adele's delicate shoulders. She pulls it around herself without noticing it. I tell her she might catch cold standing out here wearing next to nothing. She nods and then I reach into the backseat and grab the HOMELESS sign. I hand it to her. I don't want to, I truly don't, but she might need it now and I certainly have no use for it. She takes the sign like someone passed her popcorn at a movie.

"Check the pocket," I tell her. "There's something for you and Tyson."

Adele does nothing, her lips moving but no sound coming out. Finally, I dip into the coat pocket myself and pull out the hundred. I tell her there's a cheap motel by the interstate, but she'd best lock the door. It's not a great neighborhood.

While Tyson sinks to his knees and sobs, I open the trunk and haul out my suitcase. The force of its weight nearly topples me. Carrying your whole life in one bag isn't easy— every life is heavy but you can't leave it behind. I hobble a bit as I begin down the sidewalk, away from Adele and Tyson, away from what used to be my home. It's chilly, the wind penetrating to my bones. I think about that luxurious tan overcoat but shake loose the notion. Adele needs it more than me.

When my husband first drove me out to that house, decades and decades ago, he wouldn't tell me which house was ours. I had to guess. He laughed and laughed when I guessed wrong. Can't you find your own way home, he'd say and laugh. I never guessed 1249 Windfall Avenue. I guessed the one to the left and the one to the right, but not that one. I loved watching those green eyes twinkle as he teased.

I don't know if he'd understand why I did what I did. He's not here to ask.

I'm getting tired. This block is longer than it seems from inside the car. I need to rest but I refuse to sit on that filthy curb. Maybe that nice lady pruning her roses will give me a glass of water. Her house looks so pretty. You can tell a good deal about a woman by how well she keeps her home.

Children Shouldn't Play with Dead Things

The sudden noises echoed through the house, disturbing Maxine as she unpacked. The move to a suburb outside Indianapolis hadn't gone like she and Walter had hoped—amoral furniture movers, two missing boxes, broken dishes. Maxine's heart skipped to hear Persephone giggle upstairs and then the whir of wheels atop a wooden floor; her daughter had found her skates. Maxine wanted to shout at the ceiling—not indoors, we had a deal!—but she knew Walter would never back her up. She could hear him: *Let the kid have fun.* She could feel his hand upon her hip. *After all that's happened, we need to embrace the light.*

Walter had adopted these noxious platitudes shortly after Athena's death six months ago. *Heaven has a new angel;* Maxine had wept. *God brought this burden because we're strong;* Maxine had wept louder. *Everything happens for a reason;* Maxine wished she, too, had died inside that incubator, gloved fingers caressing Athena's frail form, Maxine taking a sharp breath before placing them over her infant daughter's chest. Athena's heartbeat was as quick and elusive as a series of pinpricks.

Collecting the shards of a ceramic dinner plate, Maxine looked up to see Persephone in the doorframe. The girl dug her foot into the hallway carpet, a bull eager for its dance with the matador. The skate's back wheels spun uselessly. "I'm bored. Everyone is old and stupid."

"It's only been two days," Maxine said.

"I can't text Aimee."

"You're too young to text."

"Can we have pepperoni pizza?"

"We're not getting pizza again." Maxine shrugged and tossed ceramic shards into the trash can. "No skates in the house, sweetie. We had a deal."

Persephone refused to obey, and Maxine refused to push the point. When her daughter asked to explore the block, Maxine nodded absently then started on another box. Persephone started first grade in two weeks, and Maxine seized any opportunity to distract the girl.

She's too young to be out alone, Walter would say. *It's horrible enough to lose one child.* Maxine would reply as she always did: *Darling, I'm so tired.*

Twenty minutes passed, but Persephone didn't return. Maxine, however, didn't notice, busy lining the wall over the stairs with family photos. Of course, the only images of Athena were taken from outside her incubator. In one, her rubber doll-head turned toward the lens, black eyes empty and uncomprehending, and in another, her rubber doll-fingers reached nowhere, unaware there was nothing to grab. Maxine brooded over her two daughters' similarities: the puckered mouth, goldfish eyes, bowtie ears. Persephone, too young, hadn't been allowed in the hospital's nursery. Maxine and Walter secretly agreed with the staff's decision.

Maxine felt lacking in some essential way. She'd failed to tether Athena to the earth, and now she entertained horrid daydreams: a terror-minded teen storming Persephone's classroom; a twister sucking Persephone from beneath a mattress slapped over the bathtub; a child pornographer stealing her from sleep. The girl's bedroom overlooked the neighborhood that Maxine and Walter had selected with a surgeon's precision. Still, dangers festered in other lawns, behind others' fences—dangers Maxine found so patent, her only means of coping was to swiftly deny their reality.

Why can't I see Athena, the girl had asked Maxine the day before Athena fell silent among the feckless beeps and mechanical sighs. *You promised.*

The land line's ring was foreign to Maxine—she didn't at first understand its meaning. It was Walter. They spoke in familiar, clipped phrases as if they were the leads in a screwball farce.

"Darling," Maxine said, "Persephone needs you here in the house."

"How will I pay for this house if I don't work?"

"She's upstairs sulking as we speak." The lie came easily to Maxine. Her skin pricked while she waited for him to take the bait. Her disappointment upon hearing his reply again pricked her skin, more sharply this time.

"It's a great neighborhood," he said. "Tell her to make some friends."

"We haven't been here long enough."

"This is a fresh start in a fresh place, honey. Let's stay positive."

Maxine felt alone in their large, unfriendly home with its cherry-paneled walls and dark-hued ceilings that loomed like thunderclouds. For a moment, she remembered Athena's hand inside hers, her gloved hand. Actually, she'd been able to grip her infant daughter's entire arm. She'd felt the tiny being's heartbeat, too fast and too quiet. A car horn's bleat shattered her reverie. She glanced at her watch. Persephone had been gone a half-hour.

Maxine began her search. Peaceful Acres was the sort of fabricated neighborhood Maxine had ridiculed as a girl. She didn't resent the slight decline in economic status her move here signified; at least, she didn't *openly* resent it. The rows of dull and identical two-story homes hypnotized her. She spotted a group of children huddled in a knot, as if debating the next play in a football game. Above their heads, the end of a hockey stick bobbed in and out of view. Where had they come from? Though she'd dismissed Persephone's complaint about no children, she secretly agreed with the observation. Lavender Avenue seemed anemic in the kid department. Maxine did not trust large groups of children. She quickened her pace.

As she hurried, some children urged the others to disperse. They were dressed smartly, clean with expensive haircuts. As the crowd thinned, Maxine exhaled with relief to spot Persephone among the makeshift mob. The girl poked at something with the hockey stick. Maxine's relief evaporated, however, to discover what her daughter found so compelling.

The cat was dead, dead and fat. Its belly swelled like a full moon, blackened from the road's grease and dirt. Its right eye had popped from its socket and dangled onto the creature's angular, prescient face. Blood had dried into a dark burgundy pool though Maxine didn't notice any wound. The animal seemed ready to explode, an overinflated balloon, but Persephone kept stabbing it. Maxine worried it might rupture like a piñata, the remaining children snatching the innards as it they were Easter eggs.

"What on earth are you doing, sweetie?"

"Mommy, make it live again!"

Maxine stared at her daughter, oblivious to the departing children. The cat's remaining eye gazed at the woman, accusing her. She grabbed Persephone's wrist. The hockey stick clattered to the asphalt. They began across the street. Persephone resisted, but her skates betrayed her, all too eager to roll.

"What have I told you about that?"

"I didn't touch it."

"Don't get sassy."

Persephone glanced over her shoulder. "He needs a doctor, Mommy."

"A doctor can't help him now."

"But Mommy—"

The green minivan zipped past, missing Maxine and her daughter by inches. The driver swore at them and mashed his horn. Maxine fell to her knees, clutching the girl. Terror bubbled behind her eyes, the reality of what had happened (or what *almost* had happened) detonating like a cloudburst. Her skin turned moist, her heartbeat thudded. You can lose all you love in a moment, she thought. That's all the time God needs.

"You didn't look before crossing the street," Persephone said.

Her innocence stunned Maxine, rearranged her molecules. She laughed and finally released the girl. "No, sweetie," she said, "I didn't. Shame on me."

Maxine watched the girl skate toward their new home. She was small for her age, not quite delicate but certainly not robust. She feared Persephone would be too preoccupied with her own thoughts to put up a defense if faced with danger. She was like a magnificent butterfly bobbing on the breeze toward the grill of an eighteen-wheeler. Still, Maxine would never admit *both* her children couldn't thrive in the world.

She hoped that would be the end of Persephone's preoccupation with death. As Maxine settled into the house she'd begun to resent, she shuddered to find Persephone vegetating before Headline News, enraptured by the latest natural disaster or atrocity in the Middle East. She watched her daughter stand on the stairs, gazing at the photos of dead Athena. Walter dismissed her fascination as normal, hardly worth mentioning. "We should be thankful it isn't sex," he told her, hand on her hip. Maxine was not mollified. He recommended they send Persephone to the city to visit her best friend, Aimee. "She makes our little girl so happy", he said. "Don't you want her to be happy?" Maxine sighed and flopped onto the bed. Walter's eyes lit up, amorous, but Maxine's hard glare doused his desire instantly.

"That Aimee kid is a juvenile delinquent," she said.

"Nonsense," Walter said. "She's just a bit of a daredevil."

"She set off the burglar alarm in our old condo."

Walter rolled his eyes, dismissed her.

"On purpose," she added.

He sat next to her. "It would get her out of your hair," he said. "Just for the weekend." He lightly grazed her shoulders. As his fingers increased their pressure, she recalled with a stabbing pain how she hungered for a touch that did not end in death.

"I'll think about it."

Late that night, hours after Walter sang to Persephone about a little teapot, short and stout, and Maxine looked on from the doorway, she jerked awake, startled to hear the front door close. She considered waking Walter, but couldn't bear more of his condescending "attention." Instead, she quietly headed downstairs. In the kitchen, she thought about grabbing a knife. Finally, she left the house unarmed. This was a safe neighborhood, she told herself. Persephone's boredom with it was as good an indication as any.

Lavender Avenue was abandoned. As Maxine reached the curb, she realized she'd failed to check Persephone's room. Walter would be incensed to learn that, she thought. Of course, this oversight was easily explained: Persephone had been the one at the door. Maxine had known it the moment she woke. The girl lurked somewhere in the still neighborhood.

After passing one dark house after another, too timid to step upon any lawns, much less peer into any backyards, Maxine saw a child-sized figure in the shadows between two streetlamps. As she approached, she recognized Persephone's nightgown and wild curly hair. This was the same spot where Persephone had disgraced the dead cat. The girl didn't look up at Maxine, but instead continued gazing at a dark stain by the curb. She didn't acknowledge her mother until Maxine's silhouette mingled with her own.

"What happened to him, Mommy?"

Maxine knew what she meant. "I don't understand, sweetie."

"Did it get up and leave? Is it better?"

Relief inflated Maxine like oxygen gulped by a drowning man. "No, sweetie, God took him to Heaven." She didn't really believe in an afterlife, a secret she'd hidden from Walter their entire marriage, and she was tempted to make a crack about Animal Control's slow response. She knew, however, a good mother would offer Persephone her hand and guide her back toward the house—no tears, no accusations, no anger—so that's what she did. Maxine called Aimee's mother the next morning. She insisted the girls spend the weekend in the new neighborhood. It's perfectly safe, Maxine assured the other mother.

She had rules for the girls. Failure to heed them would result in no dinner at Chuck E. Cheese and no new Pixar film. Of course, work took Walter away for the weekend. The upside, Maxine thought, was that Persephone would credit her and not Walter for this indulgence. After six hours of cackling and chattering while a storm threatened, however, Maxine made no resistance when the clouds cleared and Aimee demanded they go outside. Persephone slapped on her skates and followed her friend.

While the white noise of the house—the hums of the refrigerator, central air conditioning, and clothes dryer—soothed Maxine, she didn't truly relax until a glass of red wine. Walter had insisted they share it on a special occasion, but she doubted he'd notice. She didn't think about Persephone or Aimee, she didn't think about Athena. Instead, Maxine thought about the house, how to manipulate its domineering persona into something warmer. First, she'd repaint the ghastly ceilings. She wondered if the Addams Family had lived there before her. Her home improvement fantasies bewitched her until she heard the screech of tires and screams of children erupting directly across the street.

As if in a fugue, Maxine slowly rose to her feet. She calmly passed through the door into the neighborhood. She should call the homeowner's association about all this reckless driving, she thought. Her refusal to panic revolved around her faith that bad fortune would befall Aimee before her daughter. Aimee was reckless, insolent and rebellious; Persephone was merely curious about morbid things. Even the end of the hockey stick bouncing over the heads of another group of children didn't inflate her fear.

The kids dispersed as Maxine approached, and she was about to admonish her daughter before she realized that it was actually Aimee poking away at something on the asphalt. The girl's head whipped up at the sound of her voice. She dropped the stick and fled down the road, screaming and crying.

Persephone's body lay on the asphalt, her limbs jumbled like those of a sock monkey. At least one limb was broken, likely more. Bright red blood pooled beneath her head, the fluid oozing toward the curb. Her face was blank, as if she expected the sky to open and welcome her. Still in shock, Maxine knelt to check her daughter's breathing—there was none. *Please, God*, she thought, *not my other daughter. Not unless I can go with her.*

As Maxine choked out silent tears, however, Persephone blinked. Maxine recalled Dorothy's face as her relatives rejoiced over her return from Oz. "Mommy!" She forced Maxine's hand over her heart, the joyful muscle pounding. "I'm not dead anymore!"

The Mother of All Mistakes

Abetted by the white bulbs' sinister glow, she navigated a cornucopia of cosmetics—pale pink lip gloss, eyeliner, eye shadow the hue of bruises, rouge—with the serene confidence of a Mary Kay veteran. The focus necessary for it blunted her panic. *If Mr. Leonard won't show mercy*, she wondered, *who will help my son become a man?*

Her disguise complete, Josie Child studied herself in the cluster of mirrors. Captured from myriad angles, her face split and shifted, incompatible puzzle pieces. The surfaces collided to form a reflection of no coherence. Her mother had often told her that beauty was to women what money was to men. Clicking off the lights, she felt grateful she'd had no daughters.

The trip from her house, the spoils of a quick and dirty divorce, to Mr. Leonard's group home took less than twenty minutes. The journey from the plantation-style properties to a subdivision with just-add-water tract housing, however, underlined this stark contrast. She traveled not between neighborhoods, but discrete universes among the Houston metroplex.

She stopped at the corner store two blocks from Leonard's Place. Topping off her tank, she brainstormed how to handle the home's proprietor. He'd called her last night, irate. He'd called her, demanded that they meet today. She hoped her deep discomfort with angry black men didn't destroy her credibility as Cory's mother. As she sealed the tank, that genius response to Mr. Leonard's indignation continued to elude her. She paused to examine herself, while leaving, in a store window. *Happy Holidays* was written in shoe polish beneath her reflection. Men liked women who made an effort. Nearing fifty, however, an effort was required more days than not.

As she parked, her tires scraped the curb. Mr. Leonard's house appeared meager and generic from the street, scarcely large enough for a couple and their two-point-five children, let alone the six men he'd split between two bedrooms. Neither were larger than his abode, the master bedroom in the rear. She couldn't see inside. Mr. Leonard forbid his tenants from raising the blinds or opening the garage without his consent. The waning daylight, in that moment, seemed to Josie more precious than platinum.

After clearing her throat, she balled her fist to knock. Before her knuckles hit wood, a man behind the door called out for Mr. Leonard. She paused. Was that Emile? Or perhaps the swaybacked boy who staggered about on a crutch? Ear pressed against the door, flaking white paint tickling her cheek, she listened to the commotion unspool.

"It's Wally! He's butt-ass naked!"

That instant, Mr. Leonard bellowed for Wally to get his ass back inside the bathroom. Even through the door, Josie heard each word clearly. She wondered why he bothered with all the privacy measures if the drama inside was loud enough to draw neighbors. Stay there, he ordered. He'd find a clean pair of shorts.

Josie backed away, convinced her propriety would be noted by an authority unseen yet sentient to all her affairs, her feelings and failings. Behind her, the young man offered a bright greeting. Her breath caught. It was difficult to remember these men didn't vaporize every time she left and returned to the relief of daylight.

"I'll make sure the situation is rated PG," the young man promised. "Wait right here."

"I was about to knock…"

The young man climbed onto the porch. "Just normal pandemonium." He gestured toward a rocking chair. Josie understood she was to sit patiently while the young man, Emile, helped restore order. After a few moments, he poked his head through the doorway and informed Josie that Mr. Leonard was expecting her. "Just enough time before we start supper," the young man added.

"I should've called before coming," she said. "I wasn't sure when the best time might be."

She lightly raked her fingers through bright blonde hair, shaking her tresses in a limp attempt at informality. The pantsuit was too dressy. The paisley scarf knotted around her neck only made her more conspicuous. She had to beg a man to spare her son. He'd wind up on the streets, she'd planned to say. Of course, his bedroom at home was still tidy and waiting, but Mr. Leonard didn't need to know that.

A spindly old man with a snow-white beard drawled for Cory to come see his mother. His noxious smile unnerved Josie so completely, she failed to return it. His name was Buster…or maybe Boomer? Some name more common among dogs than men.

Mr. Leonard entered the hall, the washing machine having rumbled to life in the room behind him. The beefy black man acknowledged his guest with a curt nod. "You boys remember we got a lady in the house," he said. "No bullshit, keep it clean."

He was short and stout, his jeans pressed with creases, bare head smooth and mouth full of dazzling teeth. A silver ID bracelet, *contender* engraved upon it, wrapped his thick wrist. She'd been surprised when Cory revealed he was at least fifty-five. He'd aged miraculously well. She, on the other hand, had gone to so much trouble to look her best, but no one gave a damn.

The master bedroom hosted a daisy chain of unpleasantness among the group home manager and his clients, or the occasional family member. In the living room, a widescreen plasma television aired a *COPS* rerun. The scabby, skinny streetwalker onscreen bullshit an officer, the man she'd solicited already cuffed. Emile watched the whole scene dispassionately, sucking on his e-cigarette. The dense, bright vapor hung in the air like a lover's guilt. The other men bunched about the room like hairs around a bathtub drain. There was no Christmas tree, not a stocking, not a single string of lights.

Josie stopped halfway down the hall. "Is my…is my son already inside?" She gestured toward Mr. Leonard's bedroom.

Behind her, a sullen squeak solved the mystery. "Mom, I'm right here." She glanced over her shoulder, unsurprised yet disappointed anew in the boy dragging his feet across the shag carpet toward Mr. Leonard's lair. Cory was tall but no one noticed, his slouch too pronounced. He hadn't cut his hair in months, and he never bothered to style it. He wore a Simpsons T-shirt reading "Worst T-Shirt Ever," the artwork distended by his lewd belly. Her little misanthrope, she noted, hardly old enough for junior college.

Mr. Leonard shook his head in dismay and disappeared inside his room. Josie and her son followed. She felt a pang of sympathy for this black man forced to conduct business in his own bedroom. What if life's events confronted her where *she* slept, before the makeup, before the solace of her now-silent mornings.

The widescreen plasma television mounted on the wall dominated the entire space. His desk, a no-name laptop perched upon it, stood shyly in the far corner. A twin bed was tucked opposite that, bedspread folded so crisply that sleep seemed unwelcome. A leather recliner, beige and big, was too close to the television. The same episode of *COPS* continued. The streetwalker yelped as the officer forced her into his cruiser.

Mr. Leonard, distracted, invited them to sit. After he'd claimed the recliner, however, only a desk chair remained. Cory plopped down, the chair creaking in dismay. All that remained was Mr. Leonard's bed. Abashed, Josie sat primly on its edge. She tried to forget that this is where the black man slept.

His bedroom door remained rudely open. Josie couldn't bring herself to insist on privacy.

"Been havin' problems with your boy for a good long while," he began. "I hoped we wouldn't need to make that phone call, but this boy don't goddamn listen." Josie couldn't meet his gaze. Cory glared at the floor. The boy was stealing other clients' medication, Mr. Leonard said. He took too long in the bathroom, sometimes over an hour. He wouldn't pick up his clothes. He never helped with the chores. "And he don't seem too familiar with basic hygiene."

"Hate this fucking place," Cory muttered.

Josie blanched. "That word doesn't impress me, you know."

Mr. Leonard threw his hands above his head, frustrated. "Damn, Mrs. Child, we got worse problems than the F-bomb."

"He's my only child." *He was comfortable expressing fury*, she thought. *Don't speculate why.* "He's not used to all this…excitement."

"He had time to adjust, Mrs. Child. It's been almost three months."

Cory rolled his eyes at them both. "Don't talk about me like I'm not here! Fuck!"

Josie had quickly lost hope of steering this confrontation. He seemed in total command of this encounter, and Josie sat still, feeling silly in her peach pantsuit. She looked at Mr. Leonard while he gazed, disgusted, into nowhere.

"I come off a hard-ass," Mr. Leonard said, "but I care 'bout these boys." He rattled off a semi-coherent story about getting shot in the back over a failed drug deal. Not crack or heroin, but fucking marijuana. For over ten years, he'd lived with the pain. He firmly believed, as God had told him directly, he must guide other troubled men to a more righteous path, or his anguish meant nothing. "Take Emile, for instance. My greatest success story…"

"He's a fag, Mom."

Her voice tightened. "That wasn't necessary!" She smiled, big and stupid. She wouldn't let the black man know how her son embarrassed her.

Mr. Leonard ordered Cory to leave. Josie gazed at her son as he shuffled into the hall. He didn't return her gaze. Once he was gone, the group-home manager shut the door with a gravitas that unnerved Josie. She'd never been alone with a black man. What would Daisy—or Victor!—think? Mr. Leonard sat, delicately, next to her on the bed. He did not touch her. He gestured grandly, detailing the hopes he still had for her son. He'd seen worse boys, he claimed, and they left here great men. "Hope, to me," he said, "is anything but a luxury." He promised to keep Josie updated through text messages. They'd meet again in person, the three of them, in a week.

She offered her hand, expecting Mr. Leonard to shake it. Instead, he took it tenderly into his own, like a lover, like someone whom he would never be. The black man was touching her! His skin was rough and dry like an emery board. The shooting left him in such constant pain, he confessed, he couldn't endure normal socializing. "I miss women. You know what I'm saying…"

She knew what he was saying.

After she left Mr. Leonard's room, the door whispering shut behind her, Emile invited her to stay for dinner. Spaghetti, he said. With extra sauce! Josie was tempted, she said, but she had another engagement. She told her son goodbye. Her words traveled through the sliding glass door, opened wide, where Cory sucked down a cigarette.

"I tell him to try vaping," Emile said. "I'm saving a small fortune."

"Thank you for having me," she said absently. "I hope Santa's good to each of you."

The men in the living room—Wally, the spindly old man, the man on the crutch and the rest—stared as she left. Shutting the door, she felt their eyes on her. Her son treated his housemates with such contempt, and she wanted to believe that was an uncharitable belief. She hoped, however, no one had noticed her similar disdain.

Her son was too old for military school or anything that reputable. Her ex-husband Lyle had always chided her for failing to instill discipline in the boy. Since childhood, he'd done only the work necessary to make a passing grade. He didn't play sports, he didn't care about college, he made no effort to find a job. His friendships, few as they were, involved other sullen boys who sat with him, staring stupidly at the television, video-game joysticks or remote controls at hand. He lacked direction, she'd decided, but couldn't find any solution that didn't make her cringe: drill sergeants, uniforms, the belief that any whiff of individuality indicated a character defect. Lyle had long ago abandoned hope, and Josie feared her middle age would be spent kowtowing to her sour-tempered spawn.

Her friend Daisy had told her about group homes. These places—very private, very discreet—were where troubled young men, whether just out of prison or rehab, could bond and, together, construct a worthy existence. She'd never before insisted her son do anything. There are certain things a mother can't teach, she'd said. Cory simply muttered an obscenity and slinked back to his room. She'd packed his belonging herself.

Driving home, she wasn't surprised to hear her cell phone chime with a new text. Since Cory's departure, her social life had drastically improved. She hoped it was Victor, with his pretense of asking about their book club, his naked desire for her hardly a secret. Instead, it was Mr. Leonard. He wrote that he'd had a long discussion with Cory after she left. He'd apologized for insulting Emile. *Maybe he even meant it*, concluded Mr. Leonard.

Gazing so intently at the message, she almost front-ended a neighbor's passing car. His familiar tone unnerved her. He was speaking to her like she were his *friend*. It was Cory, though, who was supposed to be making friends.

The house, cavernous and sterile, was silent when she walked into the foyer. She'd enjoyed the novelty of quiet the first couple of weeks after Cory went to Leonard's Place. The lack of commotion had started to seem, to her, like a sort of death. Lives were noisy. If her house offered no noise, she wasn't living an actual life. She stepped more forcefully on the tiles, the *clickity-clack* of her heels comforting her. She'd turn on the air conditioner, despite the chill outside. She'd turn on the television, the station didn't matter. She would not be swallowed whole by a house full of things and other things. She hoped Victor would call.

Rising late the next morning, well past nine, two unread texts awaited her. Surely, one had to be from Victor. Instead, Daisy had asked her to join her on yet another spa weekend. Instead, Mr. Leonard had written, *Cory seemed really crabby this morning. Was he that way as a kid?* She had typed a whole response before realizing she wasn't obligated to respond at all. Mr. Leonard's text felt like idle chatter, the sort of message intended to ignite conversation. Still, it would've been rude to ignore him, and he did, after all, hold her son's future in his hands. *I guess so*, she typed. She sent the message. She waited, cell phone in hand, for several minutes. She didn't know why she waited. She'd never before waited on a black man to text or call.

"Have you thought about whether you want Cory home for Christmas?" Daisy, her sharp chin resting on the cushioned massage table, asked questions in such a blasé manner, she must've expected the answer, whatever it was, to bore her. Josie liked to imagine her friend was so disconnected that she, Josie, was free to say anything.

"I'm still debating whether I want a tree!"

"Dumpling, you must have a tree. And you must have plenty under it."

"He hasn't even told me what he wants this year."

"There's nothing a boy his age wants that a mother might have."

"I thought maybe I could send him to Lyle's for the holidays."

"Oh, dumpling! Exquisitely selfish *and* very practical! I'm impressed!"

While the tanned masseuses rubbed her back, fingers moving in slow circles, Josie kept gazing at her cell phone.

Would Mr. Leonard text again? How would she make sure Daisy didn't notice? Her friend supported civil rights for all, much like her, but there was a clear line that must never be crossed. For Josie, flirting atop this line proved a pleasant distraction from the predictable pampering. She didn't even resent Daisy's acidic glibness.

Josie didn't expect her son to pick up the phone when she called that night. He never picked up. If he needed her, he would call, his voice melodious and sweet, the boy full of apologies and promises neither of them believed. She left her usual message: how are things at the house? Are you being good? She, of course, didn't tell him about Mr. Leonard. She'd planned to tell him but hung up before saying the words.

Mr. Leonard sent a text shortly afterward. He told her what the boy was watching on TV. *All these trashy shows about trashy people*, he wrote. *Not like the shows we used to watch*. It was true that she and Mr. Leonard were from the same generation. She remembered little from her childhood except that she didn't care to remember more. She felt included, unexpectedly so, one adult reaching to another and nakedly hoping. *I don't even watch TV anymore*, she wrote back. This wasn't true, of course. Everyone watched TV. But, still, he responded. And, still, she responded to him. And then it was past ten in the evening. Hadn't Victor promised to call?

Two days before their planned face-to-face meeting, Josie received an odd message from Mr. Leonard: *don't forget to fold the laundry before you leave*. She wasn't sure how she felt about this non sequitur—Mr. Leonard didn't seem like a fan of the willfully absurd. She sent a bundle of question marks in response, and he followed instantly with an apology. He'd meant to text Emile and got distracted. She didn't know how she felt about him texting others with enough regularity to invite confusion. She'd thought *this*, whatever *this* was, was hers alone. She didn't acknowledge his apology.

Josie chose a lightweight summer dress for her visit to Leonard's Place. She'd always loved the way it clung to her breasts and hips, sophisticated yet approachable. All she lacked was someone to approach her. After parking, she realized she'd been saving the dress for the next book club meeting. It had been intended for Victor. *I'll simply wear it again,* she told herself.

Wally lumbered toward her the moment she walked through the door. He was sorry he didn't know where to poop. He was embarrassed and he was so, so sorry. She brought out her most gracious smile. She wouldn't have even remembered, she told him, had he not brought it up.

"What bullshit," Cory muttered. After a fierce reaction seen by no one but him, she and her son joined Mr. Leonard in his bedroom. She listened as the group home manager started with guarded praise. Cory was getting better at cleaning up after himself and limiting his time in the bathroom. But he couldn't seem to get along, however, with Emile.

"He's always telling me what to do," Cory huffed.

"You know he's in charge when I'm not here."

Josie, once again seated on Mr. Leonard's bed, spoke sharply. "Just because we don't like someone doesn't mean we disrespect them."

"He takes it up the ass. Fuck him."

Unlike the initial meeting, Cory's childishness seemed to deflate Mr. Leonard. Josie wondered whether he was just going through the motions. During this visit, he hadn't once mentioned banishing her son. Why was a sit-down necessary? He knew her number. *Of course,* she thought. *He wanted to see* me. After this epiphany, it wasn't only Mr. Leonard who went through the motions. Josie took turns chastising and cautiously praising the boy, but all the talk was just prologue to the moment Mr. Leonard sent Cory out of the room.

"I still have hope," Mr. Leonard said, rising from the recliner. Josie felt certain he'd come directly to her, where she sat, on his bed. Instead he opened a desk drawer. The many minor noises that junk makes inside a drawer filled the room. Finally, the crinkle of tissue paper made itself apparent. In his dark, muscular hands, Mr. Leonard held an object about the size of a baseball, wrapped in green tissue paper. He approached her. It was a gift. Yes, next week was Christmas. She hadn't bought her son a single thing.

"I saw this in Walmart and thought of you right away." He sat beside her on the bed.

She blushed. "I didn't get you anything. I'm…"

He shook his head and handed her the gift. She carefully peeled away the rustling paper. She didn't remember the last time a man surprised her with a present. Or had she expected this? She *was* wearing her favorite dress.

It was a coffee mug: white porcelain with the word MOM written in large bubble letters on its side. She hated coffee. She didn't especially need another reminder of her greatest failure in life. It was a cheap piece of crap, but now it was *her* crap.

"It's like something a child might make," she said.

"Hey, maybe a child did make it."

"Let's hope not a mistreated one from Taiwan."

His gaze went blank. "What does that mean?" He didn't sound hurt, merely confused. Josie could've dealt better with hurt.

"Nothing." She gestured at his face, fingertips safely distant, but when he flinched, the absurdity of her gratitude announced itself. "I'll bring you something next week, I swear."

"You don't gotta do that," he said casually. "Besides, that be the day after Christmas."

Her son must've seen her face. Just because Cory rarely showed interest in others' emotions didn't mean he was blind. After Josie shut the bedroom door, cradling the ugly coffee mug to her breasts, her son's glare accosted her.

"Did he give you that?" he asked.

"Yes, it's a Christmas present."

He sucked on a cigarette. "What were you two talking about?"

"What else, honey? We talked about you."

Driving home that night, she made a sudden U-turn for the mall, just a half-hour from closing. It hardly mattered what she bought her son. He took pride in how little she knew about him, and he knew that this meant any present she gave would appear thoughtless. But he was her son, her only child, and Christmas was about parents making their children's wishes come true. She strode past the stores, vetoing one after another. She couldn't buy clothing—she'd lost track of his size. She couldn't buy music—she didn't know what he liked. Finally, at the mall's far end, was a store notorious for carrying X-rated party games and lewd T-shirts. She'd never been inside. She imagined a locker room in which all the crude jocks had transformed into novelty items. Finally, she saw, tucked away on a low shelf, an ashtray with a drawing in its dish of a closed hand, middle finger extended.

It was perfect. She choked on tears. The clerk offered to wrap it in green tissue paper.

He'd wanted to call, Victor said the next night, but grading finals gobbled up all his time. "You don't want to know how many college kids can't write a basic essay." This would be there first night together, but it felt to Josie like a state visit. He flipped the omelet, the masterwork landing perfectly inside the pan. On the stove's other burner, another omelet conspired for a heavenly aroma. He had his back to Josie, hadn't turned away from his pans in several minutes, giving her ample opportunity to sneak a text to Mr. Leonard. As Victor prattled on about America's ill-fated generation of young scholars, Josie couldn't help thinking how wonderful it would be if Cory had that problem. That would've meant he was in college, and it would've meant a professor took his education seriously enough to offer criticism. Instead, she'd left the green-wrapped novelty ashtray, bought moments before closing, in the backseat of her car.

I finally found a present for Cory, she wrote.

Victor was warbling some show tune from a long-closed historical musical. *If wallpaper were given voice*, she thought, *it would sound like this*. She only wondered when this bore would call because it gave her something to anticipate and dread in equal measures, like an eclipse.

After Mr. Leonard asked what she'd found, she wrote, *It's stupid. He'll hate it.*

Right away, she received his response: *He's damn lucky to have you for a mom.*

She was so touched, it almost didn't matter that she felt like an enormous fraud. Her MOM mug sat on the kitchen counter. Victor hadn't noticed it. Even if he had, he rarely commented on what he felt was simple kitsch.

She wrote, *He's lucky to have you, too.*

And then nothing. Josie had abandoned all pretense of participating in Victor's diatribe. She snapped to attention to find him, hips against the stove, looking indulgently over his shoulder. She wanted to slap him, record the smack and then force him to watch it on an endless loop.

"Breakfast is mere moments away," he cooed.

"It's all I've been thinking about," she said, voice hollow.

"Lies and deception." He was so damn chipper, and she hated him.

Josie reluctantly gave herself over to the many tiny rituals of etiquette that governed the first time a man cooked for you. Despite herself, she was grateful those gestures and words were so easily accessed. She was sleeping, she was pretending to be awake—she'd forgotten, however, whom she wished to deceive.

I'll take him to bed tonight, she decided, right after she complimented his culinary prowess. That was the sort of thing that happened between people like them. It was foolish to pretend otherwise. Afterward, they might discuss the book they'd both been pretending to enjoy. The club met soon after Christmas. The novel was about an extended family traveling across the country during The Great Depression. Josie wondered why they simply didn't turn around and return home. California was a pathetic life goal.

The lovemaking was pleasant and mercifully brief. Victor did the proper thing and dozed off moments after their bodies separated. Josie kept glancing at her cell phone laying on the nightstand. She didn't understand how Mr. Leonard could abandon such an intimate discussion. This web she'd spun around her marathon texts with him forever threatened to tear apart. Victor snored lightly.

The cell phone chirped. She looked at the display: the land line of Leonard's Place. He'd never used that line to contact her before. After all, the phone was located right there in the kitchen, zero privacy included. And Cory would've called on the cell phone she dutifully paid for each month, convinced he'd drift into complete seclusion without it.

"You gotta come quick!" It was Wally, frantic. "Mr. Leonard's gonna call the cops!"

"What's going...Where's my son?"

"Come quick, lady, please! He's gonna call the cops!"

Men were shouting over the line, pandemonium. She tossed the phone onto the nightstand without hanging up, tugged on a pair of jeans and a jersey, and grabbed a coat hanging from the pegboard. She caught a glimpse of herself in her vanity. The mirrors' multiple angles distorted and disrupted her face. It was the same trouble with beauty she'd always had. Victor called out from the bed.

"Darling, what's wrong?"

"I have to find my son. I'll be back."

He snapped up in bed, gallantly tossing off the covers. "Let me drive you."

"This has nothing to do with you." The acid in her voice stunned Victor. He slowly reclined back onto the mattress. "I won't be long," she added softly.

Those twenty minutes from her child's only real home to her child's make-believe home, they'd never seemed longer or to begin and end with such extremes. She'd cast off her only child into an overcrowded dormitory run by an angry black man who believed the angels were on his side. Except he wasn't angry with her. Except he'd given her son a second chance. Except the shouts and chaos booming from inside Mr. Leonard's home greeted her like a wave as she dashed toward the house.

She threw open the front door, pushed through the screen door. The men sloppily circled the living room. Two chairs and a coffee table were overturned. Cory, her son, brandished a butcher knife. She'd never seen him looking so animated, so perversely alive. She didn't recognize him but knew at once this was her son. Facing off against him, Mr.

Leonard wielded a baseball bat. A large mirror hanging on the wall had been shattered. No one paid her arrival much mind; the chaos simply consumed her as it had the others.

Mr. Leonard's eyes were wide, teeth gnashed, muscles tensed. The baseball bat seemed a perfectly natural extension of his erupting temper. "Josie, you tell your son nothin' happened, all right?" The streak of fear in his voice surprised her. She hadn't known black men acknowledged fear. They never did on *COPS*. Also, who was afraid of her son? "Josie, you tell him that!"

Cory stammered, voice harsh, "Some nigger touched my mother!" Finally, he glanced at her. "How could you let him touch you?!?" He looked so horrified, she instantly knew she'd done something wrong. The fact she couldn't recall the sin in particular didn't matter a bit.

The hysteria swept through her. "What are you talking about, honey? What do you think happened?"

"Emile, that faggot, he showed me a text," Cory said, panting, "meant for you. It said, *Josie, let's not make this into something it's not.* What the fuck else could it mean?" He was staring at his mother, terror in his eyes. More than anything, her son needed an explanation that would instantly undo what was about to be done. Josie, however, was too struck by the realization that the text Emile had received by mistake was meant for her. It was meant in reply to her message: *He's lucky to have you, too.*

Her gaze flitted for a moment across the room. Arms crossed over his chest, ugly satisfaction in his smile, Emile stood apart from the melee, but she knew instantly that he was the instigator. He'd wanted Cory out of the house, the boy who ridiculed him, so when Mr. Leonard texted him unwittingly, he showed it to her son, letting his imagination do the rest. Emile, he was one of Mr. Leonard's success stories.

Mr. Leonard and Cory circled one another like gladiators in a cage, Josie rushing their circle of contention but always drawing back. She had to protect her son from the angry black man. Perhaps he sensed this instinct of hers for at that moment he lost his focus, knife dropping to his side. "Mom," he said, "just tell me it's not true."

Mr. Leonard swung the bat at Cory's hand, the one brandishing the knife, but the boy deflected the attack, his arm sending the bat directly upside his head. The sickening crack silenced the house. Josie didn't see the impact. One moment, her son was staring dew-eyed at her and the next he was on the floor, shielding his bloody head. Even with the boy plainly disarmed, Mr. Leonard wouldn't relinquish the bat.

Josie leapt upon his back, wrapped an arm around his neck. "Fucking nigger, don't touch my baby!" Those words snuffed the altercation for good. She let herself slip from his shoulders, almost toppling when her feet hit the floor. Cory writhed in pain, bleeding through his hands. Mr. Leonard stood breathless, his shoulders quaking. He gazed at Josie before collecting himself. He was crushed, and she would've rather dealt with that than this. She pulled her son to his feet, ordered him to wait in the car. Unsteady, blood streaming behind him, he tottered away.

"I'll come for his things in the morning," she told Mr. Leonard. He nodded, resigned, refusing to look at her. He hadn't let go of the bat. As she strode through the front door, oddly serene, Wally waved goodbye.

She raced toward the nearest emergency room, Cory using her winter coat to soak up the blood. He was stunned, and she worried he might go into shock. Winters Memorial was just two miles away. The sheath of silence they'd entered surprised her, coming on the heels of such violence and hate. She was proud of her son for defending her honor, no matter how brutally or mistakenly. That meant something. His room was ready at her house, their house, awaiting him.

"When we get you stitched up, I have a present for you."

Cory turned to her, and she saw the gash striped along the side of his head.

"I saw it in the store and thought of you right away."

His words barely audible, he asked what it was.

"Let's get you better first," she said. "Christmas can wait."

A pothole rattled them, Cory wincing in pain. She'd made a mistake; she'd been careless with her child. She sought forgiveness, but that unseen yet sentient authority wouldn't respond. She would give her only child an ashtray. It had a hand, middle finger extended, painted in its dish. It was a cheap piece of crap.

Learned Response

2002

That young, still in junior high, I didn't know why I was so impressed with Clayton March. I was, however, damn impressed. As he strutted toward us, his narrow torso and twitching hips lent him a tough femininity that made me think of my mom. He seemed impervious to ridicule. The words *faggot* and *cocksucker* were from a language he didn't speak, filtered out, gibberish. How humiliating that Clayton was six months younger than me.

He stepped to the table and announced in his tight, hoarse voice the start of class. He whipped out a grade book, swiped from a real teacher, and began roll. There were only eight of us, but we still called out "here." Piney Woods Day Care liked to boast how simpatico its children were, all friends, all day and every day.

"Teacher," a girl named Olive said, sniffing back snot, "can we go outside for recess?"

"If you're good children and refrain from vexing me, perhaps."

"Teacher," said a boy with a lazy eye, "Mom says I shouldn't let you be the boss of me."

Clayton slid a hand over his greasy, matted dark blonde hair. Not a single tuft rose in rebellion. "When you're with your mother, do as she says." With his red pen, he savagely marked the grade book. "But when you're in my class, I *am* the boss of you."

I could bolt any time I pleased. With my thick torso, muscular thighs and quick feet, I was always the first pick for kickball or dodge ball. Cattycorner to me, though, sat good reason to raise my hand and say please and pretend this all wasn't more than a little creepy.

Bart's chestnut locks flopped over his eyes. Every time he flipped them back, he smiled bashfully. He suffered from the adolescent affliction of believing his every gesture will be scrutinized; I knew a few things about that. Clayton lowered his eyes to inspect the grade book, and Bart mouthed those words—faggot, queer, pervert—that Clayton knew others brandished. A skilled teacher notices everything.

Bart popped his knuckles. Watching his bicep undulate stirred longings in me I didn't fully comprehend. I was strapped in a car stalled on the tracks. Intense desire for another boy's company made me a certain type of person, and my heart would've shriveled like bacon if Bart called me hurtful names. I wanted to be Bart's friend, his only friend. I wanted him to stay overnight, our sleeping bags overlapped, sending dirty texts to the girls he liked. A year or two ago, we wrestled outside on crunchy, dead grass. He pinned me against the earth, and I held his gaze for a sweet eternity until we both burst laughing.

Clayton cleared his throat and smacked a ruler against the table. "Today is your math test. If you don't pass this exam, you must explain to the class why you're so dumb."

Bart whispered, "What does he shove up his ass to get that little twist *just* right?"

I giggled, hand clamped over my mouth. Bart leaned back, a perfect passivity slipping over his features. Olive and another girl muttered excitedly about someone catching hell.

"Does math amuse you, Randolph?" I stopped laughing, dropping my hand followed by my head, and assured Clayton that I took arithmetic seriously. "I'm so glad to hear it," he sniffed and whipped out photocopies from his grade book. "You'll have five minutes to finish." He passed out the tests. Bart took one and scrubbed under his arms. Ignoring him, Clayton continued. "Any outburst will be handled harshly." He halted at the head of the table, his heels clicking together. Waiting for the Piney Woods van every day after school, he polished his black dress shoes. "Now, make me proud to be an educator," he said.

With a flurry of bobbing eraser ends, we began our fake exam for our fake teacher. All of us, that is, except Bart. With a blue crayon, he wrote nonsense like "maybe" and "don't think so" and "you suck." The test couldn't stump a first-grader: simple addition and subtraction. Clayton might've feared more difficult curriculum would leave empty seats. I flew through my test in under a minute then watched Bart deface his.

The day care center was a converted Victorian mansion in the historic district. Roads of actual brick lent what the city's tourism division called "stateliness." On a plasma TV at the end of the large playroom, most of the kids gazed like zombies at a cartoon about a neurotic sponge and his quasi-queer relationship with a dumb starfish.

Bart squeezed his thumb and forefinger together, placed them before his lips and sucked sharply. At the time, I thought he meant cigarettes. Now, of course, I know he either wanted pot or was willing to share. Then confused, I simply laughed. Guys like you to laugh at their jokes, even the stupid ones. Bart Callahan was the funniest bastard in the world.

The swift, searing pain in my left knuckles jolted me. Bart and I snapped up our heads. Clayton stood beside us, arms crossed and eyes narrowed. The ruler twitched in his hand. "Randolph, since you're the better student, I'll let you decide. Who should I discipline first, you or Bart?"

Bart smirked. "Gotta catch me first, *ma'am*."

Clayton cut his gaze to my friend then returned to me. "I need your decision."

That's the spooky thing about childhood games, the scenarios your friends invent. You're loath to give them up because of the time and energy invested. I could've told Clayton to piss off. Like most kids my age, though, I was so fucking miserable, I held fast to any fantasy offered—even a childish, unpleasant one.

A smile flickered across my lips, but Bart missed it. He drifted over to the sponge and starfish; they were arguing about something, dozens of little cartoon bubbles climbing from the ocean floor. The spell, it seemed, had ended for the other kids as well. Only Clayton and I remained, acting out our parts. His game always ended when he sought to punish a student. Not even the dumb kids wanted to peek behind that curtain. Me, though, I had to know.

How committed was Clayton to his sad, sad show? His devotion mesmerized me. He ordered me outside, instructing me to wait. I stood on the pavement, one foot inside a hopscotch square. The wind sliced through me, raw and frigid. Why couldn't this happen inside? All week, the winter haze had obscured the sun.

I didn't know where Clayton had found the paddle, or who had been dumb enough to give him one. He softly slapped the wooden instrument against his palm, stepping toward me lightly like a spider. He told me to bend over. I didn't bend far enough, so he demanded that I grab my ankles. I didn't question him. Decadent anticipation overwhelmed me, surging like an ice-cream migraine. I disgusted myself. Clayton swung and stopped inches from my bottom, back and forth, practicing like a golfer on the links.

He spanked me. He spanked me again. He kept spanking me until I cried out. No one watched. We were the only two boys in the world.

After Clayton was done, I gaped at him, unsure how to acknowledge what had passed between us. My buttocks tingled with electric warmth, every nerve ending alive and essential. I gasped, forgetting all about Bart and his unruly forelock. I massaged my buttocks, hoping the sensation would linger. It faded quickly, elusive like a dream recalled too late.

Clayton straightened his back, the paddle dangling from his hand. He suggested I come inside. It was freezing and I hadn't brought my coat. Would I like to explain to the class that I caught a cold because I'm so dumb? Clayton waited for an answer. I really didn't have one. Only one word sat on my tongue: again.

2009

I figured Shane might be there. It was the only queer bar in town, and since it was Spring Break, every faggot home from college convened at The Petting Zoo. The drag revue started in an hour. Everyone watched because they pitied the wheezy old queens.

I gazed into the mirror behind the bar. I watched my reflection drink, hoping a stupor wasn't far away. I watched other guys pretending not to watch their own reflections drink. Truthfully, I wasn't sure I wanted anyone's attention, but I still wanted Shane to pour down my parched throat.

I struck him only once, and I promise it wasn't that hard.

I was so busy watching my ex, I didn't notice anyone beside me until he cleared his throat. Startled, dreading and hoping for Shane, I twisted on my stool and saw a sinewy, gorgeous man, probably a college student himself. At least, his sweatshirt bore three Greek letters I didn't try to identify. After blessing me with a wide TV-host grin, he kept glancing over his shoulder into the crowd. Damn, I thought, he's not alone.

"Are you Randolph Fitzpatrick?" He offered his hand.

I would've shaken it no matter what my name. "Do we know each other?"

"The name Clayton March ring your bell?"

Was it possible? Had the prissy, absurd boy who introduced me to sexual pleasure matured into delectable manhood? Shane would have to understand. "We grew up together," I said. "My mother insisted I go to private school after junior high. I lost touch."

"Wait here," the handsome man said. "I'll go grab Clayton."

I had to laugh. The man disappeared into the throng of drunk, horny clubbers. I thought about that day Clayton took me outside and unveiled a foreign world. As elemental as it had proven in deciding the nature of my desires, I rarely thought of Clayton as a person. I focused on the sensations, the anticipation between slaps. I could climax if a boy swung at an ideal speed and angle.

A presence materialized behind me but refused to identify itself. He cleared his throat, and I cleared mine in response. The handsome man never returned. I kept my eyes trained on the exit, afraid it might vanish if I lost track. Finally, I told him my name and felt that lovely sting radiate through my bottom.

"Randolph, what a stroke of luck!"

I shouldn't have been surprised. The innate girlishness from junior high had not abated. Though his gestures and posture were less extreme than I remembered, no one would mistake him for a specimen of masculinity. His greasy hair still clung to his scalp like a suction cup to glass. He folded his arms over his chest, belying his friendly smile. Knowing a homely, effeminate man inspired my ecstasy didn't hasten its retreat. I offered my hand.

He laughed. "We're too young to feel this old, don't you think?"

My brow pinched. "I don't feel old."

"God, I've already embarrassed myself. I meant that seeing an old friend reminds you how much time has passed."

"That's one way to look at things."

"You look fantastic, Randolph. I really want to—"

"I go by Rand now." I lit a cigarette. Shane wasn't there to chastise me. "Just Rand."

"Another coincidence! I go by Clay."

Some gifts don't warrant thanks. Indeed, showing gratitude dilutes their worth. A few years ago, I read a news story about a young woman who befriended the middle-aged man who saved her from choking. By all accounts, the friendship was intense and all-consuming. The man and woman became so fixated on one another, they lost their jobs and their spouses divorced them. One night, they simply vanished in the man's RV. All that heartache could've been averted. Some paths run parallel and some cross only once.

I kept an eye out for Shane. If he saw me with someone so unappealing, the shame would finish me. Others considered me attractive, and I had the bedroom history to prove it, but I couldn't let *any* ex, including Shane, catch me slumming. All this time, Clayton had been recounting his high school years and his tentative dip into junior college. I pretended to listen and he seemed to find my occasional "uh-huh" and "yeah" satisfying.

"So…" He leaned against the bar, signaled for a beer. "Tell me about you." He reached for my arm, but his fingers fell before reaching it. "I'm sure you lead an exciting life."

"I'm spending Spring Break at my mother's house, staking out a shitty bar on the off-chance my ex-boyfriend shows up."

Clayton's earnest sheen withered. He inched back, didn't acknowledge the bartender when he slipped her a five for a beer. I should've been pleased. If I'd upset him, he'd leave that much sooner, but I feared that once he vanished from my life, vanished again, I'd be left with our memory of stark eroticism, a defining encounter. I'd have no one to help safeguard it from fading.

At that moment, a built blond with a stiff gait passed behind me. I caught his image in the mirror. I spun around. It crushed me to find him gone. Was it Shane? Perhaps I really was desperate to end this reunion.

"Was that the guy you're waiting for?" Clayton asked, looking sheepish.

"Yes—no, what—this is very weird, okay?"

"Please, call me Clay. I shouldn't have said anything…"

"Yeah, we were kids together, but do you remember any of that shit? I don't." My heart pounded. I lifted my mug and slurped suds. Clayton offered to buy a round and I nodded. We drank in silence for a half-hour. He never looked at the passing men and didn't look at me either.

After our fourth round, he slammed his mug on the bar and studied me like I was a bull in need of breaking. "The reason I came over, you know, after all this time…" He was slurring now, and his "proper" diction had vanished. "When you went off to private school or whatever, you didn't seem…fuck, there's no delicate way to put this…"

"Then don't be delicate." He desired me. It took him almost a decade, but here it came.

"You're openly gay, right? I mean, you're *here*, but I know a few 'out' guys still in the closet with their families and jobs." He swallowed, looked to the side and smiled like he'd embarrassed himself. Acne scars lurked beneath his cheekbones. "I just like people to be happy, you know?"

I hadn't expected that. I needed time to process. I wanted my mother.

"You don't have to answer that, you know."

Springing from my stool and digging for my wallet, I knocked over my empty mug. The clatter was so loud that you'd think something terrible had happened. Clayton remained on his stool, looking lost, maybe disappointed. "Look, it's late," I said. "This has been great. Find me on Facebook if you want."

Clayton clutched my shoulders but didn't tighten his grip when I struggled. He held me gently like an injured bird. The world spun and my shoes felt too small. He spoke to me, assuring me in soft murmurs that I could trust him. He said men like us have to be there for each other. All the trivial shit from our childhood was just that—trivial shit. Enraged, I shoved him backward; he toppled over the barstool but caught himself before hitting the floor. The hurt in his eyes excited me, it did. I wondered how else I could summon it.

After tossing two twenties on the bar, Clayton backed away, hands raised in surrender. I struggled to catch my breath. The drag show started soon. Clayton promised to pray for me and quickened his steps toward the exit. "Be good to yourself, okay, Rand?" I looked at my feet, palms pressed against my skull. If I didn't chill, the bouncer would toss me. I blessed the drinking men with a smile, hoping to ease them, but those smiles never fool anyone. I absently rubbed my buttocks, worked my way to the base of my spine.

"Don't grope yourself in public like that. You some kind of sex pervert?"

I whipped around and knew there was mercy in the world. Shane, underdressed as always in gray athletic shorts and a navy blue football jersey, was smiling and reached out for me. He stopped just short, like Clayton had. Goddamn, he's such a *man*. That's all I wanted, the company of a real man. I asked him how much he saw.

"I stopped looking after a bit," he said. "If I want drama with you, I'll start my own."

I squeezed his arms, eyes closed in gratitude. "Shane, I'm so fucking sorry, baby. You've got to believe—"

Nonchalant and saving the day, he wrapped his arm around me and guided me toward the drag revue. The inescapable bass line of some mega-mix rolled off the dance floor and into the bar. Shane liked these tacky things, all the deception that fools no one, deception so inept, the ineptitude becomes the whole joke. I rested my head on his shoulder; he was a few inches taller than me. When we reached the dance floor, I tried to kiss his neck, but my angle was all wrong. Instead, I caught, after a spotlight briefly washed us in pink, the hairline scar above his jawline. It hadn't healed as cleanly as he'd hoped. Still, he wouldn't let me hold him if I weren't forgiven.

2018

Shane said I needed to be more social, network with the other teachers. I told him it was pointless. Davenport Boys Academy didn't appreciate unwarranted ambition. For now, I was happy to eat my lunch in the front office, talking to Martha. She was like my mother except I didn't know her address.

"Siesta's over," she said. "Don't leave the kids unattended. They devour their own."

I chuckled and slipped my tuna-on-wheat back inside the brown bag. Shane insisted that he help out, no matter what the doctor said about *easing* back into minor physical activity. That afternoon, the district required all teachers show a safety video illustrating the difference between "good touch" and "bad touch." Martha told me to brace myself for lewd comments.

"Kids aren't kids anymore, Rand." She pointed a sealed envelope at me. "You're lucky to be a bachelor. I can't imagine opening my front door and hearing silence." She tossed the outgoing mail into a bin. "I hope Heaven is a quiet place."

The kids hadn't really clicked with me, and it was close to Halloween. I'm not sure what I expected. Miss Hall, who taught next door, believed their generation was ripe with autism, an army of social retards. Most days, I felt like a kennel proprietor, making sure one kid didn't bite another and that they all got to the bathroom and looked presentable at dismissal. Playing the video, I could text Shane and chat with someone who experienced puberty. I'd forgotten to check my messages at lunch.

I stopped, the first boy in line colliding with me, when I heard a child's screams piled over a woman demanding that he be still. Be still and it'll be over! I feared the commotion might block our path to the classroom. My forehead grew moist and my pulse quickened. I knelt down to the kid that hit me; he was still rubbing his nose. I told him that he was in charge and asked the class to line up against the wall. They must wait either for myself or another teacher. Did they understand? They nodded, grunted, moaned, chirped—everything but actual speech.

Turning the corner, I found Miss Hall struggling with one of her second-graders. Miss Hall wore heavy makeup and pearls to class. She didn't believe in wearing flats. I admired how ably she was staying upright in three-inch heels. It didn't register why they were fighting until I saw the wooden paddle in her hand.

A few times after leaving the bar, Clayton contacted me, usually through Facebook, a few times through Adam4Adam and Manhunt. He called once. I left his messages unopened. I didn't answer the phone unless I knew the number. Our paths were meant to part—it was the universe's decision, not mine. I turned thirty that winter.

Every time Miss Hall aimed for the kid's bottom, he jerked out of the way. I could've backed around the corner and pretended I didn't see, but she spotted me. She thanked God and called me over; I had no choice.

"Grab his other arm," she instructed, panting. "Get him by the shoulder."

"Miss Hall, you know I don't support corporal punishment."

"And I don't support standardized testing, but I do it anyway. Grab him, Rand!"

I hesitantly reached for the flailing boy. He was surely too young to experience pleasure from a spanking. I held him lightly at first, but his resistance forced me to tighten my grip.

Miss Hall and I pinned him against the yellow tile wall, his face mashed against it. Miss Hall asked if I wanted to get in a lick or two. I turned away and ignored that familiar tingling in my buttocks. I couldn't look at Miss Hall. I knew she'd enjoy this.

She spanked him. She spanked him again. She spanked him until he cried out. It was over, and they still didn't know anything about me. After thanking me, Miss Hall whooped with exhaustion. She shoved the boy, ordered him to return to class. Just before opening the door, he stuck out his tongue. "My daddy beats me harder than that!" Miss Hall brandished the paddle like a flyswatter, and the boy rushed inside. A rumble of voices echoed from behind the door.

Miss Hall smiled, twisted her pearls. "Guess you need a man sometimes, huh?"

"Yeah, I suppose."

She punched my arm. "Shake it off." She reached for the door. "I wish I could take that paddle to some of these parents. A lot of people need a good spanking."

After firing up the computer and pulling down the screen, I opened the video file and collapsed behind my desk. Some teachers liked to hold a discussion before showing the film. I instructed them to keep their eyes open and mouths shut.

Shane had left six texts, five of them within the last ten minutes. Blood raced through my veins, horrified that our arrangement had finally broken his spirit, left him mumbling in a corner, wondering why I hurt him if I truly loved him. I didn't expect to read Clayton March's name. At some point over the years, I told Shane about what happened between us, including what happened at the day care over fifteen years ago. He nodded and offered compassion; that was all I had the audacity to seek. In a series of texts, Shane told me that Clayton had been attacked inside a client's home. His head was bashed in. Apparently, he was a social worker. It was all over the daytime news. My lover begged me to call, his last text insisting we'd get through this.

You're not alone, he wrote. *You'll always have me.*

On the screen, a dumbass actor in a plush bear costume told the boys that a "bad touch" is when anyone fondles parts of your body covered by your swimsuit. I'd never thought of it that way—easy enough to remember. I didn't recall what Clayton looked like, and I didn't know which incarnation I *should* recall—the stern prepubescent teacher or the confused man who promised to pray for me. It wasn't until the boys' caterwauling reached ear-splitting level that I looked out onto the classroom. There is no mercy in this world.

Chet Bedlam had his uniform pants pulled down to his knees. He stood on a chair before the class, thrusting his hips back and forth while rotating left and right so every boy could see. His penis wiggled like a caught fish. He shouted "bad touch" over and over. Later, I wondered why he chose that phrase over "good touch." He'd rendered both absurd.

I stormed to the front of the class and grabbed his arm. Chet twisted and yelped like a barnyard sow, but he couldn't escape. I slapped his buttocks, slapped them till my hand burned. He just kept screaming. I finally stopped and sucked in some air, and he toppled from the chair, landing on his back. No one spoke, the plush bear's singsong voice filling the room. Chet at last wailed, clutching his head as if it were filled with helium and ready to soar.

Chet tugged up his pants and crawled away. My class stared at me. So much fear in their eyes, I felt myself growing hard. I almost told them about Clayton and my first bad touch, how much I liked it, how much I convinced a good boy, a good man, to like it. Chet would tell his parents and that would be the end of me. Boys needed discipline, however, they needed rules. I had a unique perspective on the matter.

Me Love You Long Time

At three o'clock, I locked the front door to San Carlos Wine and Spirits and went out the back. I shook a menthol from my pack, and I perched on the concrete stoop, waiting for the old Asian woman who enjoyed her cigarette the same time every day.

I told myself I wouldn't turn pussy. I'd ask her what she does all day, see if the rumors were true.

The heat was intense, another sweltering August day in South Texas. The forecast offered no hope of rain. In less than a minute, I was wiping my forehead with my shirttail.

I'd be pissed if the old Asian woman didn't show. Too damn hot to wait like a chump.

The tanning salon was next door. I'd smoked my cigarette to the filter when the back door burst open. Asians age more gracefully than whites and that made it hard to pinpoint her age. Still, if I had to sum up her looks in one word, I'd say *old*. Two crevices ran from either side of her nose past the corners of her mouth. Crow's feet collected around her chocolate eyes even when her face relaxed. Her forearms were neither muscular nor fat, rail-thin like a teenage girl's. She wore a green silk kimono with a large tiger embedded on the bottom. The creature snarled, bared its teeth. Julie would like that, maybe for our first-year anniversary. I wanted to ask the old Asian woman where she bought it.

I fired up another cigarette, glancing at her. I needed an excuse to stay outside. No sane person would sit in this heat without reason. Each time I looked at her, I couldn't speak. What do you say to a woman like her? I tried to imagine her laugh, whether she laughed at all. She looked severe and humorless, like a state trooper.

It took me a moment to register that she'd asked me a question. How long you work at liquor store? Startled, I tried to smile, like the Southern boy I hopelessly was. A month, I said. You like it, she asked. She puffed a long, slim cigarette. Man who own store not nice man, she said. He give girls evil eye.

Girls, I thought. How many worked in that place? I don't see him much, I said. Most days, it's just me. She nodded, her gaze so potent I couldn't turn away. You come in soon, she said. Girl make nice with you. I chuckled and stared at my black Converses, mumbled that I had a girlfriend. The old Asian woman nodded. She said, Some have wife. Some have girlfriend. We very discreet.

I felt seduced by proxy. It wasn't arousing, unless you count my curiosity. I dashed back inside, never glimpsing behind to see her reaction. I didn't want to hurt her feelings.

Mr. McEntire told me about Tokyo Tan when he hired me. I'd heard the rumors, like all the students. Most of us thought it quaint that a small-time whorehouse operated in the shadow of multi-story residence halls. From the outside, it appeared no different from the other ragtag buildings on San Antonio Street across from the strip mall housing a Kinko's and the off-campus bookstore. Not even San Carlos' oldest residents were certain when Tokyo Tan opened its doors or why it never popped on the sheriff's radar. Perhaps local law enforcement found it too pathetic to bust. Students sometimes reported seeing homely Asian women entering and leaving and white men even more often, but no one I knew had actually gone inside.

I still didn't know the old Asian woman's name. Julie would've asked. My girlfriend was fascinated that I worked next to a genuine slut shack. I flirted with making up stories just to please her. Until now, my interactions with the Asian woman had been G-rated. Why proposition me? Did I seem like the type who frequents sad little sex dens? I was happy with Julie. We hadn't made love in over a week because of her condition, but what kind of sad sack uses that as an excuse to fuck around? I wasn't some high school shit who had to bust his nut right now.

Unnerved, I lit a cigarette and searched for the ashtray. I zipped back to the register when the cowbell rigged to the door announced the arrival of Felix and his faggot friend. Felix wore a T-shirt two sizes too large and pajama pants he'd hacked off below the knee. Felix hadn't turned nineteen, hence the presence of the fat faggot with bad teeth and a receding hairline.

Russell, he cried and marched to the counter, his arms thrown wide as if he wanted to embrace me. It was surprising after less than a month how many regulars knew my name. I laughed and hauled the vodka bottle up to the register. Felix's shirt bore a picture of Charlie Brown missing a baseball pitch with *I'd Hit That* written in block letters beneath.

While I rang up the purchase and the faggot scooped a wad of bills from his jeans, Felix smirked and waited for me to react. It's a sex joke, Felix said. You get it? I'd hit that...? I grinned and nodded. Yeah, I got it.

The faggot was kind and meek, like a new kid in class. His voice barely above a whisper, he asked if that was enough money. Sure, I said. You don't have to ask every time.

I bagged the bottle and handed it to the faggot. Rules are rules, I said. Felix brayed like a donkey, kissing my ass. He asked if I'd seen anyone enter Tokyo Tan today. He said he passed a guy three days ago, a loser in a blue business suit. Felix leaned over the counter. Would you let those chink whores anywhere near your dick? The faggot switched the bottle from one hand to the other, mumbled to Felix it was time to go.

Julie lived in the south side of town. She complained about driving all the way across town for school. But the rent was cheaper there than close to campus. I'd been debating whether to ask her to shack up.

We cuddled on her unmade bed watching a *Real Housewives* rerun. Those women are whores, Julie said. They marry these poor assholes for their money and then bitch about the whores who found an asshole with even more money.

Maybe they're really in love, I said. Julie laughed and patted my chest. She kissed my forehead. Every time we had sex and I climaxed, she kissed me there, like a mother comforting her child. People with that much money never find love, she said. They stop believing.

She gazed at me with sharp, gleaming eyes. I knew our friends envied us, what they believed went on when we were alone. I promise we'll fuck soon, she said. I grinned and took her hand. No rush, I said. I'm having a great time just like this. It wasn't a lie, but I suddenly wanted to leave. There was nowhere to go, however, so I stayed.

The next day, I sat behind the register reviewing college algebra when the cowbell announced a customer's entrance. The girl looked so young, I almost started my spiel about no one under 21 being allowed. She approached the register so meekly, her black eyes shimmering. Her subservience spooked me, so I said nothing. She was Asian, even thinner than the older lady. Dressed in a neon pink tube top and denim cut-offs, her thighs were no wider than her shins. When she reached into a tiny backpack she'd slipped from her shoulder, I spotted a butterfly tattoo on the inside of her wrist.

She handed me a crinkled slip of paper. Written in a scrawled hand was the name of our most expensive champagne.

I asked her name. Shii Ann, she said. Mr. Lee send me for good stuff. I waved the scrap of paper like a winning bingo card and entered the aisles. When I returned with the bottle, I went to tally the sale. Her eyes widened and she cried, No money! Mr. Lee give me no money! I held out my hand to calm her, explained that even merchandise given freely must be entered. I had no clue if she understood. She calmed down when I handed her the bottle and receipt. She let the scrap of paper flutter to the floor. At the door, she gave me a stiff, brief bow. Thank you for help, kind man. Her smile reminded me of my kid sister's Christmas portrait.

It was almost three o'clock when she left. I didn't want to talk with the old Asian woman, but she'd be disappointed if I didn't show. Julie loved to tease me about always putting the other guy's wants before my own. If I didn't, maybe she'd love me less.

The old Asian woman stood on her stoop. She'd smoked her cigarette halfway to the filter but never flicked her ash. I lifted my chin to acknowledge her presence, a gesture I typically reserve for guys. The woman glared at me as I sat upon the steps. She wanted something, but I had nothing to give.

Shii Ann my girl, she finally said. You not see her again. I handle business, not her. I felt like I'd broken curfew. She seemed like a sweet kid, I said. The woman's smile unnerved me. Perhaps you can see girl again, she said. I pretended my cigarette required my full attention. I didn't look over, afraid she might be like Medusa, able to turn me to stone. But once I grew a pair and glanced her way, the stoop was empty.

The electric company started rolling blackouts that day. I offered to let Julie spend the night, but she refused. My roommate blatantly stared at her tits. It's not my problem he's sexually deprived, she said. We spent the evening in her bedroom. She lazed on the windowsill in her bra and khaki shorts, fanning herself with a program from *A Doll's House*, the last show she did at the university. I wish I was a slut so I could parade around half-naked, she said.

I wanted to invade her, make her call my name like I was running from the law. After I quickly pawed my crotch, she gestured for me to approach. Part of me had hoped she missed the gesture. I grazed my fingers along her collarbone, down her sternum. Anxious like a teenager, I wanted to bury my face between her breasts.

The sound of a slamming car door ejected me from my daze. Anyone in the parking lot two stories below could see us. Blushing, I withdrew my hand. Why did you stop, Julie asked. That felt tremendous. The doctor said we have to wait, I mumbled. The look on her face puzzled me. Even after nearly a year, Julie knew how to surprise. I imagined how I could seduce Shii Ann, seduce and protect her. The two could not be separated, like links in a chain.

Julie resumed fanning herself. Doctors, she said. I wish people believed my word like I was God. I promised to call later. She didn't watch me leave.

The rest of the week I went to class and work, and cuddled with Julie in front of the bullshit reality shows she adored. Customers came and went, including Felix and his faggot hostage. I continued my three o'clock smoking ritual. The old Asian woman hadn't spoken to me since her vague suggestion about Shii Ann. I'd lost my confidence, allowed the minutes to slip away.

I spent Saturday looking forward to a house party one of the seniors was hosting. The theme, according to a flier posted in the greenroom of the theatre, was *Can't Beat the Heat*. The host encouraged guests to attend in their swimsuits. I looked forward to all the stares Julie and I would collect.

At three o'clock, I locked the front door and headed back. I smoked in silence, relieved the old Asian woman hadn't shown. As my cigarette burned to its filter, a loud female voice emerged from the salon. It was the old Asian woman. A higher, piercing voice followed, also in a foreign tongue. Was it Japanese, Korean, Chinese? Common sense urged me back inside to let the ruckus next door resolve without me.

But all I could think was that Shii Ann might need me. I hurried to the back of the salon. I pressed my ear to the door—as if that would make them easier to understand. The blazing sun blasted crippling heat. The argument escalated, punctuated by a thump, making me think one of the women had collided against a wall. A harrowing cry erupted, abruptly ending with a loud smack that must've been a slap to someone's face.

Without thinking, I threw open the door and stormed inside.

So many rooms! How could all these doors lead to different rooms inside this rinky-dink building? I imagined brittle-boned Asian girls getting fucked while they stood because there was no room to lie down.

It took me a moment to register the old Asian woman was shouting at Shii Ann while shaking her. She held the girl's wrists, slammed her repeatedly against the wall. A thin, elderly Asian man watched with no emotion, like he was waiting for the bus. The old Asian woman spoke quickly, an odd melody to her words. They didn't notice me, so I called out.

Only the old Asian woman looked. Shii Ann kept her gaze riveted to the woman. You not a customer, the woman said evenly. You pay Mr. Lee or leave now. She wore the kimono with the snarling tiger stitched along the bottom. I noticed two scratches on Shii Ann's cheek beginning to bleed.

I knew I was all that stood between Shii Ann and more abuse. I bolted toward them, ripped the old woman's hands away from the girl's wrists. It took more strength than I expected. The woman's grip was strong. I extended my arm and slammed it against the woman's shoulders, her back smacking against the wall.

I comforted Shii Ann. I brushed the hair from her face, looked into her eyes and tried to smile like someone trustworthy. Are you hurt? Her jaw jerked and she made only a high, startled cry. The woman remained against the wall, watching us with the smugness of a Persian cat. I guess it was too much to hope she'd fear me. I told Shii Ann to follow me outside, draping my arm around her shoulders. The sidewalk seemed safer. The older woman couldn't start shit out there— too many people passing by. Indeed, she did nothing as I led Shii Ann down the hall and past the old Asian man. I assumed he was Mr. Lee. His eyes were glassy, unfocused. He made no move to stop us.

Outside, I embraced the girl. Her arms bunched to her chest. Tell me what happened, I said. Where do you live? I feared she'd never manage a coherent word. After a few gulps and jerks, she said, You save me, yes? You like man in movie with bam-bam and ka-boom. You my American hero. She wrapped her thin arms around me.

We hugged like long-distance relatives reunited for Christmas. Her naked need sent a near-electric charge through me. This was what every man desired, right? More than love, more than sex. We're small boys imitating TV superheroes, bed linens as capes.

I doubted she understood, but I kept talking until a familiar, strident voice shouted my name from the liquor store. A rattle followed, the front door's deadbolt thump. Felix needed his fix, but the faggot wasn't with him. I shouted that I needed a minute. He whined, said he was late meeting his girlfriend. I couldn't believe the drunken bastard had one. Shii Ann needed me far more badly, but I didn't know what to do. Haggling with Felix, at least, seemed an easy task. I kissed the girl's forehead, brushed the hair from her face. Wait here, I said. I'll be two minutes. Do *not* go back inside. Promise? She nodded, tears streaking her cheeks. After I unlocked the store and Felix stepped inside, I glanced at Shii Ann one last time. She gazed about as if San Antonio Street were an alien planet.

Once I was behind the counter, Felix smiled bashfully. The dumb kid was trying to charm me. He began a detailed sob story about the faggot's new demands. He wanted me to suck his dick, he said. Despite his venom, the little smirk never left his lips. I said I couldn't sell to him. I went into the spiel Mr. McEntire taught me the first day. If I made one exception, soon every underage alcoholic in San Carlos would demand likewise.

Felix whined that he'd go nuts without a few stiff shots. I reminded him about the party. You'll find plenty of hooch, I said. This was taking longer than I'd planned. I could've told Felix to fuck off, but I didn't want to snap at the poor kid. Julie was right—I'm a pushover, the designated nice guy. Felix rolled his eyes, muttered *fuck this* and stomped away.

The moment he disappeared, I bolted outside. No one stood in front of the salon. The whole block was empty. I peered through the salon's front window, but it was too tinted to see inside. I tried the door, but it was locked. I could've tried the back entrance, but the shitty thing about failure is how it kills your imagination.

* * *

The party wasn't as scandalous as the host had hoped. After five minutes of judging our half-naked friends, the novelty wore off. Julie held court in an upstairs bedroom with two girlfriends. She expected to be admired and envied. She was pissed when I declined to join her little display. I told her to find me when she got bored. I'd said nothing about saving Shii Ann. After midnight, Julie tugged my arm and said some creepy guy kept telling nigger jokes. The last one was kind of funny, she whispered. I took her home. She offered to suck me off, but all that near-nudity soured my mood.

At home, I wondered where Shii Ann slept. Was she heartbroken I returned too late? *You my American hero.* I wanted someone to tell me I'd tried my best, but that would mean reliving my fuck-up. My roommate asked why Julie had stopped coming over.

The next day, I took my smoke break at two, not three. The old Asian woman never appeared. It was another sweltering day. When I was about done with my cigarette, I heard glass breaking inside the store. Shit! I'd forgotten to lock the front door. This was why I believed in rules. The moment you break one, your world gets fucked.

Opening the back door, I heard glass break again. Some asshole was trashing the store. If it were Felix, I'd kick his scrawny ass. But when I dashed down the aisle, my urge to fight vanished.

The old Asian woman methodically pulled one whiskey bottle after another from a storefront display, smashing them at her feet. Her face was blank, her eyes small and black. What the fuck are you doing, I shouted. She stopped calmly as if I asked the time. She stepped over the jagged dark glass and approached. She wagged her finger in my face. You not come back, she said. You not pay for girl. You take her like wife. She grew louder, more intense. You never return, yes? Tell me you know this!

If you break one more goddamn thing, I said, I'm calling the police. The woman rocked back on her heels then smirked. You call police, Shii Ann say you rape her! She know men like you. I tell her men dishonor you.

Not sure if she was bluffing, I didn't risk it. By keeping this secret from everyone, I'd unwittingly made my behavior suspect. If you leave now, I won't tell anyone, I said. Please, ma'am. I slid my hand through my hair. I promised she'd never see me again. After a long silence, the woman broke into a loud, cackling laugh.

She was still laughing when the cowbell announced her departure.

It took me twenty minutes to sweep up the glass and mop the floor. The heavy musk of the booze filled the store, giving me a headache.

At Julie's I called Mr. McEntire and quit. I concocted some bullshit about my tough course load. He didn't try to change my mind. He asked me to collect my last check, but I told him to mail it. The thought of returning there mortified me. After I hung up, Julie asked why I'd lied. I told her it was complicated. She approached me, cupped my face in her hands. You're a complicated cat, Russell. The power was out again. I was shirtless; she wore a bra and cut-offs.

That night, we finally made love. I never asked if her condition had cleared—her eager hands were answer enough. As always, she kissed my forehead after I came inside her. We lay atop the sheets, her head nestled upon my shoulder. I wasn't tired. Neither was she. I wanted to ask her something. I wondered what I would do if I told Julie to wait for me on the sidewalk and returned to find her gone.

Sweetie, I said, do you need me or do you want me? Stillness swallowed my words. She gazed at me with a dropped jaw then roared with laughter. Did those chink whores give you a joint after they sucked your dick, she asked.

The next morning, she asked me if I ever learned the secrets of the tanning salon. I shoveled runny pancakes in my mouth. After swallowing, I smirked. We weren't in danger. I'd given the old Asian whore what she wanted. I told Julie there was a sign in the salon window. New Girls Wanted. Apply within. Julie rolled her eyes. I stopped sucking dick for money after high school, she said. I chuckled at first, but it escalated until I almost hacked up the pancakes. She demanded to know what was so funny, tapped her foot. I was still laughing too hard to speak. The girl I loved servicing some middle-aged goon—impossible. Julie grinned and challenged me to guess her identity. She crossed her eyes and babbled in broken English. Fifty dollar, fifty dollar! Me suck you good, me suck you hard! Fifty dollar, fifty dollar! Me love you long time! Doubled over, I tried to control myself. This was funny shit.

After she finished, she warned me about all the whores in the world. They're worthless cunts, she said. They belonged in dark rooms sucking fat cocks and never asking names. She forced my hand between her legs. Later, when I surged inside her, I found myself eager for her kiss on my forehead.

The Gospel on Giving Up

Angel Heinz considered calling him. She felt she deserved credit for at least that. She knew, though, that Mr. Northam would deny her request. Her probation sentence stipulated that she never spend the night away from her group home, Safe Haven, once a retirement home, shut down by the state after an old man died from five hundred ant bites.

At any given time, three to four dozen residents played their tacky games: smuggling booze inside soda bottles, making out in the laundry room, buying synthetic weed after their dealers finished football practice across the street. Esther, the manager, watched them like a skilled broker would the stock market. In fact, she was too busy defusing an argument between tenants, however, to catch Angel skittering into the lobby, out the door and into Lisbeth's waiting car.

The two women, Angel and Lisbeth, strolled down one of the wine aisles at the Spec's nearest to Lisbeth's house. Spec's was the omnipresent liquor retailer in Houston and its suburbs. The chain had its own mascot, a bespectacled white rabbit with perfectly erect ears. Lisbeth held out a bottle of red for Angel's approval.

"Get what ya want, honey. It's your money."

"Oh, I know." Lisbeth smiled. "It's just been so long since I played hostess."

A second and third bottle followed. Angel was surprised. Lisbeth typically hid vodka in her backpack at the day program. More than once, Angel had seen it. While Lisbeth chattered about this guy at the program whom she was certain wanted to flirt with her. Angel casually placed a six-pack of her favorite Belgian beer in the cart. She didn't ask permission. It would've been rude to interrupt her friend.

At checkout, Lisbeth handed the cashier a credit card but never lost focus on the tabloids' headlines of misfortune and mayhem desperate for her attention. Watching her friend, Angel tried to simmer her roiling envy. Lisbeth knew nothing of government assistance, and the carousel of shame it demands you board. She'd never have to lie about her teenage son in order to bilk enough benefits from the food stamp program.

Thirty-six years of frequent-flier miles and cash-back incentives: in a perverse way, breast cancer seemed a fair price for Lisbeth to pay. The ill woman glanced over her shoulder. "Monday in group, we'll give them the G-rated version of this weekend." Absently, she shook her leather handbag the size of a throw pillow. "That goes double for Deborah." Angel chuckled at her friend's shudder. *Lisbeth can be herself around me,* she thought. *Can't say that about the others.* Angel took the bags of booze, allowing Lisbeth to lead them out of the store.

As they crossed the lot, a young black man passed. His hand dove for his crotch when turning back to admire the women. If the forward young man in the striped Hillfiger and low-riding cargos had lewd intent for only Lisbeth, her friend wasn't worried. She had a pretty face, and now that she'd started the Adderall, the pounds would soon depart. It had taken nearly a month of whining about racing thoughts, impulsivity and an inability to focus, but the program's harried psychiatrist finally caved. When Angel reclaimed her focus, Lisbeth was wiggling her maroon-tipped fingers at the black man. She laughed and slapped her thigh.

"C'mon, Sunshine," Lisbeth called. "My buzz is wearing off."

When Lisbeth had asked Angel at the beginning of that week whether she could "babysit" her at Daniel's apartment that weekend, her first instinct was to say something rude but funny enough that Lisbeth would laugh and drop the subject. In the moment she actually considered the offer, however, Angel imagined two days spent in a life the state of Texas had made certain she'd never achieve. She didn't want the whole apple, just one crisp bite, the juice dribbling down her chin. The logistics of escaping Safe Haven for a whole weekend never occurred to her. Even then, she figured she would simply pack her bag and walk out the door. She craved freedom and opportunity, and those things never fall in your lap; you must take a risk. Also, of course, it was her only chance to survey Lisbeth's vast array of pain medications.

Angel noticed that her friend had removed the silk scarf from around her head. At the program, she steadfastly refused to expose her decimated chestnut locks. The scarves were almost sheer, blending with her remaining strands instead of obscuring them. Several therapists had asked if they were expensive. In the Spec's lot, Angel witnessed how fully Lisbeth's hair had returned. She made a mental note to ask if she might be parting ways with them.

"We haven't made plans for dinner," Lisbeth noted, her car chirping as she unlocked it.

"I thought you were on a liquid diet."

"The fuller your belly, the more you can drink."

Angel shrugged and smiled sadly. "Anything's fine."

"I'm serious, Sunshine." Desperation flickered across Lisbeth's face. "This weekend means so much to me. Tell me how I can make it special."

There was an Italian place on the city's west side. Angel knew Esther, the group home manager, took her married boyfriend there on her nights away from Safe Haven. *Your tax dollars at work*, she thought. She wanted to see the look on that bitch's face after her lowly tenant had dinner there.

"Sounds terrific," Lisbeth said.

Angel quietly shifted in her seat. "Remember, it's your money."

Turning the ignition, Lisbeth grinned. Angel felt wholly responsible for her bouncy spirit. "It's my money," her friend said brightly, "but it's *our* weekend."

The Secret of Sicily prided itself on a cramped dining area. Lisbeth called it "intimate," but Angel was reminded of quickie shelters erected after major disasters. She imagined Esther letting the married guy slip his hand between her knees. Diners bumped against their table, trying discreetly to pass.

They never got around to dinner. Lisbeth ordered a dirty martini and insisted Angel have the same. They tasted like old pennies. Warm and crackling like a campfire, Lisbeth kept repeating their drink order. Their plain waitress, more disconcerted with each return, finally asked after Lisbeth's sixth order if she could verify the merry woman's credit card.

"This is a man's name," the waitress said.

"I'm on the account," Lisbeth said. "Check with Capital One." The waitress scurried to the bar, Lisbeth barking their next order in her wake.

"Does Daniel care that you're buying me drinks?" Angel asked. Lisbeth lived with her older brother in a penthouse overlooking all the urban rot that living in a penthouse spares you. His business took him overseas for two weeks at a time. Lisbeth grew lonely, she told the group. Lonely and scared she'd get sick again.

"My brother's a peach." She tried to light a cigarette but Angel snatched the lighter and pointed to the "no smoking" sign on the wall, a homemade thing with ornate font. Lisbeth cackled. "My whole family is simply divine."

Angel looked sharply at her friend, the inspiration obvious in her eyes. "May I use your phone?"

Lisbeth gulped, as if the question shocked her. "You know what the judge said, Sunshine."

"Lisbeth, give me your phone." Her tone had turned hard. "I want to call my son."

Outside, the headlights, the streetlamps, the neon, the windows' warm glow—it was well after nightfall, but the city was as bright and alive as a pinball machine. Gripping Lisbeth's cell phone like a weapon, she tried to enter the crowd but soon retreated back toward the restaurant. She knew her son's number. Brody lived with one of Lisbeth's elderly aunts. The old woman believed no criminal should have contact with children, including those she birthed. Angel didn't have a cell phone. After missing payment after payment, no carrier would touch her without imposing monstrous fees. She was too scared to call her son from Safe Haven or from someone's cell at the program. If the old bitch grew angry with Brody, he'd wind up in foster care.

She'd fully intended to call him when she asked Lisbeth for her phone. Once it was in her hand, however, and she'd left the cramped restaurant, the whim's absurdity shamed her. She watched a couple, both dressed in pressed denim, pass. Their clasped hands swung back and forth, a metronome of safety.

She thought of Esther, likely furious that she'd gone. Holding Lisbeth's phone to her face unconsciously, as if someone on the other end had her total attention, Angel did the math and figured she could still make curfew if she and Lisbeth left right now. But she was drunk. *I've already snuck out*, she told herself, *that's the true insult. Does it matter when I return?*

Back inside, Lisbeth's head listed as she propped it up from the tiny table. Weaving through the other tiny tables, apologizing and wishing all these rich bastards would die and let her watch, Angel pondered wasting what cash she had on a cab back to Safe Haven. Brody was right—one day she'd have to become his *mother*, not just in name but in deed. Her face relaxed, eyes growing dull.

She didn't notice Lisbeth's watery glare until the woman spoke. "Did that bitch ever return my credit card?" Angel squeezed into her seat, missing the silent interest from the swarthy young men in polo shirts beside them. Lisbeth grunted. "It's like Daniel always says, the best way to make money is to take it from someone."

"Should we go vomit now, or can you make it back to your place?"

The first time Lisbeth had disclosed during group therapy that she called her brother's high-rise apartment building Nosebleed Heights, Angel and the others chuckled. They knew Lisbeth wouldn't continue her story until they offered some sort of reaction. Even Deborah had managed a tight smile that stopped at her eyes.

Angel clutched her friend to her side, Lisbeth's arm slung over her shoulders, her feet dragging the polished marble floor until they tumbled from her pumps. Daniel's apartment felt like an aquarium, floor-to-ceiling windows inviting the darkness. Angel had always fantasized about living in a space so opulent. She smirked wondering whether chocolate mints perched atop the pillows of the made beds.

"Which way to the bathroom, honey?" Angel hefted her friend higher against her side. "I'm not saying you're heavy, but I could use a little break."

Lisbeth's head twisted this way and that, in mock awe at her brother's shrine to his financial prowess. A stranger might've thought it was Angel who lived here. Lisbeth flailed her hand forward and slurred instructions to head toward a doorway spilling soft amber light.

While Lisbeth retched over the porcelain black toilet, her distress echoing through the apartment like a whole sorority losing its lunch, Angel's gaze fell upon the mirrored medicine cabinet. She didn't know whether this was Daniel's domain, abdicated to his sister, or shared by the two. Lisbeth made no effort at discretion when discussing her various narcotics for when booze couldn't blot the pain. Angel hadn't heard some names since her summer giving head to the janitor at an urgent care facility. The evening had been an arduous trek across a game board of distressing real estate, but that medicine cabinet was her Boardwalk.

The vomiting subsided into a series of spits. After that, Lisbeth carefully lifted herself to her feet, clutching the bowl for leverage as she stood. She announced that she always slept in Daniel's room when he was away. "You can sleep in my room." Lisbeth embraced Angel, the purulent spittle on her chin staining her guest's blouse. "My bed is extra comfy." Trying not to recoil from the warmhearted but foul assault, Angel promised to cook breakfast in the morning. She was banking on Lisbeth not remembering this; she feared the elaborate kitchen might mock her.

Angel waited at least a half-hour, Lisbeth's shallow breaths never breaking rhythm, before she crept into the bathroom. Once inside, she moved quickly. Behind the mirrored door, a cornucopia of pharmaceuticals greeted her, and she was shocked to discover a couple of names unfamiliar to even her. She'd planned on swiping a sample, like the pills were on a buffet, but realized she could swipe a whole bottle and Lisbeth wouldn't miss it. If she did, Angel would suggest that she'd lost them during a blackout. She touched a finger to each label and spoke the names silently, unsure whether to trust her luck. She finally grabbed one when Lisbeth's breaths had ceased. The apartment was silent like the bottom of a sea. She froze before the medicine cabinet, pill bottle in hand, and waited for some sound to reassure her. For a few moments—minutes?—she stood motionless, Lisbeth's muffled voice trailing from Daniel's bedroom. "You have no idea what I'm going through," she cried from Daniel's room. "Don't fucking pretend you do. I'm tired of your holier-than-thou shit." Her voice grew louder, more strangled. "Why answer the phone if you won't listen to me!"

Angel stood silently until the call ended with Lisbeth in helpless sobs. Slowly, a flush of heat expanding inside her, a feeling others might call shame, Angel crept back into the room on loan from her host. She crawled into Lisbeth's bed and looked out Lisbeth's window. When the immense night proved too stark, she stared dumbly at Lisbeth's walls until sleep came. The pill bottle resided at the bottom of her cheap canvas bag.

Angel woke, a dull ache webbed across her forehead, to find Lisbeth standing at her bedside. In a blue satin dressing gown with lace trim, she held a wide breakfast tray: coffee, toast, eggs, bacon and a newspaper folded so that the horoscope greeted her guest. Angel had forgotten her own empty promise to cook breakfast. The glass of orange juice emitted a familiar odor.

"No hangover is a match for a good screwdriver."

Angel slowly scooted to a sitting position amid the pillows and allowed Lisbeth to set the tray before her. "You're unstoppable." She felt compelled to say it again, but her host's smile signaled that Lisbeth wasn't there to listen. Angel downed the screwdriver in one gulp, her hangover departing like low morning clouds before a spring day. "I'm not sure food is such a good idea."

"When Daniel's here, I always make breakfast."

"That's…very thoughtful."

"Actually, that reminds me of what I wanted to discuss."

Chewing eggs surprisingly rubbery and salty, like fat, Angel listened, wanting to distract Lisbeth long enough to make sure the pills were still in her bag. Did her host rummage through guests' belongings while they slept? Long ago, when Angel had her own place, she didn't hesitate to comb through suitcases, backpacks, purses. It was a good way to collect pocket money. "You make me feel like we're in group." Angel chuckled, but it sounded small and dead.

"Daniel is thinking about getting a bigger place." Lisbeth rolled her eyes. "Yeah, I know. He hardly lives in this one, but that's not the point. He's offered to let me take over the lease, but there's no way I can afford the rent myself, not even with my savings." Her lips remained parted, poised to speak.

Angel could see the end of this exchange barreling toward her like an avalanche. The little bitch didn't have a clue, Angel thought, how desperately she scrimped and saved to sustain herself in Safe Haven. In Lisbeth's world, the beautiful and confident exchanged properties and cars like elementary children's lunches. Angel wanted to throw her tray against the soothing walls and scream. Instead, she smiled and nodded, a signal for Lisbeth to continue.

Her host beamed. "Sunshine, you wanna be my roomie?"

She had to live in a group home until her probation ended in three years. Mr. Northam tolerated no bullshit. Esther became a group home manager because busting the disturbed and indigent gave her a surge of power that some married dick never would. The day program was filled with people like Angel. They were desperate and clawing, knowing the dirt cascaded from above far too swiftly. Those pills in her bag were the only good things left in the world. These were just some of the things Angel Heinz believed.

From Lisbeth's bed, Lisbeth's guest nodded, a wide smile slapped across her face. "Slumber party!" She slid the breakfast tray from her lap and threw open her arms.

Lisbeth insisted they spend that afternoon shopping. She wanted Angel to pick out furniture and "accents" that made the apartment more hers. "I don't think that Middle-Aged Banking Savant is a good look for us," she confided as Angel struggled to keep up. The two women breezed through high-end furniture stores, making small talk with high-heeled salesladies, giggling in the car as Lisbeth did wicked impersonations of those same salesladies, and snacking on meals they ordered knowing they'd eat only a few bites. Angel tried not to imagine how far all that bread and beef and fruit would go if smartly rationed.

Several times during their forcibly carefree outing through Houston's upscale retailers and restaurants, Lisbeth's cell phone rang. She didn't answer, after the third time didn't acknowledge the sound. Inwardly panicked, Angel wondered if perhaps Esther or Mr. Northam had acquired her host's number and was trying to reach her. In her weakest moment, her mind bobbing inside the current of martinis, she wondered whether the caller was her son, Brody. *Mom, where have you been? Mom, it's been a long time.*

"It might be something important." Angel self-consciously gripped a handbag Lisbeth insisted perfectly matched her eyes.

"More important that you? Not likely, Sunshine."

"Is it Deborah?"

"This weekend is a Deborah-free zone."

"What if it's your brother?"

Lisbeth's gaze darkened. "What if it is?"

"Something might be wrong."

"When you shit money into a pot every damn day, everything's wrong."

"I just want this day to be perfect." Angel stunned herself—she meant every word.

Her eyes flickering again with benevolent fire, Lisbeth placed her hand on Angel's shoulder, stilling her. "Then let me worry about everything. This weekend is all about you."

Back at the apartment, all the dainty shopping bags surrounding them, Angel embraced Lisbeth. The gesture was genuine. Her opportunism was not a constant presence, but more like a blip on radar, blinking in and out of existence ad infinitum. Lisbeth smacked her friend on the cheek and announced that she needed a shower before they went out for dinner. "Not that damn Italian place again!" she called from another room. "Did that bitch ever return my credit card?" So encased in ecstasy, regardless of how quickly it would end, Angel never answered. The water jetting against the shower walls broke the spell.

Knowing she had only a few minutes, Angel dashed to the bedroom and dug through her duffle bag. Hallelujah! Painkiller Whatever was present and accounted for. She decided to down a few for levity's sake but needed a glass of water, or wine. As she scampered into the kitchen, a ringing phone startled her. It wasn't Lisbeth's cell but a sound more insistent and jarring. Daniel still had a landline!

After blundering among the knickknacks and small appliances littered over the tile countertop, Angel located the telephone. It was bulky and black. It had been ringing for eons. She didn't pick it up, though, trusting it would at some point stop, and it finally did. She backed away, as if the phone was a growling mutt, but when the ringing resumed, she snatched the receiver and whispered hello.

"Where the hell have you been, Lisbeth? I've been blowing up your cell all damn day!"

"Um…this isn't Lisbeth. It's…"

"And who might you be?" It was a man's voice, authoritative and hard.

"I'm her friend, Angel." The words fell in a torrent, useless and essential. "She invited me to stay this weekend. She was lonely. She always talks about how lonely she is. We had fun. She wants me to move in after you're gone. Isn't that nice? No one's ever asked me to—"

"Please stop. This is her brother. I just…need you to stop."

She almost hung up out of shame. She was relieved to hear the shower still running. What would Lisbeth do when Daniel told her about this conversation? Would she be forced to rescind the offer Angel couldn't feasibly accept for longer than this magical weekend? Her palms were damp and the night outside opened like a mouth.

"My sister doesn't need a roommate, Angel."

"But she said—"

"She went to the clinic last month. The cancer is back, spread everywhere." Daniel paused. "That little program helps her forget things. Angel, my sister doesn't need a roommate."

"I'm sorry, I—"

"She has three months if treatment goes well. If not…"

After hanging up, Angel gazed at the phone as if it were new and frightening technology from a parallel world. She could call Brody. Some nights, she wondered whether she remembered his voice or had simply invented one to soothe her anguish.

"Sunshine, why the long face? We out of booze?"

Angel spun around slowly. She muttered a weak excuse about looking at the skyline, but Lisbeth's attentions had already settled elsewhere. She straightened up a few throws pillows, flattened stray wrinkles in the runners covering pathways through the space. Angel watched her, willed herself to imagine this immense apartment without Lisbeth's presence. She pictured it collapsing, slowly and grandly, like a parade blimp with one tiny, tiny hole in its seam.

After waiting for Lisbeth to pass out in Daniel's room, Angel pulled the prescription bottle from her duffle bag. Growing up, whenever she heard her father or a teacher urge her to do "the right thing," typically after it was clear she would not, Angel always envisioned a small child slurping castor oil from a spoon. The right thing—how unpleasant. She downed a half-dozen pain pills then slipped into the bathroom and replaced the bottle in the medicine cabinet. After closing the mirrored door, she gazed at herself. Already, she saw a narrowing of her cheeks, a reduction of the bothersome bulge beneath her chin. If she could avoid Esther's wrath and Mr. Northam's revocation forms, the Adderall would bring results in just a month. She hoped Lisbeth lived long enough to see her new body.

Sunday morning, Angel woke to hear Lisbeth gabbing on the phone. Unlike her breakdown Friday night, today her friend sounded bubbly, her end of the conversation punctuated by piercing giggles. After climbing from bed and wincing to remember her beloved pills were no longer safe inside her duffle bag, she crept toward the den, Lisbeth's voice growing louder and merrier. She doubted her friend was speaking to Daniel, but who else could it be? Someone she called *sunshine*.

Angel halted, startled to hear her nickname tossed in the air for someone else to catch. She peered around the doorway, into the den, and found Lisbeth in her blue silk dressing gown, chattering while twisting her body as if warming up for aerobics. She was telling the caller how easy it would be to get her name on the lease. Her landlord, she assured the unknown caller, was very laissez-faire.

"It'll be wonderful, Sunshine. I'm talking to Daniel about it the moment he walks in."

Lisbeth's face fell after catching Angel in the doorway. Angel felt a series of weights flee from her, like pebbles plucked from a beaker, water filling all the resulting space. This revelation had accomplished the impossible: For a moment, Angel forgot her friend was dying.

"Sunshine, I'm sorry," Lisbeth said into the phone. "I have to call you back." Her friend rushed to her, hands actually clasped at her breasts, her diseased breasts, in search of forgiveness. She hadn't put on her makeup. Angel was amazed at how young and fresh-faced she appeared. "She's just a plan B," Lisbeth insisted. "You're the one I *want* to live here."

"Who is it?"

"No one. It's—no one, really. Someone from group."

"Who is it?" The panic in her heart didn't materialize in her voice.

"It's Deborah, Sunshine. I'm sorry I wasn't entirely truthful with you."

Angel shrank back from the doorway, the wall blocking Lisbeth from sight. She abruptly turned and rushed toward Lisbeth's room to toss clothes Lisbeth had bought into the canvas bag left on Lisbeth's floor so they could head back to Safe Haven in Lisbeth's car. Her friend lurked in the doorway as she numbly packed her things, and Angel wondered what had possessed her to give up those lovely, lovely pills.

An hour later, outside Safe Haven's busted double-door entrance, Lisbeth rammed her head through the driver's window and called Angel's name. She didn't turn around. She heard Lisbeth like she heard the traffic crossing the interstate a half-mile away, like she heard a rap song blaring from a second-story window. Lisbeth called her name again. Angel was too tired to resist.

"I'll see you in group tomorrow, right?"

Angel nodded. She wasn't sure if she would or not. It all depended on Esther.

"We had a good time, didn't we, Sunshine?"

Angel waved limply. Lisbeth's car zipped away as she entered the building. A few residents sat limp and dull among the foyer's ragtag furnishings. Dazed, Angel climbed the shuddering stairway to her room. She didn't glance over her shoulder as a second set of footsteps rushed to catch up.

"Where the hell have you been, Miss Heinz? I left a message with Mr. Northam last night, another one this morning. You better get ready to kiss some ass if you wanna stay in this establishment!"

Angel unlocked her room, shutting the door behind her. She knew Esther was too cowardly to force a physical confrontation. Her canvas bag dropped to the floor. She gazed about her small, colorless room, a space that cost most of her monthly government check. The one window looked out on a rusted, abandoned barbecue grill. The greasy sheets covering her flat twin mattress never looked clean no matter how often she washed. Unlike her neighbors, she saw no point in decorating. All that hung on the wall was a Polaroid of her son, Brody, in his white band uniform, proudly holding a tuba. She didn't look at the picture but trudged toward the window where she sat every night. While waiting for Esther to go away, she watched black birds atop the grill shake water from their feathers. The manager was still shouting outside the door, indignant about the many indignities of her life. *Let the bitch keep yammering,* Angel thought, *I pay my rent.*

Ten Bucks Says He Beats Her

So, I'm just standing there behind the register, and I'm wondering if Dex saw my new dye job on Twitter or Instagram or maybe Snapchat. I can feel my heart act the fool in my chest, and my skin gets hot. My hair is long and black, like the crazy chick from that old horror movie, *The Ring*. Seriously, I could be the girlfriend of some mass shooter, the one who knew what would happen but just stayed home and watched *The Price Is Right*. I think Dex will love it.

Wade hasn't mentioned it. He says I should, like, pay more attention. I've been here over a year, he says, and I've totally taken orders from baby-rapists and armed robbers. Maybe even a murderer. It's simple statistics, he says. He can't believe I'm not curious about the losers that want a cheeseburger and a shake. It doesn't matter. The child molester isn't molesting *me*, the armed robber isn't robbing *me*. Wade looks at me like I'm some pathetic freshman, still wearing Affliction shirts. I feel bad…or maybe I feel nothing. It's, like, the same sensation.

Anyway, while I'm thinking about Dex, I notice Wade staring out into the dining area. He asks me, he says, do you think that dude with his three kids is on meth? Before I turn to look, I roll my eyes and agree.

I took his order. He was sweating like a fat-ass in gym class. Even his wife-beater hung from shoulders, like he'd lost a lot of weight just last week or whatever. And when one kid opened her trap, he turned to the wrong kid, thought it was *her* talking. Oh, totally, I tell Wade. You should see if he wants to party.

Okay, fine. I'm a bitch. I know Wade is trying to live clean. I always imagine some Mexican maid when I hear that: *live clean*. All my thoughts and prayers are with him, but he was eye-fucking that speed freak. Seriously.

That old fossil, Eileen, shuffles our way. She's a team leader, *not* a manager. She's either too brain-dead to know the difference or she has major control issues. Have those feed-sack tits ever pointed out instead of down?

So, Wade asks Eileen if there's anything we can do about Father of the Year, and she says no. He might sue. Oh, and two of the kids are totally sobbing now. The other customers stare, but think about it: do you care who's watching when you're high? One customer glares at me, so evil, like it's my fault the crying won't stop. I'm, like, eat your burger, bitch. Not really, that would be super-dumb, but when I imagine myself doing it, I feel badass.

Now Wade's waiting on some Crossfit creature and his skinny little slut. She won't look at anyone but him, and when Wade asks her what she wants, he totally answers for her. So, like, they go find a table, and Wade leans over and whispers, *Ten bucks says he beats her.* Hell no, Elmo! Some asshole hits me, I go into bitch mode.

Loser Eileen hasn't left. She whispers to Wade that she'll take his ten and raise him another ten. Like, why hasn't she left? She tells us her ex-husband used to slap her around and call her a whore. That was a total over-share. You don't tell your friends that personal crap, and we're not even her friends. She says women who stay with those types of men secretly like it. I'm, like, go away, Eileen!

The phone won't stop ringing. Cashiers don't have to answer, and that gives the other losers who work here one more reason to hate us. If I could answer, I'd say, this is Busy Burger, what the fuck? Actually, it's my mom on the line. I bet she and Eileen talk about how old and sad they both are. I'm totally kidding.

So, anyway, my mom can't pick me up from work. The next shift will be here in half an hour. I'm totally fucked. Wade's the only one who can help. Everyone back in the kitchen ignores me. So fucking rude. Just because they're no good at English and I'm an actual American. Anyway, Wade has a cow when I ask for a ride. He says his boyfriend is waiting, and he can't be late. If he can't drive me, I tell him in my little-girl voice, I'll have to walk home in the dark. Men in cars might slow down, lean out their windows and call me *baby*. They might rape me, and my friend in biology says rape sucks in ways you can't even imagine. He finally says okay, but we have to go to his place first.

* * *

I've always wondered how Wade landed such a sweet ride. It's some tricked-out Corvette that's older than me. It feels awesome outside, but he won't take the top down. He'd die if any of his anal-entry buddies knew he worked at Busy Burger. He won't even friend me on Facebook 'cause why else would he know a sixteen-year-old girl.

I ask if we can have some tunes. This dude totally still listens to actual radio stations, like, with towers and contests and shit. Doesn't he know satellite radio is so much better? He gets this really annoying look. He's reminding me that he's the adult and I'm not. I just keep smiling. It doesn't fucking matter 'cause the news is on, so I space out for a bit. I hate the news. It's just a bunch of sad and scary crap that happens to people I don't know and never will.

Ugh. Some Marine walked into the mall in, like, Omaha and just went thug-life on everyone. Thirty-five people are definitely dead, but a few more might bite it in the hospital.

Wade's looking really serious right now. He's having a grown-up moment and I'll never get it because no grown-up will explain them. Seriously, I'm not sure he even remembers I'm here. He's pretty cute—and a year older than my dad in Florida. I've never met my dad, but I've seen pictures. Wade's arms are stringy but his legs are thick and have sexy tone. He calls it the Busy Burger workout. That's funny. He has a kind face, but Mom says gay dudes can be tricky and I should watch out.

I hope she's okay. Whenever she calls at work with whatever excuse, I can't make myself believe her. I try real hard and I try to remember all the cool things my mom has done, but she's a total liar. Seriously, my mom is kind of a whore, but whenever she calls and Eileen answers, I'm just glad she remembered me.

Fuckin' people, Wade says, what's the goddamn point? The sun's setting, and the glare's a bitch. We're both squinting, and we can't really see each other. I think that's a good thing right now. When I finally find his face, it's so heartbreaking. He's trying so hard not to cry, but seriously, mass shooting bullshit has been happening, like, since I was in diapers. This is America. Some people win the lottery and other people get shot in the face. It's all luck. Seriously, build a bridge and get over it.

I check my phone. No texts from Dex. Hey, that rhymes. I'm badass like that. I'd love to be his play-cousin, but thinking about the whole fucking script every high school girl has to play out just to get a guy—it makes me tired. That sad and empty feeling sneaks up on me.

We exit the freeway. I don't know Wade's telling me a story till, like, he's already started. He was a grad student at, like, that big-ass university in Austin. He lived in a co-op, which sounds like a dorm except you can visit any room you want. Sweet. Wade had invited some random dude to spend the weekend with him. He had his own room. His name was Duncan. Wade announces that he loved him, but I don't believe him. Seriously, I don't think he believes himself. They were flipping channels and all the big networks and cable news were airing video from a big, ugly school in Colorado. It looked like a prison, he says. There were tons of cops, high school kids filing out holding their hands together behind their heads. It sounds like a rap video, except everyone is white because it's Colorado.

Columbine, he says, was the first major mass shooting at an American school. The news couldn't stop blabbing about it. They dug up dirt on people who just happened to know people from there. Six degrees, you know? Wade says America lost her innocence that day, and—I can't help it—I laugh like a retard. For the first time since he started his story, he looks at me. He doesn't, like, look hurt or whatever. He just looks *done*.

I remind him that the Omaha shootings were in a mall, not a school. Also, and I'm not trying to be a bitch, but no one's gonna miss a few Kansas rednecks, anyway.

He sounds big and hollow, like a drum. Omaha is in Nebraska, Nikki. Nebraska, not Kansas.

He pulls in under a carport, parking in a numbered slot. This complex looks major shady. A few tenants, none of them white, not that I pay attention to that kind of thing, pretend they're not watching. Horrible Tejano music thumps against the passenger window. When I step out, it feels like the woofer is right beside my fucking head.

Two toddlers are playing in the tiny-ass yard in front of his neighbor's unit. Even their Barbie dolls look ghetto. Most of the hair is pulled out and they're naked. While I'm watching them, one kid takes her doll, with its pointed feet, and stabs the other in the eye. Seriously, it's fucking disturbing. I'm practically up Wade's ass, I'm so scared. The toddler who got stabbed in the eye screams for mommy. The trashy bitches watching me and Wade the whole time, none of them give a shit.

Wade pulls me inside and slams the door. It has four separate, individual locks.

As he slides the last deadbolt into place, I totally remember my fucking phone. It's still in the passenger seat. Seriously, I tell him, someone could steal it. What I don't tell him is I'm still hoping Dex will call. Wade shushes me, like, actually shushes me like I'm a baby, says we have to talk quiet. Chuck is resting down the hall in their bedroom. Five minutes, he says. Just give me five minutes and I'll take you home. Promise? I know when my mom makes a promise, it means zippo if a man calls after that. I need to think of some bullshit story for why I'm getting home so late. Wade promises just five minutes. He kisses my forehead and it's, like, something a dad would do. I mean, I'm not sure about that. I've seen it on TV.

He gently takes my hand, like I'm blindfolded or whatever, and we enter a dark room. He guides me to a recliner. I can make out just enough to see a lamp beside me. When I reach for it, Wade smacks my hand like I'm five and he's the boss of me. Hell no, Elmo! I call him an asshole. Seriously, I'm not quiet about it. The Tejano music bleeds through the walls. We should keep things dark, Nikki. Just trust me.

I sigh, make a big deal out of it, and fall back into the recliner. His footsteps fade down the hall. I hear a door open and shut. Five minutes. I can totally handle five minutes. I've always wanted to know how faggots decorate their homes. Seriously, I've heard rumors. I'm tempted to turn on the lamp anyway.

You goddamn cocksucker, what did you promise me?!?

Dude, from the room at the end of the hall! Shit just got real. The voice is so hoarse and strained, I can't tell if it belongs to Wade. I wouldn't know if it's Chuck. A few bumps and screeches. Whatever it is, it's totally gotten physical.

One man shouts about why something shouldn't make a difference, and the other says that he didn't marry some bathhouse slut. A thump, and then a real weak yelp. Seriously, hit a guy just right, any guy, and he'll whimper like a girl.

One man slaps the other. Palm against cheek, like, you can't mistake it. Fuck this shit. I switch on the lamp. Big-ass framed pictures on the walls kinda look like art—or, like, what grown-ups call art when they don't wanna look dumb. The furniture matches. I'm totally afraid to touch anything.

This must be Chuck! I check out a framed portrait of Wade, smiling like a total idiot, embracing another man. He's not smiling. Not at all. The picture stands inside a bookcase filled with no actual books. Chuck, tall and built and intense, like, reminds me of pictures in my history textbook, the ones of Vikings out to rape and pillage. Wade's gonna get his ass kicked! I need a weapon. The Tejano music sounds so goddamn happy. Seriously, Mexicans don't have that much to be happy about.

I scoot my way into what seems to be the kitchen. When I find the light switch, there's a butcher's knife lying beside the sink. Grabbing it, I'm ready to kick, like, some serious ass. I step deliberately down the hall, closer and closer to the bedroom at the end. Now I can hear the whole conversation.

One man, crying out, says in a pleading voice that he was lonely. Jesus, why do old people always complain about being lonely? Seriously, if all the lonely old people hooked up, it would solve so many problems. This doesn't sound like Wade. The voice is higher, more girly, but maybe that's just because he's upset. But what follows is, like, definitely Wade. He asks how many bitches have been in their bed. I assume *bitches* still means men. There's an awful silence, broken only by whimpering and the Tejano bullshit. There's another smack, but it's not palm against face. I've got my ear to the fucking door, my free hand inching toward the doorknob, like I totally have a plan once I'm inside. Please, one man begs— I can't tell who anymore—the bleeding won't stop.

That instant the door swings open, and I stumble into their bedroom. It was dumb, like, to put all my weight against it. I still have my knife. I'm still ready to kick ass. The bedroom looks sterile and scary, like a museum that isn't free.

This must be Chuck. He's definitely the man in the picture, the one not smiling. He's not smiling now, either. Someone, like, split his head open. His blond hair is drenched with blood—it's streaming down his face. Seriously, he's on his knees, and he's reaching out to me. Why? He doesn't—no, he's reaching to someone behind me.

Wade holds the golf club like I'm holding the knife. We're both ready for action. But the look on his face—I don't know if it's, like, meant for me or Chuck. His eyes are alive but totally cold, his nostrils flared, teeth bared. Finally, I notice blood dripping from the club, oozing down the shaft onto Wade's hands. Seriously. Five minutes, he says, still glaring at Chuck. I told you to give me five minutes.

Fuck my life.

Chuck reaches out again, this time definitely to me. He begs for help. I'm backing out through the doorway. I, like, totally want my mom. I know Wade will keep beating him. I'm still holding the knife like I plan to do something badass. I haul ass.

The knife clatters to the floor. I hear the golf club strike poor Chuck two or three times while I unbolt all four of the locks. Seriously, part of me is convinced that when he's done with Chuck, he'll come after me. I'm, like, a witness, right? I had no idea gay guys beat up one another. I thought they were, like, too busy fucking. I tear open the door. That's when I hear Wade, still in the bedroom. Nikki! He sounds normal again, the guy who bullshits with me at Busy Burger—but I am *not* taking that chance.

I dash into the parking lot, totally freaked. Oh, fuck. Wade drove me here. I don't know this part of the city. Seriously, where the fuck *am* I? I'm sweating and shaking. I need to call someone…my phone! I rush over beneath the carport to his ride, and for real, like, there's my smartphone lying on the passenger seat. I press my hands and forehead against the window, like a father admiring his newborn in the nursery. It's, like, ringing. That's what the screen display means. The caller is stored in my contacts, so I see only his name: Dex.

* * *

So, I was helping my friend, Angelique, vomit into a plastic wastebasket when I met him. The party was last weekend. Seriously, I only knew half the kids there.

Me and Angelique were in a bedroom on the second story. I, like, knew it was a boy's room: a basketball team's schedule and roster were tacked on a wall, several posters of various players at the hoop. He had *Star Wars* sheets and pillowcases. I wanted to meet him. He was either too good to be true or too much of a loser for words.

She threw up again. In between episodes, she moaned. Like, why am I such a slut? Her head, like, rolled to the side, vomit spraying everywhere. I held her up. I don't even like sex, she said. I almost said maybe she was doing it wrong, but I heard a boy in the doorway.

He asked if he was interrupting anything. I said yes and thanked him. He laughed, and I totally got a little excited inside—but just inside. He asked if I needed help. Seriously, I'd been thirty seconds from letting her drown in her own vomit, but I knew sticking by Angelique's side would impress him. Loyalty means so much more to boys than girls.

We traded our names and all the basic, party-talk crap. We went to neighboring schools, so it was weird we'd never met. It totally bummed me out I might never see him again. Already, I was, like, starting to mourn.

His lips were so plump, I wanted to laugh. He had one hazel eye and one green eye. Seriously, he said they both changed color depending on what he wore. I really laughed this time, for real, and called him a liar. He smirked and insisted he take me out and prove it. Our heads edged closer together, our eyes closing and lips parting. We were seriously going to make out.

Angelique's head, resting on the wastebasket's rim, slipped off and hit the floor. Hell no, Elmo! I was so bummed, I wanted to, like, smack her. To be continued, Dex said. I asked if he wanted my number. I was so fucking pumped, I rode that wave all night.

* * *

So now, in the parking lot, I'm watching my smartphone click over to voicemail. Dex's name, like, disappears. I think I'm gonna cry. I'm totally going to sob.

There's a sharp stab in my hip and I glance down to see Psycho Toddler, like, poking at me with her broke-ass Barbie. You don't live here, she says. You're a stranger. She repeats it over and over, seriously, like it's some sort of spell. I'm backing up, like, deeper into the lot, resisting the urge to smack her because I totally couldn't handle jail. Her face is scrunched so tight, her mouth and nose and eyes all jam together. She keeps stabbing me with the doll. I totally tell her to stop, and she totally ignores me.

Wade is in his front yard, calling to me, before I realize he's outside. I start, like, backing up faster. A blue Tahoe honks at me then swerves around. Seriously, does he not see me? Wade is apologizing. Nikki, please. He says Chuck is totally fine now. He says he'll, like, take me home. The girl won't stop. *You don't live here. You're a stranger.*

An old black Buick screeches to a stop beside me. A heavy Mexican leans out of the driver's window, asks me if I'm okay. Seriously, he calls me *baby.* He shifts his gaze to the little girl and his voice gets totally gruff and scary. He's, like, speaking Spanish, I guess. Anyway, the girl gets spooked and runs off.

Now Wade is coming closer. He's limping. Maybe Chuck, like, got in a shot or two during his beating. I totally hope so. In English, the Mexican asks if this man is bothering me. I dash around the hood to the passenger side, throw open the door and hop in. I lock the door just as Wade reaches the car. Seriously, he pounds on the window, blood streaking from his hands. I hear him saying *sorry*, like, over and over again. The Tejano music has totally stopped. I don't know exactly when. The Mexican asks if I need a ride. I should totally be scared, but all I can see is Chuck, bleeding from his head and reaching. I tell the Mexican to, like, just fucking go.

His name's Fidel. We're almost to the freeway before he asks my name. Alison, I tell him. Alison, he repeats with what I'm totally sure is a smirk. Seriously, he doesn't believe me. He clears his throat, I guess to change the mood or whatever, and asks if that man, Wade, *touched* me. I finally turn to him and, like, scoff.

He switches on the radio. I'm hoping for some tunes, seriously, but it's an all-news station. He, like, totally doesn't do the satellite thing, either. Omaha this and Omaha that. Now thirty-eight dead. I wanna turn that shit off. But, seriously, he'll think I'm a heartless bitch. And maybe I totally am. I think about Chuck reaching out, like, first for Wade—and then for me.

Instead, he talks over the announcer. He deals with a lot of young people in bad situations, he says. It's, like, his calling. Ever since his little sister was strangled to death by her boyfriend, during his senior in high school, he's totally made it his mission to save *troubled*—he hits that word hard—youth from terrible fates. Seriously, I guess I could've asked more about his sister, but then he totally would've told me, and I for sure don't wanna know.

He tells me to look in the floorboards. I noticed getting in that there were two shopping bags full of loose papers. Keeping my eye on him, more to convince myself that, like, I was worth harming than out of a fear of being harmed, I pulled out part of one stack. Missing posters, like you find stapled to telephone poles and bus stops. I flip through the stack, every sheet a totally new face, always smiling. Seriously, why do missing kids always know to smile before they disappear? That's cool, I tell him. That sadness and emptiness are totally eating at me, stronger and stronger the longer we drive.

You gotta tell me your address, he says, so I can take you home. You *can* go home, right? It's a safe place? I've, like, never thought of it in those terms, and I nod because I totally didn't wanna start thinking about it now. He'll enter the address in his GPS. I'm seriously gutted. I can't face my mom if she's there, and I can't face the house if she isn't.

You don't live here. You're a stranger.

I totally remember Dex's address. This could totally work out. He's already been calling me. Faking a yawn, totally stretching to make it look good, I tell Fidel that I'm gonna sleep, like, until we get to my house, really Dex's house. He switches off the radio. Omaha goes back where it came from. I'm not tired, for sure, but I shut my eyes. There's nothing to see but, like, streetlamps and billboards.

* * *

So, I wake up and pink and green neon totally blind me. It borders each window and forms the letters spelling out Busy Burger. Seriously, we were parked where I worked. Shit just got real. My armpits are damp and gross. For a second, I'm fucking clueless about who brought me here. That's when I see them.

Fidel's suit is two sizes too small. I can't believe his wife, like, let him out of the house. He has his back to me, chatting up that crone, Eileen. For real. She hands him a bag of food and cardboard drink carrier holding two cokes. She's laughing, she slaps his arm. God, she's a loser. It must totally suck to be old and still needing to flirt. Like, each rejection could be your last.

I'm freaked she'll glance outside and see me. I'm literally, seriously fucking shaking. It's way past midnight, and this is the only fast-food shitbox still open. Fidel's Buick is the only car in the lot. I, like, sink deeper into the passenger seat, my feet fighting those creepy MISSING posters for space. Inside the car, I can't hear a damn thing until Fidel opens the driver-side door. He's trying to be quiet. The dumbass must think I'm still asleep. The food must be for me, too, the trashy skank from the suburbs who was stranded in a seriously shitty neighborhood. I need a fucking telethon!

He eases behind the wheel. You must be hungry, he says. I smile, but it's totally fake. Not even fake-real, just fake-fake. He says he's sorry, he knows Busy Burger is kinda nasty. I wanna defend this hellhole, but it's probably just the urge to defend myself. Fuck it, the sooner we're back on the highway, the sooner we get home—well, you know, what this enchilada thinks is my home.

He hands me a cheeseburger and strawberry shake. I guess it's time to, like, say thank you. Fake-real, not fake-fake. I seriously don't even notice Eileen standing outside the driver-side door, at least not until her weak-ass knock on the window.

Fuck, fuck, fuck! There's no time to hide. Fidel rolls down the window. Won't get far without this, she says. She's smiling, the cow totally can't stop flirting. She's, like, clutching a leather wallet, handheld up for the dumbass to see. Her feed-sack breasts, like, push against the door. He thanks her. Of course, sir, I'm just glad I caught you before—

Shit, she spots me. This night is such a clusterfuck. No doubt, she doesn't expect to see one of her workers, like, riding shotgun with a fat Mexican in a jacked Buick. Fidel can't see me slowly shake my head, my signal for her to seriously shut the fuck up. Her face falls and she, like, ages five years in two seconds. She, like, wishes us goodnight. Well, she wishes *him* goodnight.

We back out of the lot, and I seriously keep my eyes on Eileen. She's watching from the side entrance, pink and green neon making her look like a Glo-Stick at a fucking rave. This is totally, seriously, for sure beyond fucked. I'm already thinking of explanations for when I see her again.

Fidel holds his cheeseburger in one hand, steering with the other. The GPS tells us to exit the highway. Dex lives close. As we enter the neighborhood, fancy two-story homes lit up by streetlamps, fear explodes in my chest, my heart totally pounding. I'm, like, staring at every house on every block, seriously, like I don't know his address by heart.

Nice neighborhood, he says. This tamale doesn't even know my name. He doesn't have a fucking clue that part of me wonders how it feels to see your own face on a MISSING poster, and, like, you can't remember why anyone would look for you. We pull up in front of a house when GPS tells us we're there. Seriously, there's nothing left to say.

Dex's house is made of bricks, the windows tall and slender, like dominos. Lights glow in every one, and I remember Dex's room: second-story, last window on the left. The night we met, when I was babysitting that fucking lush, Angelique, it seriously exists in a far corner of my mind. Is that because it's precious or because it's, like, meant to be forgotten?

I push open the passenger door. He asks if I want him to wait and, like, make sure my ass makes it inside. My mouth is totally dry, and I'm suddenly aware of everything, every fucking star, every fucking blade of grass. My dad is a little racist, I tell him, my voice seriously shaking. He'd freak if he saw me get out of a Mexican's car. I totally say it nice, though.

His face goes hard and spooky, like a mask. Racist, huh? Must run in the family, he says all hateful. What a douche!

His tires screech as he speeds away. For real, I thought he liked me at least a little bit. He was hating on me all the way from the city. Being shady about it, too. I don't get people. Wade's voice is, like, in my head, telling me to wake the fuck up and pay attention. My eyes are tired, and I want to rub but it would totally ruin my makeup.

I take a deep breath and, like, let it out slow. I knock on the door, softly, like I'm afraid of hurting it. Then I notice the doorbell. Even though heavy footsteps clomp down the stairs, I seriously press it anyway. Rich people have the most complicated doorbells.

Dex's chest is, like, heaving and his cheeks are totally flushed. He seriously looks like the answer to any question ever asked. Hey, he says, and I can see it in the blankness of his face: he doesn't fucking remember me! I'm totally crushed, but I keep my shit together. I don't know what else to do. Then he blinks and swallows. Like, there I am. I've landed in front of him, like a spaceship.

Oh my God, Nikki, what happened to you? You look…

That's right. My hair, my totally black hair. I'm, like, the mass shooter's girlfriend. Actually, I'm no one's girlfriend. What're you doing here? I shake my head and can't look at him. Seriously. Look at me, he says. He totally says that to me. His face is, like, a bonfire and I wanna stay warm. His mismatched eyes, those lips that for sure make me wanna laugh. What did you do to your hair, he asks. I hope my face isn't asking the question, too. You don't like it? I twirl in place, like I'm showing off a new dress. My stupid black hair fans out and slaps him in the face. Seriously, he laughs. You can stop now, he says. We smile at each other and the whole night seems, like, totally worth it. I might never go home.

I totally don't hear her slipping down the stairs. What the hell? I hear her screeching voice from above. It's Angelique. She's upright. Fucking bitch. No wonder she hasn't been returning my texts.

She stands still behind Dex, her hand on his shoulder like he's her child. Her face is, like, hard and still like a frozen pond. Dex never looks back at her. I totally think about the Crossfit asshole and his girlfriend from Busy Burger. We're just watching some DVDs, he says. Wanna hang out?

Angelique grabs his arm and hisses his name. I'm invisible and unavoidable, like, at once. I tell them I have to go. I don't have a car, but I'm already backing off the porch. I almost fall on my ass. *You don't live here. You're a stranger.*

Right then, sprinkler heads pop out of the lawn and begin to fucking spit, long and fast. I'm, like, soaked within seconds. Dex tries to help, but my bitch ex-friend grabs his arm. I totally should've let her drown in her own vomit. He calls after me as I sprint across the grass.

The neighbors' porch lights are flashing on, and I realize how seriously late it is. What the hell was I thinking? Wade was right. I don't pay attention.

Ten bucks says Dex fucks her. Ten bucks says I cry like a baby.

Fuck my life.

The night feels cool against my skin and wet clothes. My feet throb from running in sandals.

I slow down. There's a serious knot in my chest. I don't know where I am. It's totally a neighborhood just like Dex's— same nice houses, same starry sky. My phone is for sure gone by now.

I'm walking downhill on some street when, like, headlights appear at the hilltop. They're fucking spooky. It's a car, and it's totally slowing down. I recognize its light green body, the grill seriously gunked with dead crickets and flies and beetles. The Pontiac almost comes to a stop as it pulls up beside me.

Eileen asks if I'm all right. Baby, she says, you're soaking wet and it's late. I, like, don't look at her. If that fossil figures out I've been crying, she'll wanna know why, and right now? I totally might tell her. C'mon, she says, get in the car. I tell her I can't go home and seriously pick up my pace, even though I still feel that knot in my chest, that sad and empty feeling that never fucking disappears completely. We're not going to your house, she says, we're going back to work.

While she drives us back to Busy Burger, I wait and wait for her to bring up Fidel. She must, like, think I'm a total slut or maybe even a real-life hooker. Instead, she tells me the graveyard cashier flaked. Eileen rolls her eyes. Her feed-sack breasts press against the steering wheel. I dry my hair with a SpongeBob beach towel she keeps in the back seat. I swallow, my damp hair tumbling down my back. Instead of a pity fuck, I'm getting a pity ride. I thought she was gonna ask me to sub for the flake, and I guess I'm disappointed that she didn't.

You hear what happened in Omaha, she asks. That's in Nebraska, I answer, and I'm totally proud of myself. We're getting into town, the strip malls all dark despite the halos of light from the streetlamps. Fucking creepshow. Hell of a thing, she says. You kids think this is normal, but I promise it's not. I'm totally, seriously, for sure tired of hearing about Omaha. I got tired of hearing about Orlando and Lafayette and Sandy Hook and Dallas and Blacksburg and San Bernadino and Columbine and—

Our sudden stop in front of the restaurant jolts me. Pink and green neon reflect of the hood of Eileen's car. Seriously, what am I supposed to do while Eileen works, while all the alkies and dopeheads and losers order their burgers and shakes? Welcome to Busy Burger, now fuck off!

Did he *touch* you? She's smiling at me, but it's a different kind of smile. I totally wanna trust it. I think of Chuck bleeding from his head, reaching for me. Shit's been real the whole fucking night. I think of Dex flinching as my stupid black hair slaps his face. I slowly shake my head. It's not true. At least, tonight it's not true.

Eileen guides me through the dining room, her totally wrinkled fingers clutching my arm. A ring with a slim band and a small, clear stone catches my eye. Seriously, I thought she was divorced. Her husband, like, beat her, she sent out a group email. She shuffles away, calling out for coffee, leaving me in a corner booth. It's for one of the sketchy customers, I guess. Instead, she returns and places a steaming cup on the grimy table. My hands slip around it, like, seriously eager for warmth. She asks if Mom lets me drink coffee. When I shake my head, she totally winks at me and returns to the register. I guess she's being nice to me because I'm a total joke, but right now, that's fine by me.

I gaze out at customers, some of them washed in pink and green neon from the windows, making them look like video-game characters. Attention, Wade said I didn't pay attention. Fuck him, I'm totally paying attention now. My gaze leaps from, like, one customer to the next, and I'm deciding, deciding...

My attention zips to a couple stomping through the glass entrance. Well, the chick is stomping. Her light blue clogs seriously pound the linoleum. Black nylon stretches over her scrawny arms and legs. Her fingernails and toenails are fucking black, too. Jesus fuck. Corduroy short-shorts, like, ride up her ass. On her T-shirt, a flurry of small, pink hearts fall behind the words **Kiss Me Goodbye**, the phrase distended beneath her bobbing breasts.

The guy trailing her is a total afterthought. His dark green letterman jacket seems to be wearing him. He's gotta be at least thirty. Seriously, I should be taking notes. I'd fucking rub Wade's nose in them until the ink, like, smudged and shit.

In front of Eileen's register, she orders for both of them. While she barks her order, the man sneaks a look, across the dining room, at me. I'm totally not going to break my stare. The woman keeps changing her mind and bitches at Eileen when she can't keep up. Marching into the dining room, the stupid bitch doesn't even check to, like, make sure the guy hasn't bailed.

With her black fingernail, she points at a booth in a corner of the room. We're separated by several tables. The man makes a last glance, seriously asking for help, totally desperate just to be seen.

I keep staring. I pay attention. I make up my mind.

My black hair is fierce. When Eileen asks if I want a refill, I whisper, *Ten bucks says she beats him*. Eileen, like, totally laughs and slaps my arm. Oh, gross, I think we're friends now. She pretends her hand is a gun, one finger pointed at me and her thumb raised. It's like we've worked together for years, and this is our shtick. She winks and fires. That bitch seriously shoots me in the face.

It Starts with a Girl in Trouble

Buzzcut: The Massacre Begins

Ruth and the other kids screamed at her to run, but Candace was already running. She ran faster than Ruth had ever seen. From inside the school bus, she watched her best friend gasp for air. Her small breasts jiggled beneath her tattered T-shirt. The masked psycho must've ripped it somewhere in the woods. You could see her bra. Dear God, Ruth thought, she'd be so embarrassed to die looking like that.

The kids in the bus sucked in their collective breaths, the surprised air whooshing inside them, as Candace stumbled and groped blindly for the ground. She recovered. The masked psycho was catching up, his chainsaw wielded casually in one hand. Its roar might be the last thing Candace hears, Ruth thought. Her mother had warned her against this trip. Panicked anew, Ruth screamed for her to run faster, she was almost safe.

The masked psycho was clever, though. He'd been slaughtering barely-dressed teens for years. As Candace leapt over a dry ditch, a few hundred feet from the bus, the psycho hurled his chainsaw. Candace was slim and strong. Ruth often complimented her figure. But the weight of the chainsaw, its mad spinning propulsion, was too fiendish to escape.

There was a burst of blood, followed by Candace's startled yelp. The kids on the bus couldn't stop watching. If they defied this horror by not turning away, perhaps it would vanish. Ruth, however, turned away. Her screams hadn't helped, so she stopped. In the field, Candace cried out in agony. Soon enough, though, she didn't. The kids kept screaming. Ruth wished they'd be quiet. She worried that every time she remembered Candace, she'd hear only the screams.

Masquerade Madness II: Butcher in Disguise

No one expected Ruth to dance. She was the sort of girl who looked at the popular boys a moment too long. Notice them, Candace had urged, but don't *stare*.

The two girls stepped cautiously through a darkened doorway allegedly leading to a bathroom. Candace had big news and Ruth knew she'd be the first to hear. A cackle erupted from a dark corner, and Candace grabbed Ruth's arm. The scared girl was obligated to be scared—she was dressed like a Japanese schoolgirl. Ruth placed her hand over her friend's, promised it was just a cat. Something smells rotten in this house, Candace said, the scare forgotten.

The girls found the bathroom. It was small and the exposed bulb cast long, dripping shadows over their faces. A green vinyl curtain obscured the shower. Anyone could be waiting to leap out. Grinning and clapping, Candace told her best friend that Brock finally said he loved her. Isn't that the best! I was starting to worry!

Ruth was still worried. That ugly sound hadn't been a cat—she just hated seeing Candace scared. Something did smell rotten in this house. While her friend's face froze in bafflement, Ruth ripped open the shower curtain. Enough grime for ten showers, all of it green and brown and clinging. That's fucking gross, Candace said. Ruth agreed but relief washed over her anyway. Ruth knew it was her job to point out things only a plain girl could see. She had opinions about

Brock, but they could wait. She was dressed liked a doctor, complete with white lab coat. Her mother thought a nurse's outfit would make her look cheap.

Relieved, Candace opened the bathroom door, and Ruth watched the meat cleaver sink into her face. Too shocked to scream, she watched Candace twirl around the bathroom, blood spraying in jets, arms flailing she sank to her knees, to her hands and then flat on the tiles.

Ruth hadn't seen the psycho. He remained in the dark, in the adjoining room. It never occurred to her the psycho might kill her next. She knelt beside Candace's corpse, her lab coat soaked with red. She started to cry, wondering how she'd break the news to Brock.

Maniac Inside Me III: Weekend Cabin Nightmare

Ruth read quietly in the den. It was a Western, one she had read before. She liked confronting moral ambiguities safely wedged inside an alien world of dust, pistols and sassy madams. Finally, she placed the book face down on her lap. She'd read the same page five times.

She was kidding herself trying to concentrate on anything, anything but Candace's whispered confession at the bonfire that she and Brock planned to finally have sex that night. He won't wait much longer, she'd said. Besides, maybe I'll like it. Ruth had smiled and hugged her friend. She knew Brock had already scored two blowjobs that weekend from sluts now upstairs having sex with their actual boyfriends. She knew to hold her tongue.

Just as the two girls started back toward the bonfire, the class trickster popped out from behind a tree. He wore a rubber werewolf mask and snarled. After they recovered their breaths, the girls laughed. After he pulled off the mask, Candace pecked his cheek. From that moment forward, Ruth didn't exist for him.

She jerked in her chair upon hearing Candace call her name. She followed the voice and found Candace on the upstairs landing, leaning over the banister and dressed in a paisley silk robe. Ruth's mother forced her to wear a flannel nightgown to bed. As her best friend cooed about her wonderful night, Ruth smiled. There were things Candace needed to know, but she didn't need to know them now.

Just as she started describing how Brock had decorated their room, a masked psycho reached from behind, grabbing her head. He'd waited in the darkness. Ruth gaped in shock as the masked psycho, with his grimy hands, twisted Candace's head until her neck broke. The only thing louder than the *snap* was the silence that followed.

So quickly she rushed upstairs, Ruth didn't think to beware the killer. She gathered Candace's body beside the banister and cried. She cried, waiting for their friends to hurry out of their rooms. She waited a long time.

Babysitter's Blood IV: The Line Goes Dead

Ruth hustled down the lane, past one tract home after another. How would she find Candace? All the streets looked alike. They were all named for trees that didn't grow anywhere near. The cell phone clutched to her ear, she promised Candace that she'd be there soon. If she didn't make it, the police surely would.

Her best friend whimpered like a scared little girl. She was a scared little girl. He's going to kill me, she cried. She had locked herself in the closet, but the killer was already in the house. Ruth, gasping for breath, asked if she'd seen his face, but Candace was so terrified, she started rambling. She kept saying I love you, but Ruth had no idea who she wanted to hear it. She didn't think it was her. Candace had never said that before despite Ruth saying it the one time Candace talked her into drinking a Hurricane.

The night was chilly, the streets empty, but beckoning rectangles of light poured through the windows. Her mother had wanted to live in a neighborhood like this, but she settled for what life gave her. Ruth's face brightened when she saw the two-story tan house with the blue shutters. She yelped in relief and told Candace to run out of the house. She'd brought her pepper spray. What if he catches me, Candace gasped. Ruth promised that wouldn't happen.

The line went dead and Ruth pushed herself to run harder. She was about to barge through the front door when she heard a terrified scream from upstairs. She looked up at the windows, finally finding Candace. Someone was strangling her with his bare hands. Ruth felt sick, wanted to storm the house, but the front door was locked. Helpless, she stumbled back out to the front lawn.

The struggling twosome stumbled into the light spilling from another room. It was Brock, handsome but nothing else. He stopped choking Candace but kept her throat in his grip. He glared down at Ruth. The window went dark.

Slumber Party Slaughter V: Can't Stop the Carnage

Ruth watched a slasher movie on basic cable. It was old and unloved. All the commercials were for party lines and household gadgets that could be hers for three easy payments.

Candace hadn't come back downstairs. She'd mumbled something about a shower and left over a half-hour ago. Ruth was slightly relieved. She didn't know what to say to her best friend. The only thing she knew about boys was that they knew nothing about her.

Sometimes she wondered why Candace was so loyal. She was pretty and friendly and smart and caring. Everyone at school adored her. Her perfection was so benevolent, not even the bitchy girls could bring themselves to hate her. They told her Brock was a fool who liked to break hearts, and Ruth watched Candace smile sadly, pretend to believe them.

On TV, a masked psycho chased some dumb girl with big breasts as she raced toward her friends waiting on the school bus. Dumb bitch, of course he'd catch her. Men always catch girls like that. After a mouthful of popcorn, Ruth decided to check on her. Walking upstairs, she wondered what she'd tell her mother. She didn't like Ruth staying over all night, convinced there would be drinking, convinced there would be boys. She wished more than anything her father hadn't left. Things would be different. Maybe not better, but different.

Through the bathroom door, Ruth heard the shower's steady rhythm. She knocked and called Candace's name. Nothing. After thirty seconds of knocking and calling, she opened the door. It took her a moment to realize the blood wasn't supposed to be there. It took her a moment to realize Candace had lost too much to live. The wounds on the insides of her wrists looked like matching mouths, always hungry for more.

Ruth backed away, trembling. She dashed to the banister and called down for Candace's mother. She was probably passed out drunk in her sewing room. Ruth scrambled downstairs and dialed for an ambulance. When the operator asked her address, she reddened with shame, unable to remember the street number.

Father's Day VI: Girls' Night Out

Candace liked to make fun of Ruth, already eight years old and still afraid of the video store's horror section. They're gonna getcha, she teased. They're gonna cut you to itty-bitty bits and pieces. Ruth blushed and followed, her shoulders slouched. She was worried Candace would figure out she was a dweeb, so she didn't say how wonderful she felt.

Candace tugged on the coat Ruth's father wore while he paid for the rentals. In his warm voice, he chided his daughter's friend for being so cruel. He might leap from the shadows when she least expected it. I'm not scared, the little girl insisted, chin thrust high. Ruth watched her, making meticulous notes.

He asked Ruth if she knew Candace was kidding, and she nodded her head. Videos in hand, he knelt before his daughter, put his arm around her. Still smiling, he told her not to worry. Anytime you get scared, he said, I'm right here.

Nurse

Helen has been in the bathroom for fifteen minutes. Her limit is ten. She knows this. I have the contract in my purse, next to her caddy of anti-depressants and stabilizers. I will show it to her once she returns and say, "What did we agree upon last month? I know you like this restaurant, but if I can't trust you here, we can't come anymore. Do you understand?"

I watch for other women to leave the restroom, to catch the clues not even an accomplished talent like Helen can hide. Older women, their faces pinched sour with disgust and the younger ones, especially in the summer, who bolt from the room with whispers and backward glances. Poor Helen. Like most unfortunates in her position, her hard, impenetrable blindness prevents her from knowing the effect she has on others. In some ways, I prefer our afternoons or mornings in public to the interminable days in which her paranoia keeps us trapped in her home. Aided by the indulgence of others, I can trace her movements and perform my duties more easily.

I check my watch. Twenty minutes. No doubt Helen would implore me in her singsong voice, pale blue eyes darting like goldfish, that time had escaped her. This is nonsense. Those afflicted with her condition, in addition to her myriad other difficulties, have few skills, but they do possess an inborn awareness of where they are in time. This knowledge they rarely apply to their own betterment, but it is a unique gift, a grain of sand's awareness of where the tide will next fall.

Helen's salad sits rearranged, uneaten. One of my coworkers once joked she couldn't understand these women who regurgitated their meals yet never ate them. What were they vomiting? You can tell from this ignorance my coworker is a poor nurse. For unfortunates like Helen, eating, like most intimate activities, was something she only could do alone. Perhaps that is what was taking so long. I believe she was at the point in her illness where she took a perverse pride in the fact she could continue her behavior without anyone trying to stop her. After all, if one makes it her mission to destroy another, someone usually will step in, but if one decides to destroy herself, most will just step aside.

My sister, Carol, the real nurse, travels to a large white building advertised on television instead of crumbling brownstones and ruined, inherited single-frame houses. She put it to me best: We let them go sometimes. It is best. Too much morphine. Fail to report a matching donor. Let the call button go unanswered for a minute, perhaps longer. I knew of the ways. But these means were not available to me. Besides, Carol told me, I was lucky. People like Helen were not truly hopeless, not forsaken by God, merely themselves. They are not lost, she said.

We both remember what it is like to feel the sunken certainty one experiences in the presence of those truly bereft of all hope and time. Our grandfather, so tall and proud, once sipping whiskey and puffing smoke in my direction but never Carol's, lay dying before us. He refused the hospital. All those bitches in white, he said, they don't care. You're not their family, you're not their friends. You're a dollar. The morphine drip stood at his side, not to be controlled by him, we were urged, but of course, grandfather insisted. Technicians, he said, never had the smarts or the money to become a real doctor, but they don't mind giving orders like one.

Carol and I stood around his bed and watched the stunted, ragged breaths struggle to run the length of his lean body. The cancer, the kind that grows back at twice the speed it can be removed, the stomach kind, the kind no one "deserves," had reduced him to one hundred pounds. He was watching the Cowboys game. They were doing well for once, which would happen only two or three times again that season. Our parents insisted he was not aware, but Carol and I knew differently: the truly sick always know.

Helen emerges from the bathroom. Thirty minutes. But for once she does not look away when I hold her in the fierce gaze. Despite myself, I feel relieved. Perhaps she experienced other troubles. When one's diet is as disastrous as Helen's, the menstrual cycle can be affected as well.

She rejoins me at the table and smiles, her wan grin that seems pretty and open in the retouched photos cluttering her parents' walls, but in person is a halfhearted appeasement.

"I'm sorry," she says. "I really am. I was having," and she looks around as if someone might hear, as if someone might take an interest in this bony woman-child, barely ninety pounds with limp hair and a floral dress that clung to her. "I was having problems," she says.

"Were you bleeding?" I ask. When you are in my position, you can inquire about such things without seeming rude.

Helen nods then bows her head, keeps it fixed on her plate as if solace beckons from inside. To feel shame over such a natural occurrence but not over her constant need to rid herself of the very thing keeping her alive, amuses me. Myself, and those in my profession, must be very rational. The occupation demands it. And yet, we are constantly surround by the most irrational society has allowed to survive. I could not help but think Helen would be better off surrounded by those who could follow her pretzel logic, shimmy down its twists without complaint until they arrived at its only true conclusion: *I know they want to hurt me, so I must hurt myself.*

That is when I smell the odor. Rank and vile, like garbage. She had done it. She had done it, and then looked me in the eye. Like I was her doctor. Her mother. Nothing.

"It is time for us to go," I say.

Helen jerks up, startled. Usually, after she vomits and I chastise her and she swears never to do it again and she really, really wants to stop, we talk for a few minutes. This, I have been told, is therapeutic. This, I believe, is to give Helen the illusion of friendship, because all the other people I mentioned who might feel a kinship with this poor woman are, as she is, too terrified to seek it out.

Helen slips into her bulky wool coat, which swallows her, gives her the illusion of normal weight. I wonder if she never bought a smaller size because the experience of a mall would be too much for her or if some dim corner of her mind begged her not to forfeit.

When Helen's parents hired me two years ago, they were frank about their expectations. "Our daughter will not get better," her mother said, with the same finality of the doctor who had informed my family of grandfather's cancer. She held me steady with her eyes, pale blue like Helen's, but with the sharpness of a bright, condescending child. She was a former smoker, I could tell. Her right hand erect, resting on her elbow, fingers crooked in position. She knew discipline and knew my only purpose was to "make sure nothing happens to her," her father explained. He remained behind the couch seating Helen's mother throughout my only visit. She never once looked back at him.

I have been stalling other people's deaths for over twenty years. I could decipher the code. Let nothing happen in public. Already, Helen had run into mid-morning traffic, naked, begging to be hit, screaming in frustration that the street was so congested that she had no hope death. And there had been other attempts, less dramatic, but just as embarrassing. Like all clients with Helen's predisposition, there were attempts made in sincerity and others made for attention, where the only thing preventing death is the fear of the performance's end. Each time I encountered a patient after one of these escapades, I caught a glimmer of fevered release in her eyes, the thrill from an actor as he watches the audience rise for an ovation.

Helen's parents were busy people, their condo rarely inhabited. Helen would give my check twice a month, at the end of the last appointment for a particular week. She had never lost the money, spent it, insisted I hadn't earned it, like some others. *You don't need it,* they cry. *You don't deserve this. You don't love me. Nobody loves me.* I grip those checks tightest during my trips to the bank, hand thrust deep in my purse.

Even though I wear an overcoat warmer and more fitted than Helen's, the crisp whispers of winter creep inside my bones, and I imagine Helen shivering in the balmiest of rooms, her own body unable to protect her. It is the scrubs. Not that noxious pink the nurses Helen's age prefer, but blue-green. Neutered. I insist on wearing them, and leaving my coat open during the winter months so anyone on the street will not misinterpret my relationship with a patient. Helen is not my daughter, my niece, my mismatched lover. This is not to embarrass those in my care. It is for clarity, order. I cannot abide misunderstanding.

Helen begins to lag behind, gape at the impervious skyscrapers above her that ceased to fascinate me when I was still a child. Grandfather took me on the scaffold while he washed windows and jiggled the platform, harder and harder, heckling me, *Gonna fall, girl, better hold on!* I begged him to stop, cheeks hot and raw from wiping my tears before he noticed. I extend my arm and stretch it around her tiny shoulders, feeling both blades protrude against my coat. Helen starts to curl herself into me, as if I were her childhood plush doll, but I stiffen my arm. What have I told you about that? I remind her, in my pleasant, professional voice I practice when salesmen or my sister call.

She twists her head. This is a familiar routine. Helen will now require a comfort. Despite the catastrophes marking her life, she has a mind for others' routines. She knows my next appointment is not for another two hours. I cannot refuse her.

"Will you make me a smoothie?"

She tilts her head and when I cut my glance to her, I catch those translucent eyes, wet and dirty with need, and I want to gouge them. Twist my hand on her shoulder until the joint snaps like a struck match. Yank that awful coat from her, expose her as a wastrel, a degenerate, shove her into traffic, still steady and lethal before rush hour and shout, *What are you waiting for! Nobody loves you!*

"Yes," I say. Calm, smooth. I picture Helen drifting backward, arms overhead, into a pasture of blue and orange silk. "Do you have everything I need to make it how you like?" Helen nods, proud of herself and no doubt overjoyed to be posed a question she can answer without calculation.

Her apartment is always clean, like the solution of a mathematical equation. All my coworkers complain if it weren't for the patients, the kids, the husbands, the boyfriends, they would clean. Spotless homes, no apologizing for messes. As Helen hustles past me to the plaid couch where I find her at the start of nearly every visit, I let a grim smile widen my lips. So this is how one gets the time to clean.

Helen clicks on her game shows. A whole network devoted to them. Reruns of shows from decades past. I remember them from training in the ward, the electronic beeps, applause and excited screams cranked up to drown the moans filtering from the hall. She watches them, rapt, abbreviated human drama all she can digest.

"Do you want your pills separate or mixed in?"

I turn to her, awaiting a response. The answer is always the same, but I must ask. On the television, an elderly woman seems hardly aware of the camera mere feet away, ogling her bewilderment. Helen croaks out advice to the contestant, urges her to pick the window cleaner. Certainly, that's where the prize hides. I've never seen anyone win this one before, she cries, hands bunched over her puckered mouth. I look back at the screen and the old fool scans the audience for encouragement, helpless amid the battling suggestions, and I imagine Helen there, under the clinical glare of the stage lights, her pale features washed into a white visage, a mask upon which one could rewrite her fate. *Tell me what to pick*, I hear Helen call. *Tell me how to win.*

The old woman clucks the name of a sandwich meat as if her tongue and jaw were not in sync. Helen was right. The host pulls a WIN tag from behind the window cleaner. The old woman allows the host to kiss her cheek while she still gazes into the audience, as if the game were not over. After a nudge, she wanders out of frame.

"Put them in the smoothie," Helen says.

I break away from the set and take in my charge. Her eyes shock me with a precision I have not seen before. Like always, she says and smiles as if I were silly to ask. I imagine Helen as old as the contestant on television, but she is not the infirm, pitiable creature oblivious to the production taking place. She curls into herself on a heap of soiled and rancid sheets, entranced by her piecemeal wisdom, waiting for comfort. Carol tells me the terminal patients that worry her are not the ones who look away when she injects the syringe, not even the ones who watch the penetration. No, they look her in the eye.

My sister and I had no way of knowing that holding vigil over the bedside of the doomed would become our twin calling. Our parents had exhausted whatever optimism they possessed. As a twelve-year-old girl, I was transfixed by what I knew only then as the "painkiller machine." I had watched the technician show our parents how to operate it, spied my grandfather dope himself when mother and father were gone, his empty gray eyes fixed on me, not worried I'd tell, but curious why I'd bother to watch.

Now the cancer had made even this meek rebellion impossible. Moans like sandpaper over his workbench filled the small, mildewed room in which grandmother had set up his deathbed because, she said, "it was all too much, and we need to rest, please, girls, you must rest."

"You know how it works," Carol said. The morphine dispenser. Just press the lever and keep your thumb drawn tight, fast as you would against your first boyfriend's hand. With a desperation she had since eliminated from her personality like a childhood stutter, Carol grasped my hand with both of hers. As if I were the synapse between my sister's will and my grandfather's fate, I pushed the lever.

"Those old machines were so inefficient," Carol complains.

It does not take nearly as long now. Both of us, and it seems so absurd to believe now, were afraid to take his pulse, afraid to touch him, afraid we would not take it correctly and his withered finger, steel gray bristles at the knuckle, would emerge from our closet one night, tapered to a pinpoint: *murderers*. We waited until the wheezes subsided. Silence filled grandfather's room, the new resident. In the commotion of the following days, no one inquired about the bruise Carol had left on my hand.

My purse stays with me at all times. All those pills, it is simply the responsible thing. I rinse the blender though it has been lying in the sink since my last visit two days ago. Helen has never prepared a meal for herself, but her kitchen bustles with greens, fresh fruit, meat labeled and packed in the freezer, cracker and cereal boxes in the pantry. I suddenly want her check in my fist because that means it is time for my next appointment, an infirmed gentlemen who only requires for me to turn the television from one station to the next at precisely four-thirty. And then home.

I hold the apple cider bottle over the blender, and the thought of home makes me flush. I recall no detail of it. Well, of course I do, but they just—my purse on the counter. Open. I immediately think of Helen, but I no doubt would have seen her. The pill bottles rest atop my things. I need to put them back in her bathroom cabinet before I leave. I realize the stupidity of keeping them from her for the duration of my stay when she has whatever access to them she any other time. But, like pressing the lever, I never question it. I felt it as surely as my sister's hands cupped over mine.

The insane beeps, the applause, the dumbfounded contestants' yammering continue from the living room. I picture Helen enraptured, life on such a minute scale it is tolerable to her. Five minutes a game. Win or lose. Try and succeed. Try and fail.

I do not pay attention to which pill bottle I first empty into the blender. They plunk into the cider, zigzag to the bottom, a trail of tiny bubbles wiggling to the surface. I dice up the plums, the bananas, the strawberries. It is her favorite show, and there is a half-hour left. I have enough time. I press the button and the blender roars to life.

The traffic outside the second-story window whizzes below me. I imagine how my life might appear to Helen, to all my patients, a figure who appears twice, three times a week, disappears without remnant or complaint – a house cleaner, a home shopper, an exasperated parent, a disinterested spouse.

The sudden bleat of a car horn breaks me from my daydream. I gaze down to the street. Cars stopped, some askew, so it is not a traffic jam. I hear a woman's scream, but not the aimless kind I have heard so often. This was a scream thrust upon its source, not welling up from within. While the blender rumbles, I drift through the kitchen toward the living room.

Surely not during her favorite program.

Gonna fall, girl, better hold on!

On the screen, the silver-haired host tries his best to combat a large-breasted college girl eager for a kiss. Helen would have laughed and applauded. I think she imagines the young, beautiful contestants to be fun house versions of herself and cheers them on. And now she missed it.

The front door stands open to the hallway; she wanted to make certain I knew. The clarity in her eyes. I will not tell Carol about that. She will say that was my warning. And how she lied to my face about the purging! My breath runs short, my eyes moisten and I blink rapidly, unsure of what to do, unable to blot out the only thought that hurtles through my mind, like the morphine into grandfather's veins as the scaffolding shakes like the very earth even as Carol grips my hand in both of hers: *This wasn't your choice to make! You bitch! You goddamn ungrateful bitch!*

The blender whir softens, having broken up every solid, even the pills. I shut off the television, feel naked, like a caught burglar. I look over to where she sat, last looked into her eyes and realize now I had envied her certainty, even when

I had no idea what she had planned, likely had planned all afternoon. The smoothie meant nothing to her. She wanted me gone. Like her mother. Like everyone.

The check lies on the coffee table. I collect it, scan the area around it for a note. Nothing – neat and orderly as always. It occurs to me that once I dump the smoothie and take my check, it will be like be like neither of us arrived.

I trudge down the hall, purse slung over my shoulder. So no one can see my eyes, I wear the sunglasses I use only for driving. I hope my mood, this unexpected rising, passes before my next appointment. Sunglasses are unprofessional, and I have my duties. The door shut behind me, I hear the faint whir of the running blender as I head for the stairs.

The Profile Pic of Dorian Gray

One young man kept coming back. Dorian and the young man didn't stop tricking even as Dorian's eyes shrunk into his skull. They didn't stop after Dorian stopped keeping house, food scattered atop furniture not commonly associated with meals. He came back as Dorian's skin tightened around his bones; the obvious fallout of all those missed meals. The crystal meth, procured to convince his tricks to stay, proved too tempting.

The odd thing, the frightening thing, was that Dorian grew, if not older, at least *weathered* at a much faster rate than warranted since he stood before the mirror three years ago and took the pic so many men admired. Always the story was the same, told more emphatically with each passing month, when a trick's face fell in disappointment after Dorian answered the door. It was a trick of the light, Dorian insisted. I took that picture just last month.

He turned thirty-eight last summer but once was mistaken for fifty.

Corey knocked each time, three soft beats, like a pencil against a desktop. Did Dorian love this boy? This boy who had retained his puckish, beguiling beauty while Dorian's quickly faded? At least, faded everywhere but upon his Adam4Adam profile. He didn't think of the question in those terms, but nothing scared him more than silence. The boy indulged Dorian's desire for foreplay, and he couldn't say that about any other trick.

Dorian's initial forays in online hook-ups left him devastated. Some men actually lied about their appearance— a false age, the body pic of a porn stud, sometimes a pic over a decade old. Swallowing his pride and occasionally his bile, he'd stayed with these men, sucked them and teased them, bent them over and pretended each encounter meant everything until climax reduced it to nothing. Part of him, perhaps a naïve part, believed he'd accumulated such glowing sexual karma, the men he lured to his own studio apartment would treat him with kindness, misleading profile pic notwithstanding. At least, he hoped, they'd show him mercy.

While Dorian waited for Corey, he clicked on his own Adam4Adam profile and studied the foreground pic, larger than his body shots and cock shot. Unlike the latter shots, this profile pic could be seen by Adam4Adam users on their iPhones. The face, he believed, was the invitation; to what, he didn't always know, but he avoided men who showed everything *but* their faces.

In the selfie, Dorian's cobalt blue eyes glimmered like coals deciding whether to ignite. His lips were full, his dimpled chin wide and commanding. His dirty blond hair bucked and curled in an appealing skirmish. His tan, applied to his face despite warnings about spraying near the eyes, lent the photo a nice sense of cohesion, of unity. Not one feature drew desire at the others' expense, but they all—hair, nose, eyes, lips, chin—executed their tasks with brilliant efficacy.

He'd stood shirtless in his tiny bathroom, the track lighting bright over the mirror, and clicked. The simultaneous leer and faraway gaze took a few tries, but Dorian knew to be patient. The email had promised total satisfaction if he followed instructions. After posting the pic, however, he couldn't back out. The email explained that such a gift could only be given if the man offered it was *truly* serious. He often believed something sinister spawned the email, but doubts did him little good. Dorian focused on his future, regardless of its oddly accelerated pace.

"Some bitch almost sideswiped me on I-45." Corey slipped off his sneakers and flopped down on Dorian's bed. There was no frame; the mattress rested on the floor.

"I'm glad you made it."

"I have no doubt you're glad I made it."

"I'll load the pipe. You relax."

"I'm good, Dory. But don't let me stop you."

It disconcerted Dorian, like attending an orgy peopled by men wishing only to talk, when a trick refused his chemical refreshments. Did their jobs test for drugs? Were they one of those self-righteous "straight-edge" kids that lurked online for anonymous sex among men they disdained? Dorian wasn't sure he could perform without the meth. He certainly couldn't silence the clank of emptiness awaiting him if he tried.

"When we're done," Corey said, "I have something to show you."

"If it's dirty, show me now."

Loading the pipe, Dorian didn't register what Corey said. Instead he thought about the bargain he'd made. Logging in these last three years, bartenders and club kids and gym rats all clamored for his attention. Killer smile! Fucking gorgeous! Get over here now, hot stud!

Corey laughed gently. "Don't shoot before you score, old man."

Those proclamations, the surge of confidence constantly renewing itself, made bearable his humdrum life of serving overpriced Vietnamese cuisine and returning to his studio apartment to watch basic cable. The tricks' reactions upon discovering his withered appearance were a necessary codicil to the bargain his vanity had deemed irresistible. The online lust of ten men far outweighed the face-to-face disappointment of one.

"Finally," Dorian said, tossing the tiny plaster sleeve of crystals, "the party can commence."

"You hear me?"

"What's that?"

"After we're done, I want to show you something."

Dorian chuckled. "Boy, you better show me now. I told you before…"

Corey grimaced, a flash of pain informing his smile. He'd fantasized about asking the young man to move in, perhaps be his houseboy. Wasn't that what older queers of more considerable means called their conquests? Dorian imagined waking at night, after the jerky, feverish sleep that followed a tweak trip, and finding him lying there like a loyal hound. His dark, longish face and lithe body—all natural, all bestowed by a God that Dorian refused to believe gave a damn. Surging inside Corey while the young man cooed and bucked, he recalled the few times his guest had stayed after the assignation, the pretty little grunts escaping his lips.

Then they were done. Lewd compliments led Corey to grin at him from over his shoulder, asking if he'd come hard like last time. At least, that was to motive Dorian assigned his lover. Dorian remembered nothing of the encounter just completed. No doubt, however, he'd convince himself otherwise in order to soothe himself when the parade of deceived tricks resumed its march toward his door.

Dorian heard paper rustle. Corey stood nude, hip thrust forward, eyes wide with impatience. He held a printout of some kind. By the size and layout, Dorian thought, it must be the hard copy of an email. While Dorian frankly envisioned nestling with Corey like mice inside a tenement wall, he couldn't help fretting that his time ticked away. He wondered how much was left.

If I've aged five years every six months over the last three years…

Corey smirked. "Amazing how some people abuse their imaginations, huh?"

"Who wrote that? Another trick?"

"Aw, don't be jealous." Corey tapped his chest, after rolling up the message, and reminded Dorian that he remained nude. Somehow, Corey had slipped on his jeans and green long-sleeved jersey without his host's notice. "It's probably some scam. I'll have to buy hundred-dollar face cream once a month till I die."

Dorian asked Corey what precisely the email said. Instead of answering, he lazily spun around and drifted toward the bed. The printout uncurled and threatened to flutter away beneath the revolving ceiling fan. These young guys, Dorian thought. They think all you need is a big dick or a tight ass, and you can waste anyone's time. Don't they realize we're dying? Corey grinned and gestured for Dorian to read the printout himself.

Before finishing the first line, he knew what the entire message promised.

Tonight was remarkable, he read. The moon, Neptune and Venus aligned in such a rare way that you had to pounce. Take the photo one second too soon, or too late, and the image would bear no magic, forgettable like those parents on Facebook posted of their small children. Display this picture to the world, the email promised, and you will be desired for eternity. Age was the one indignity no gay man escaped. The young twinks at the bar spurned you while the men your own age chased those same twinks, their desperation close to crescendo.

One picture, it instructed. Seize your romantic destiny.

"It's a crock of shit, right?" Corey asked. His voice had lost its confidence.

His dry eyes red and blinking, Dorian crumpled the paper. "Of course it is," he said. "If this were legit, every fag in the city would be taking a selfie in…"

Corey checked his watch, also reclaimed outside Dorian's notice. "Four minutes."

"You sure you don't wanna hit?"

"Smoke too much, and I might start believing this voodoo."

Scooting back on the bed, Corey propped himself up with misshapen, soiled pillows. He looked bored. He didn't try to hide it. At that moment, Dorian despised him. Corey always bent over without complaint. Maybe, though, he had another trick, up the highway, waiting for his text. Maybe Dorian was no more special than a cage in a zoo. His skin prickled and his breaths grew short. The meth distorted and muffled emotions so ruthlessly, he'd years ago stopped monitoring his feelings.

"I don't think it has to be a selfie," Corey said.

"What're you talking about?"

"Maybe *you* should shoot *me*."

Dorian's tone flattened, his eyes brightened. "Don't say that, Corey."

"You've done it before. My whole sexual oeuvre is on your laptop."

Dorian paced. How could he explain the email was more than the work of a sociopathic cyberpunk? The half-eaten pastrami sandwich discarded on a stereo speaker had turned. Three half-finished Coke cans balanced precariously upon an end table. Dorian struggled to reveal the truth without telling the truth.

Corey climbed across the bed, arching back and ravenous eyes tempting Dorian. His guest offered a trade: if Dorian took the pic for his profile like the email instructed, then Corey would suck him off. His host could take as many pics as he liked of the act. On hands and knees upon the corner of the bed, Corey gazed up at Dorian.

The goddamn certainty enraged Dorian. No matter what happened tonight, tomorrow would come and Corey would still be desired, able to charm any man.

A small mirror in a beaten brass frame hung over his laptop. Knowing he'd despise what he saw, knowing the only way to stay sane was to pretend the online selfie spared him the humiliation of growing old, of younger men witnessing him age. Dorian gasped as loneliness engulfed him. He missed every man he'd ever fucked, from a neighbor boy at age fourteen to Corey ten minutes ago. Frowning, he created even more lines in his face and thought how easy life must be for the blind. He'd have to trash that mirror. Trash all the mirrors.

Corey bounced on the bed like a toddler. "It's almost time, Dorian! I wanna do it!"

Looking away from the glass, Dorian spoke plainly. "Take off your clothes."

Dorian asked Corey to stroke his erect cock then curl up on his back, exposing his asshole. Without pornography, no gay man would know what's sexy. The mini-shoot commenced. Corey implored his host to photograph him sucking cock, but Dorian said it didn't matter anymore. The aspect among those three planets had passed, and the universe once again was connected by nothing more than hope and heartbreak.

Walking Corey to the door consisted of less than five steps. Dorian promised to email him the "best" shots. Corey clung to the doorway as if drunk, his wide grin piercing Dorian's heart. What had he done? He could've still warned Corey not to post the pictures—the bargain required each man to make his image public. Corey would've dismissed him, maybe never return. Dorian slid his arms around the boy and kissed his forehead.

"You ever think about fucking me sober?" Corey asked.

"If I were sober, I wouldn't call it fucking."

The door clicked softly behind Corey, his footsteps fading. Hopping back on Adam4Adam right away seemed rude, exposing a lack of gratitude. Ten seconds passed before Dorian felt compelled to click on his profile. A blinking graphic in the upper corner of the screen denoted new messages. So much more exciting than sex, he thought. He knew the other men regularly online agreed—but only behind the protection of locked doors and intricate passwords. Still, they were junkies for any bawdy compliment tossed their way.

When would Corey realize what eternal online youth had cost him? Would he confide in Dorian? The older man might be so ruined by then, a recluse surrounded by take-out containers and burned porn DVDs, even Corey would reject him.

He'd learn when he saw his reflection—Dorian was sure of that. It was why he'd taken those pictures, why he'd condemned to despair the only trick that treated him like a person. One day, he knew, Corey would be too decrepit to find dick, and he'd knock. They'd embrace and bemoan the injustice of growing old, swap stories of hot studs in cyberspace fooled by their forever-young profile pics. Just for grins, Dorian would answer Corey's messages while Corey posed as Dorian. He'd ask Corey to move in, and the young man would say yes. After all, hadn't the email promised Dorian he'd be desired forever?

Death by Misadventure

It's my second, and surely last, visit. Curt has made his decision. The school has been informed. A lawyer lurks in the wings. It's a goddamn shame. His complex is airy and scrubbed and reasonable. Best of all, you can lose yourself among the units. But there's no time for discursion, however badly I wish to wander. Five-thirty, I promised Curt. I trip upstairs to the second-floor landing. My high has dissipated but refuses to depart. I tell Curt the whole truth, but incidentals waste his time and sour my breath. It's my second, and surely last, visit.

My polite rat-a-tat knock wins no response. Neither does my stronger staccato. I pound the door with a flattened palm. Often, at other men's doors, this moment implodes beneath the weight of panic. A wrong address given in cruel jest. His peephole preview of me failed to impress. Men are fuckwads. Men are carnival hucksters. I go home because nowhere else does a door promise to swing open.

But the panic never descends. I stand, my hand still flat against the door, unsure what to feel.

Dominic is with him. If not inside, they must be littered about the pool. Our first visit, Curt took me there. He seemed so proud, I cackled that I wasn't in the market and didn't need a hard sell. It's September in Austin. It's warm and stale. The pool, of course. I hitch my overnight bag higher upon my shoulder. No one need know I tried his apartment first.

Crossing the lot, it occurs to me what all this means. No panic, no enraged texts. I trust him. I fucking trust the bastard. I forget the heat. I forget the stiffness seizing my lower back after three hours on the road. Faith is a tricky fucker. Easily, it's mistaken for density—of the mind, I mean. My intellect resents any emotion that forbids thought. Faith. Even the tweak can't scramble the signal. Curt has no faith, no god. I concur. Gladly—to him, to anyone.

Actually, I do believe in God. He has a plan for me. It sometimes reveals itself, but only after I snort. I know I disappoint Him.

The pool awaits at the center of the complex. A whirlpool bubbles in a far corner, an afterthought. An iron fence, waist high, surrounds both. Deck chairs and wobbly tables topped by dust-plagued umbrellas. A recent Fall Out Boy jock jam pervades. I spot the Boise speaker Curt adores instructing—if it's your job to listen, you're sure to hear more than you expect. I spot the open cooler. The Shiner's bitter bite, I crave it. I spot Curt. I spot Dominic. I watch them longer than any stranger should, failing still to prepare myself for two who knew me before I wished to be known. I holler their names and break the spell.

"I still can't believe you don't own a bathing suit," Curt cries. He's from Bossier City—originally. Meeting him, you wouldn't need to be told. I've never asked when he grew the beard. His thinning hair remains a vibrant yellow, but his whiskers shimmered copper and gold when, last visit, we sat on his balcony, drinking Shiners in the afternoon sun. His body has softened and thickened. Still, middle age has yet to blunt his expansive gestures or chasten his bayou brio. He views chaos as an unending opportunity. Each absurd risk serves as an emblem of faith in his ability to survive—absent any god's largesse. When his watery blue eyes shimmer, I believe.

There's a latched gate, painted the same indifferent shade as the fence. I love this complex. They realize and respect no one cares about color or style or slant. But the gate, it demands either a key or combination. The panic I was certain I'd eluded? It crests with the sleepy certainty of a lounge singer pinpointing her pianist's key.

Being the sole faggot among straight dudes comes with perks that don't require me to fall to my knees. We're free to feign helplessness over the most mundane tasks. No one calls bullshit. A few wisecracks, maybe a smirk—nothing a red-state queer can't handle.

Curt sends Dominic to facilitate my admittance. We haven't seen each other since graduation, twenty-five years ago. He's smiling, complacent and complicit. He's handsome—laugh lines and crow's feet have besmirched his good looks, not vanquished them. Should you encounter him at a used car lot, he'd no doubt sell you a lemon, but the guilt would shatter him. Same hairstyle—wayward waves of shiny copper, a few strands, moussed into obedience, dangling to his brow. He's grown an impish belly. Frankly, I prefer straight dudes' backhand embrace of middle age and its mockeries. I've always wondered why I never desired him— not as boys, not now. The gate yawns open before me.

Curt leers from the far end of the pool. "What happened to sisters are doing it for themselves?"

I strut past his friend. "I can still diagram any sentence. You can't strip me of that."

"Bald is beautiful." Dominic always sounds like he's rehearsing lines for a show with no audience. "I told Curt the same thing."

"Did he suggest you go fuck yourself?"

Dominic tosses a towel over his shoulder. He smirks, his only response. I know to glance back for it. This aborted banter, you might mistake us for friends—or enemies. We sat beside one another in Algebra II. Some friendships need only proximity to bloom while others require spilled blood. Curt, too, smirks as I approach. I was foolish to expect the same candor I savored during our last visit, no remnants of our boyhood spare those invoked.

"Curt tried to catch me up on your life."

My old friend drapes his frame atop an innertube. He flips over to his belly. Squeaks and splashes. I don't recall last time seeing an innertube stored in his apartment. This gap in logic distracts me, and I ought to thank him for that. I do not, however. Expressed gratitude never sounds sincere unless it's not.

Dominic settles at the pool's edge, water lapping his shins. "You really write dissertations?"

"I write dystopic fiction," I tell him. "Stories about worlds where life sucks, but in ways you'd never expect."

Curt spins around. Squeaks and splashes. "One story is about a world where sex is just another chore. You know, like an oil change." He sounds repulsed, yet eager to make the repulsion known. He hasn't read a single word I've written. Still, his pretense touches me. I trust him. I trust the fucking bastard. "No one gives a fuck about fucking. Soon, people stop wearing clothes. No point in marriage. Crazy fuckers start communes. No one has kids…" Curt seems content to drift. "So much depends on a simple orgasm…"

I roll my eyes. "Thank you, William Carlos Williams."

"Curt told me about your fiancé." Dominic isn't smiling now. "What kind of cancer was it?"

The thick-armed girl's head turns this way then back. She can't determine which of us deserves the spotlight. I keep forgetting her cowed sidekick only to refresh my perspective, now tinted with guilt. I have a duty to the discarded. It's why I picked up the phone when Curt's number flashed across my screen last July. It's why we spoke for two whole hours, confessions and recollections and the sweet, sad, sobering fact that Curt Broussard had resumed his long-departed orbit around my fucked and feral world. I take my duty seriously.

"Ack!" Dominic finally finesses his lips into a familiar shape. "I'm sure you never thought we'd have this conversation…"

"Hodgkins," I say. "Spread to his lungs. So fucking quick. I thought we had time. We'd grow old and have affairs and relapses and screaming matches. And I wouldn't wonder whether it's appropriate to call myself a widower."

The water has stilled. I perch upon a deck chair. For a moment, I am alone inside a complex of derelict design, wishing it might consume me. Still warm and stale. It remains September. Austin. I do not live here. Curt watches me. Dominic watches me. I'm so tired of this tale, the role I must play. Grief is mere pantomime—the words excluded ought to be shouted in rage.

"They were engaged," Curt informs Dominic.

"Crumbling Christ, I am so sorry, Jebediah."

I chuckle. Good to know my past bears a name. All I must do is utter it. "Jeb is fine. We're too old for all those syllables."

Dominic tells me about his older sister. Her husband died just two years after they wed. He was drunk, she was furious. He scaled their claptrap rental home, vowed to walk the roof's perimeter. Because he could. He most trusted her love whenever she feared losing him. Straight dudes from shitbox East Texas can't resist high stakes. A wife in tears is a wife for life. The fuckwad fell and broke his neck. Dominic smirks before going on. He doesn't seem to care I notice. I've never liked him more. The coroner, he said, ruled it "death by misadventure." A finding no less official than homicide, accident or natural causes. Ask my sister about it now, he adds.

She'll tell you it's doubletalk for dying because you're a dumbass.

I remember Josephine, his sister. Junior-year chemistry. My straight-A streak showed little chance of surviving the onslaught of protons and electrons, beakers and burners. Josephine embraced the dirty thrill of helping the class brain cheat. Also, she bought me Marlboro Lights. Seeing a boy compromised offers far greater insight than simply watching him strut and surpass.

"Curt found himself a maiden." Dominic seems tickled. He kicks his feet at the water's surface like a child. Curt hasn't drifted far. His friend's splashing jostles the innertube carrying him. He tries to sip his Shriner. The suds soak his chin.

The thick-armed girl laughs. Her derision ricochets about the complex. Dominic and I laugh, too, but it goes unheard. So many moments in a friendship aren't shared. They are cherished, they are mourned, they are the first moments to fade. I never fight. I respect how my life seems fated to vanish even as I live it.

My first visit, Curt bemoaned his bedroom, so barren of women, even transient lovers. I told him my last fuck was two weeks prior. He marveled at gay dudes' talent for fornication. Blowjobs for breakfast, ass-pounding a certainty. I lay beneath the roof of the unpainted gazebo, worried the abrasive cushions might incite a rash. I wanted to tell him I didn't enjoy it. I wanted to tell him I was already confusing it with other fucks. But a man who gets laid proves so easy to admire, and everyone needs a hero. His Boise speaker offered tinny validation.

Dominic and I watch Curt flirt. The thick-armed girl titters and smirks. Curt refuses to lift his shoulders or even head from the innertube. He courts her with words spoken to the sky. Her male sidekick, I haven't forgotten him—I suspect he needs no help with that task. The girl hoists herself onto the pool's edge. She gestures somewhere far away, some unit somewhere else. Curt paddles back to us. He's elated. He chuckles. I don't recognize the sound.

"She's going to meet us at the bar."

I haven't dropped my overnight bag this entire time. "You breeders and your courtship rituals."

Dominic reminds him our arrival time isn't definite.

"Make sure you're back here by eight," Curt says.

He'll no doubt ask if I need dinner. I haven't eaten in three days.

Dominic collects his towel, slips a T-shirt over his head. His girlfriend needs something. She won't be joining us at the bar. She works in marketing and has a daughter in junior high. Dominic divulged the basics of his Austin existence while Curt heeded his dick. I almost told him my dead fiancé's name.

After Dominic departs, Curt and I make our way back to his apartment. The sun sinks, but the heat persists. Curt can't stop talking about the thick-armed girl. Her name is Glenda or Galen or Gilda. He tells me what he'd like to do to her. He doesn't use the word pussy. He uses words that make me nostalgic for pussy—the word, only the word. I warn him that pretty strangers break promises even more often than unhappy lovers. The gold-colored form clipped to his door holds his attention so briefly, I at first dismiss it, but the word EVICTED, its bold font, startles me.

Unlocking the door, Curt explains. "I'm moving across the globe in two weeks. Why pay last month's rent? I'm leaving anyway. Let the fuckers evict my ass."

The apartment's floor plan makes no concession to ingenuity. The kitchen, dining area and living room meld into a single airless vacuum. A balcony beckons from the side. The bedroom and bath oppose one another at the unit's far end. If there ever were furniture, it was scrapped before my first visit. Curt is packing. Heaps of clothing, documents, and objects whose purposes mystify me litter the floor. A cache of family photos, unframed, seems destined to get lost. One is a school portrait of Curt from maybe second grade. He smiles like no one ever gave him reason to stop. I want to steal it, but then I'd be obliged to look at it forever.

Curt fusses over one of the packaged dinners from the HEB across the interstate. Exotic foods, squash and curry and udon, foods you can't procure through a loudspeaker. He mentions once again that my diet disappoints. Our first visit, I insisted on Sonic and Chicken Express. He cracks open a Shiner, offers me one. I don't often drink, but the thought of him drinking alone craters me.

We relax on the balcony. He eats his dinner as if apologizing to it. Would I like a bite? C'mon, Jeb, he says, you should try new things. I decline. I need to survive the emptiness another night, maybe two. I know what he's doing. His concern is sincere, but its potential to distract has not escaped him. We need to talk about Taiwan. Two more weeks. The police lie in wait at the airport. I need to discuss this with him. Again. It's my second, and surely last, visit.

"Have you heard from the lawyer?"

Curt asks me for a cigarette. I've taken only a puff or two from the Camel wedged between my chapped lips. I pass it to him, the cherry bright and private. He takes it without comment. Whenever I'm flirting with a dude, I light the cigarette as if it were my own only to relinquish it. I like men thinking about my mouth, despite what awaits them there. But this is Curt, and I never fuck a dude I actually like.

"Fuckers don't have any evidence." He holds his cigarette like a blunt. "No real evidence, anyway."

"Dude, this is Taiwan. Didn't you see that Claire Danes movie?"

"Who the fuck is Claire Danes?"

"And the whole world hates Americans."

"Do you know how many yellow chicks I'm Snapchatting at the moment?"

"Your online harem unnerves me."

Curt pops up from his seat. "I left Miss Nasty inside. Be right back."

This is what he calls his Boise noisemaker. Returning, he sets the speaker on the dusty Plexiglass table separating our two lawn chairs. He demands Bob Marley. As boys, we got stoned and listened to those goosestep baselines.

"It's just something I have to do," he says. "A man faces the music." The bravado drops from his tone. "It took me a long time to call myself a man."

"If you get stuck in the clink, it'll be like solitary confinement. None of those dudes will speak English."

"Is solitary confinement really that hardcore?"

I wield the newly-lit cigarette clenched between my knuckles. "Man is a social creature. Spend too long alone, and your mind devours itself for sport."

"What do you want me to say, Jeb? It's something I have to do. Taiwan is home. It's time I went back home."

A couple of years ago, long before he resurfaced stateside, Curt was busted with a brick of marijuana. It weighed as much as a newborn. He managed to skip town thanks to several improbable windfalls he never adequately detailed. Always, he finds the particulars of any past scrape too mundane to recount. All I know is that he expects to face arrest the moment he steps onto the tarmac. He insists the incarceration is a mere formality, unlikely to extend beyond a week. But there's always a chance—a chance of what? Even with the backing of the elementary school where he taught, and plans to return, disaster remains far from impossible. Ignore Claire Danes at your peril.

"What does Dominic have to say?"

Curt shrugs. "Says I should follow my heart."

"Dope smugglers don't get to follow their hearts, friend."

A half-hour before Dominic is due to fetch us, Curt hops in the shower. It tickles me watching straight dudes preen and primp for a night out. I see no reason for such rituals. A breeder bar, one Dominic proudly labels a "dive," seems an excellent place to nurse a Jack and Coke while fading into the walls. Curt promises karaoke. That's the principle difference between bars straight and queer: at one, the patrons burst into song, and at the other, patrons watch men in evening gowns mouth the lyrics to songs carved into their psyches. When Curt emerges from the bath, the new-car aroma fills the apartment like the ring of a call no one intends to answer. He's trying a new beard oil. The thick-armed girl will surely spread her thick legs. Right, Jeb? I'm no good at reassurance. I find the truth too tempting, its potential for devastation an elixir more potent than even primo speed. We shouldn't keep Dominic waiting, I tell him. I have to remind him to lock the front door.

Dominic drives a Jeep Cherokee that might have once passed for black. To my surprise, Curt concedes shotgun. From the back, he strokes his oiled beard as a lover might. We zip out of the lot and onto the access road. Interstate 35 slices Austin down the middle. A stone barricade running its length, at least as far as we can see, compresses the freeway down to just two northbound lanes. Cones and reflectors, all neon orange, litter the lanes. The city is widening the interstate, Dominic informs me. No one knows when the expansion will finish, and no one can recall when it started. It's after seven on a Tuesday night, but the traffic bottlenecks before we reach downtown. The radio plays so softly, I wonder whether I'm hallucinating. Speed concocts fake voices to blot out the real ones urging you to stop. Dionne Warwick croons that's what friends are for.

"I don't sing," I inform them. "Don't even ask."

"C'mon, Jeb," Curt brays. "I need backup vocals."

Dominic chuckles. "I'm sure they have some Madonna."

"That's not only offensive, it's unimaginative."

Curt and Dominic drift into a conversation that doesn't involve me. We pass sign after sign: DETOUR, LANE CLOSED, EXPECT DELAYS. I'm listening to my friend and his friend speaking as if alone. The subject is girls. Our junior year, Dominic took out my old friend, Corrine, took her for an overpriced dinner at Chili's then to the opening night of *Wayne's World*. She excused herself after the first reel. Ladies room, she said. She never returned. Cell phones, of course, didn't exist back then, so Dominic never learned her fate until the next school day. Indigestion, she swore. So humiliating. MERGE RIGHT, BE PREPARED TO STOP, TRAFFIC FINES DOUBLED. When my focus returns, I hear Curt teasing him about his girlfriend. Was she ready to assume the mantle of Ex-Wife Number Four?

I turn to Dominic. "You've been married three times?"

Curt snorts. "Didn't invite me to a single one."

"Guys, marriage is difficult. You wouldn't understand." He winces the moment he finishes. I could've made an effort to conceal the wound. Then again, my only shot at compassion resides in the souls of others. I spare none for myself. "Jeb, man, I'm sorry. I didn't mean—"

Curt swoops in to rescue one of us, or perhaps both of us. "Dude, it gets better." He tags Dominic's shoulder. "C'mon, man, tell him their names."

"Fuck off, Curt."

"You can't fathom the hilarity."

Not even a quarter-century has lent their friendship a richer dynamic. They make each other laugh, and I suppose that's enough. A man who can't rouse even a chuckle from his intended ought cancel the wedding at once.

"Fine." His gaze penetrates me. Should I return it? "Belinda, Becky, and Bess."

Curt preens, victorious. Dominic concentrates on switching lanes to breech the exit for MLK Boulevard. He seems, still, to wish for consolation, some promise that the next woman he weds—sure, she'll be the one. This hope announces itself in his lifted brow and tremulous jaw. I say nothing. The unsavory view outside my window offers needed distraction. Concrete swatches imbedded within asphalt roadways; patrol cars boasting their red-and-blues, light pulsing atop traffic, but bereft of sirens; mounds of damp sod; and a slew of workmen unmistakable in ill-fitting vests of fluorescent orange.

"Jeb, take another whiff of my beard. Tell me you're not aroused."

My cheek presses against the window. "Austin keeps evolving, but its dwellers never do." The silence greeting my observation must be filled. "I'm goddamn wet, Curt."

I do believe in God. He has a plan for me. I know I disappoint Him.

It's been many years since my doctoral days at UT Austin, too long to warrant even a moment's marvel at which landmarks and businesses have endured and which succumbed to the same impetuous expansion afflicting the interstate. Are we jumping puddles far beyond Sixth Street and its array of queer clubs? If not, are we mere blocks away from my fuzzy and fair-weather social debut? I snorted my first line of coke in the men's room of Oilcan Harry's. The memory crests so sharp and certain, it demands I unveil it— but I deny myself. Dominic skirts one pothole only to jolt the whole Jeep upon striking one deeper and wider. Curt asks where the fuck we're headed. My head lands upon the headrest, and I allow my eyelids to slip shut. Dominic calmly reminds Curt this dive bar is no different from the one they trolled back in July. When he first entertained me, a childhood friend from a presumably more delicate tribe of menfolk, Curt gladly escorted me to Oilcan Harry's, to the side bar located in the billiards room. Several men, as the hours grew heavy, asked whether we were lovers. Curt didn't notice, too drunk for such mundane inquiries. I didn't tell the entire truth. I didn't know the entire truth. I may never know—the truth, I mean, the truth of this life, of the lesson Curt offers that no other man can. This is my second, and surely last, visit.

Have I slept? That small, sad ache I experience upon waking pangs the back of my head. Life missed, the lives of others, the life I've navigated by depicting worlds both more dire and more desirable than the one I currently share with Curt and Dominic.

He won't stop stroking his beard. "Why are we parked under an office building?"

"I told you about this place," Dominic replies.

I take in the unlikely view. "Surely, this wasn't always a bar."

Dominic chuckles. "It's Austin. It's a bar. I thought you did grad school here."

It appears to be the size of a small-town meeting hall, but dive bars have a way of obscuring their true floor size. No windows, walls painted so darkly, they could be plywood or brick. A few dozen vehicles shine sickly like wax fruit beneath bare fluorescents that illuminate all the scene's worst details. Pierced and preening, kids smoke cigarettes and scan the lot. My beers with Curt have dulled the edge, but I mustn't lose myself. He's clearly bombed, shuffling alongside us, his gaze snatched then dismissed by sights I have no faith exist. Still, I have a duty to the discarded.

When we reach the entrance, a heavy oak door bearing an airbrushed heart cracked down its middle, an emo dude steps before us. It takes me too long to realize he's the bouncer. No bigger than Dominic, this rodent. But his smile is wide and carries no hint of irony. He hands me a perfectly bloomed red rose. It's perfect because it's not real. Curt and Dominic take their roses, baffled.

"When you find a lass at last," the bouncer purrs, "do what any gentleman would do."

"Eat that pussy with a spoon." Curt's beard oil mixes with the dense aroma of Axe body spray, its many insistent varieties. Breeder boys always wind up smelling like a single-bed room rented by the hour. Dominic stammers an apology I miss. The tone tells me enough. I don't see the point. The more Curt debases himself, the more quickly I can disappear.

The bouncer bows grandly, arm extended. "Enjoy your night at Chivalry."

Curt cackles. "This place is called Chivalry?"

In grad school, my choice queer bar was named Male Call. When drinking, I prefer limp wit to tone-deaf sincerity.

As we enter, the bouncer delivers a final bit of advice. "Don't surrender your blooms too soon." I surrendered my bloom to

Harrison Murtz in the scene shop a week before finals my junior year at Texas State. He's married. I'm not. He's happy. I hold a rose I can't give away without giving away myself.

Curt lurches ahead. "Where the fuck do you sign up for karaoke? Jeb, sing us some 'Vogue.'"

"Don't make me kiss you," I mutter. "Then no lovely lass will take my flower."

Dominic grins. It doesn't occur to me to ask way.

There's a stage, festooned with generic Valentine's Day trappings: hearts pierced by arrows, cherubs grinning, unnumbered calendars all flipped to February. A dumpy woman writhes while never quite keeping up with the beat to Rhianna's "Umbrella." Billiard tables, two of them, stand in the back. Enough room for dancing onstage. No one dances. Maybe five dozen breeders, sardined among the plastic bake-sale tables, sit atop what reminds me of piano stools. To the side, the only bar, the requisite looking glass stretches behind two unsmiling bartenders. I can't help speculating how often they're mistaken for lesbians. In my head, I name one of them Sunshine and the other Sourpuss. Already, I'm liking them more.

Dominic and I wedge ourselves between two patrons, each of them already listing and heavy-lidded, at the bar. Dominic's body radiates an oddly paternal heat. My appreciation of this warmth sparks not a desire for sex, but a desire for home. Not my current Houston abode, shared with no one and greeted by visitors who rarely stay over an hour, but our home, in East Texas. Shitcan, backwood Pineknot.

"Jeb, wake up, fancy man." Dominic stumps for my attention. Who knows how many attempts he's made? "We're in a bar, but we're not drinking. You're the brain. How do we redress such bullshit?"

He calls out for Sourpuss, calls her *lady* instead of *ma'am* or *miss*. Whenever a man calls a woman *lady*, I think of all those Jerry Lewis films I learned about during childhood, how I made no effort whatsoever to sample them. Sourpuss doesn't simply stop before us, she strikes a pose, making no secret of her indignation. Dominic orders two Jack and Cokes, one of them, I assume, meant for me.

"How did you know what I drink?" I ask.

"Oh, yeah, sorry." He chuckles, visibly flustered. "Usually, I do the ordering, I forgot that…"

"You forgot I was a dude."

"Nothing personal, Jeb."

"What do I owe Employee of the Month?" I fish for my wallet.

With a quick, decisive gesture, Dominic stills me. He's paying for the drinks. Curt paid for the case of Shiner meant for the three of us this afternoon, and, later, just him and me. Curt also footed the bill during my first visit. Once I'd filled the tank and hit 290, my obligations were met. My company, I strain to convince myself, is all Curt expects me to provide. Well, he does find my Camels hard to resist. Most men, I know, wouldn't see the point in dissecting a generosity so benign, free of undercurrents or subtext. It's my second, and surely last, visit.

I sip from the glass Sourpuss slams in front of me. I spit the instant it desecrates my tongue. "I didn't order tequila! Sourpuss! Over here!" Jesus fuck! Dominic is too busy watching a dude with a belly too bulbous for his chicken-bone arms and shins. He's singing "The Shape of You," that Ed Sheeran staple that always imbues me with hope. If that ginger joke can get laid, hope remains. Just offstage, Curt bounces like a child eager to conquer the wildest ride at Six Flags. Dominic takes a long sip, makes no complaint.

"Excuse me, miss. I think you switched our drinks. I'm pretty sure this is whiskey."

I turn to my right. A pocket has opened between the dude speaking and myself. He must shave twice a day. A dark, porous shadow reaches high, just beyond his cheekbones. He's slicked back his dirty blond hair, but his curls will not be denied. His eyes are kind. Men with kind eyes don't know how to fight. Not for lovers, not even for levity. But his soothing tenor secures Sourpuss' attention right away, and she trades one glass for another with grand gesture. I suppose this dude and I could've done that ourselves. The fact neither of us made an attempt might indicate a rare but serious shared character defect. He absently twirls his fake rose between his thumb and outstretched fingers. I think about his mouth. I then recall what's so, so wrong with mine.

I return my attention to Dominic. "The Shape of You" clip-clops through its last chorus.

"Please tell me he chose a song from this decade." I need a cigarette.

"That ain't how we do it."

"You're no help."

Sunshine hands Dominic his credit card, a long and fluttering receipt wrapped around it. He pockets the card without giving it a glance. He's smiling, complacent and complicit. The receipt cascades from his breast pocket.

"That was a clue, Jeb." The following silence takes me by surprise, my eyes narrowing as if Dominic were out of focus. "I'm trying to play fair."

There's a meaning implicit in his confession. It shouldn't surprise me he and Curt discussed how we'd function as a trio, perhaps brainstormed several strategies to neutralize me. This is likely to be, however, my only chance to educate him on the treachery perhaps awaiting our friend overseas. Casually, I ask whether they discussed his kamikaze impulses before my arrival.

"I just want to give him enough good memories to last him however long he needs."

"Dom, we both know Curt is impulsive, foolish." I wonder if he realizes those same descriptors could glibly label me. He watches Curt climb onto the stage. The breeders hoot and cheer, and my naïve, nihilistic old friend pumps his fist to encourage them. "Fond memories won't keep him sane. They won't keep him alive." I gulp from my glass, set it behind me on the bar.

Dominic jerks his head to the side, perhaps too irritated to counter. On instinct, I grasp his shoulder, my other hand falling upon his thigh. These aren't inappropriate flirtations, but rather unwelcome evidence that I now consider Dominic *my* friend as well. He's given me no reason to expect any such latitude.

"Lasses and laddies," a middle-aged MC announces from the stage, "Chivalry is proud to welcome Curt Broussard." Catcalls, hoots and stomps. "He's an English teacher in—wait for it!—Taiwan!" The crowd schisms: some groans, some cheers. Some asshole shouts, "Buy American!"

The MC cracks a lame joke about his surprise over meeting anyone blond from that part of the world. Curt snatches the mike and lurches forward. "My stage name is G-Dog Sizzle! I am here to *represent*!"

My upturned hand catches my head. "Dear Christ, it's just like high school except I have to smoke outside." Dominic roars with laughter. I'm not the friend Curt needs right now.

The MC scuttles offstage, and the music bursts from the speakers. Cheap karaoke approximation, an impromptu band composed of cake tins and crockpot covers and myriad kitchen utensils. It sounds cheap, the kind of cheap that takes perverse pride in its half-assed efforts.

Montell Jordan was a one-hit wonder who blipped on pop radio's radar sometime during the nineties. Too accessible to be termed a "rapper" without drawing mockery, but certainly not a singer, either. The song is called "This Is How We Do It," a painfully ordinary paean to the party life. I remember white boys, nervous that their racial heritage was nothing but an echo chamber, lined up to emulate whatever black musicians offered the tricky cocktail of "legitimate" and "bland." Dominic, himself, mouths the lyrics. I need whatever's left of my drink.

A fake rose, its bloom collides with my nostrils when I tilt back the glass. I glance up at Dominic, but he's too busy manufacturing memories to notice. Obviously, I was intended to find the flower—but I'm not a lass. I just cry like one whenever Green Day catches me unawares.

I snap my head the opposite direction, the back end of the bar in full view, a narrow hallway branching off from beside the bar and leading somewhere unknown. A man hustles toward that unknown. His dark blond curls raise even more ruckus than when I first saw him. I must follow. Nothing to do but mourn my boyhood friend's freefall. I've trained my gaze elsewhere since the dinky instrumental track started.

"Jeb? Dude! You're missing Curt! He wanted you here! What the fuck?"

The hallway dead-ends, safely from most barflies' vantage, into twin restroom doors, each airbrushed with the same enormous, breaking heart that afflicts the main entrance. Inside the men's room, I'm relieved to note the bar's suffocating whimsy has not followed. Three stalls, three urinals, a mirrored bank of sinks. It seems empty. I know better.

"Hurry, bud. Someone might catch us." His voice, it's scratchy and emphatic, as if puberty still has a trick or two in store. He clears his throat. Last stall in the trio. Pacing toward my fate, I listen to my footfalls' pissant echo—they ricochet but rubber soles offer too little racket. I push open the door but stay rooted at the threshold.

My admirer stands atop the toilet, bending at the waist just low enough to avoid detection by any third party needing to piss. His shorts and boxers are collected at his ankles. His shirttail hangs so low, it grazes his erection. He's not fully hard, and I'm not fully sold. It's thick and mercifully cut, and I can't help admiring a man who proudly eschews all foreplay and banter. Again, he urges me to hurry. I lock us inside the stall.

Once inside my mouth, he thickens a bit more, and hardens more than a bit. I have rules when sucking off strangers. These are not the same rules I follow when sucking off men whose pleasure I place above my own. Despite his awkward positioning to avoid being caught, he allows himself to moan, even mumble a few banal vulgarities. Thankfully, he doesn't call me *bitch*. I can't stomach that word, at least not when it disparages a man.

"Ow, ow, ow. Careful there, bud. I feel those teeth."

I should address this obstacle now, but I don't. Even after losing my last one, I still assured myself that nothing in my life, not even sucking dick, need change. I apologize and adjust the angle of my jaw. Moments later, the same complaint. I hate to disappoint, especially with something so simple as another man's orgasm, so I slip him from my mouth, reach into my own and pluck out my bottom denture. Into my pocket, it disappears.

I do believe in God. He has a plan for me. I know I disappoint Him.

"Ask me even one question about my teeth, and you'll have to get yourself off." It's the first time I've glanced into his eyes since starting to suck. "Is that unambiguous enough for you?" I can't help smirking to watch his head jerk as he, frankly horrified, nods in agreement.

Like shame, I didn't lose my teeth all at once. Any tweaker will tell you that hygiene rarely troubles the spun. It's not a matter of demolishing your teeth, it's simply a matter of *forgetting* them. Starting in my early thirties, they were excised individually, or in small groups, until so few remained, my dentist suggested a humane end for that embattled crew. I didn't care. I wasn't pretty. It thrilled me to witness the erosion of my physical self. Alas, sucking dick, the vacuum that forms inside your mouth, readily uproots a lower denture from its precarious position upon the gums. Incidentally, I've been forced to jettison from my diet popcorn, gummies and corn on the cob.

Minus that distraction, time unravels only to then congeal into blocks of eventfulness difficult to measure, impossible to mourn. Have I been sucking this dude's dick for three minutes, or fifteen? Finally, his moans grow louder and deeper, and his hips start to buck back and forth. We'll be done soon. I contend that debauchery, sex—especially impromptu sex—is our tribe's sustenance and salvation. All such fucks are triumphs for any man who desires other men. He doesn't whine or haggle when I slip him from my mouth before orgasm, and I am grateful. From my knees, I rise.

"What's your name...? That was..." He shoves his shirttail into his khaki shorts.

I grin. I've been hoping for this chance. "William," I tell him. "William Pope."

The eloquent bouncer, that emo rodent, lunges for me the instant I leave the men's room. "Whoever your friend is, you need to take his ass home." His spittle spews forth. "The police are on their way." He grabs my arm, pulls me down the hall toward the barroom. This boy is steeped in alarm, and he wants company.

"Which friend?" I call out, unsure he hears me. "What exactly has he done?"

Fucking Curt, I knew I shouldn't have left him on a stage with a means of public address. No doubt Dominic finds his man-child madness utterly charming. I'm beleaguered by bothersome boys. The bouncer releases me and fades into the swarm of patrons. I scan the stage: no Curt, no one at all, actually. I missed his performance. I'd love to lie, but I tell that man the whole truth. Always. He's nowhere among the crowd.

"Give me back my fucking card, you fucking cunt!"

Not every man can be identified from his raised voice. It's coming from the bar. I hook to the left, the patrons casually clearing the way. Part of me persists believing it's Curt who must be corralled. Not until I see Dominic, tendons stretched along his neck and his frame angled over the bar, bellowing at Sourpuss, or maybe Sunshine, can I admit my error. In fact, Curt tugs at his elbow, like an ignored child desperate to steer his father from temptation

"You think I'd let my name appear on some Discover card bullshit!"

Ah, yes. The credit card wrapped inside an endless receipt. He never looked closely. At least, not until now, apparently. Police sirens, afloat upon the melee like motor oil atop puddled rainwater. There isn't a moment to lose. I shoehorn myself between my two friends and shout my warning inches from Dominic's face. The cops, I inform him. Even a minor legal complication might prove one complication too many for Curt. I don't know how true this might be, but I'm hoping Dominic secretly aches to bail. Whether it's Sunshine or Sourpuss, her blank façade hasn't shifted once.

Dominic pulls me closer, his voice dropping to a whimper. "That bitch stole my credit card—and she won't give it back."

"Cancel it with your phone. I'm sure your bank has an app." I never learned that guy's name, the one with the crown of unruly curls. Then again, he never learned mine.

The sirens fade. This relief, however, surely won't last.

"C'mon, Dom, I need to get home." Nice to see Curt has co-signed my script. I want badly to glance over my shoulder, eager to know if the patrons, in a sort of osmotic solidarity, watch our enfeebled exit. But I don't. We shuffle out the door. The din resumes before it can swing shut behind us.

Kids, more than before, still loiter in clots, smoking and judging. But there's a young woman, dressed in black denim hot pants and a low-cut blouse that first knew life at an Army/Navy outlet. She watches us skitter toward Dominic's Cherokee, keeps watching long after the kids lose interest. Her arms are quite thick. No garment could distract from those tree trunks. Of course! It's her! From the pool. She seems to recognize me, too. But I do not alert Curt, and I never again look over my shoulder. I'm tired. I'm strung out. And distractions are the last thing I need.

My duty to the discarded never outlaps duty to myself.

"Why'd you skip out on my karaoke?"

"I was sucking off some strange dude in the men's room. He left his rose in my whiskey."

Dominic veers left onto the interstate. The late hour has thinned traffic. No bottlenecks, no substantial delays.

We'll be home soon. At least, if my recollection of this city can be trusted. Home. A funny word I chose. Austin hasn't been home for nearly two decades. Curt can't wait to leave this city far, far behind. I suppose Dominic claims this place as his own, but I find myself too stingy to include him in my semi-conscious doodling. These thoughts distract me while I pretend to fight sleep. Curt and Dominic bicker about the nearest Whataburger locale, whether the construction might play spoiler.

"Isn't it kind of dangerous, Jeb, skipping off with some stranger, telling no one you're gone?"

Their voices, I can't quite discern one from the other, but Curt never moralizes. Not to me, anyway. I don't respond, and Dominic lets the matter drop. I'd be curious to meet these ex-wives, or maybe eavesdrop on his last blowout with each.

Back during the summer, my first time to visit Curt, we stumbled out of Oilcan Harry's not long after midnight. He stumbled, I steadied him. It took him far too long to recall his iPhone's passcode, but the Uber app presented no trouble once located. Still, Sixth Street bustled with vagrant, visceral life—taxis and bar-hoppers and sporty rides headed nowhere near. I fretted we'd miss our own ride. I demanded that Curt share this burden. He instead threw his arm over my shoulders and muttered how I hadn't changed since Pineknot and how deeply that touched him. I was strung out and somewhat drunk but knew, like I know tonight, that Curt couldn't truly enjoy his oblivion without supervision. Our Uber driver spoke with an accent. His skin was a deep brown, but the passing headlights and streetlamps left unknown the finer points of his identity. He tried to chat. I wasn't interested, and Curt wasn't coherent. Not long before we reached his complex, however, he announced that I was a real writer, that people paid to read the endless ways I imagined our world might fuck itself. Curt hasn't read a word I've written—for him, the words don't matter so much as the audacity required to write them.

Dominic's Cherokee idles in the cul-de-sac separating the gated entrance and exit of Curt's complex. They banter and curse. Curt clutches a take-out bag from Whataburger. After my brief doze, I no longer feel the least bit tired. A whole night staring into the ceiling atop Curt's air mattress in his ransacked living room does not delight me. Dominic bids me farewell. I wave and smile. I'm still furious he turned out to be more complicated than I dared wager.

"How did that man convince three separate women to marry his ass?"

Curt shrugs. "They were all bow-wows, every last one.".

The hydraulic gate slowly shuts behind us. We amble deeper into the complex. My deep appreciation, my juvenile love, for this complex renews, no doubt compacted by the certainty my love matters not a bit to its units and standard-issue amenities. Again, I want to lose myself among them. My complex boasts just a dozen buildings with scarce parking after the late news. I've always wished to show Curt my home, to discover where he'd choose to sit, which of my blu-rays he'd ridicule first. This is my second, and surely last, visit.

Once inside, I beeline for the fridge. Another beer offers my only chance of sleep. I sit at the kitchen island and drink while Curt throws on flannel lounge pants and a Nike tee. He grabs a beer and sits across from me. He asks for my rose. I can't recall what I did with it, those pissant plastic petals. Maybe it lies unnoticed on the dirty concrete floor in the men's room. Maybe my curly-haired trick wanted a memento. Maybe my name wasn't enough.

He chuckles. "Fuck if I know where mine went either."

"Theme bars are the worst."

"Shit. Almost forgot." He tosses the take-out bag upon the countertop. Grease stains smatter the white, orange-striped paper. Curt and his crew loved Whataburger in high school. Sometimes my crew encountered his. Curt and I exchanged hellos unobserved. "Bacon and cheese, no tomatoes, right?"

I don't bother to conceal my amazement. "I've had boyfriends who never learned that."

"You haven't changed a bit since school." His smile flattens. "Eat your dinner."

A sour, aggrieved ache blossoms in my gut, but even the thought of flavor, of chewing, of working my jaw for ten, maybe fifteen minutes sickens me. I tell him I'm not hungry. He should eat it. Whataburger tastes delicious when you're smashed.

"When was the last time you ate, Jebediah?" I open the bag slowly, as if wishing to avoid crinkles. "I hassled you about this last time." I glimpse inside. Large box of fries, perhaps cold by now, burger below, wrapped in yellow paper. "Stop staring at it. Every Texan knows what comes in those bags. Eat, motherfucker."

I pinch a single fry—soggy, not quite cold—between my thumb and forefinger. Flummoxed, hoping I might make Curt laugh and lighten up, I drop my jaw as far as I can. My bottom denture, confused, disengages. I then maneuver the limp fry over my gaping mouth, like a songbird feeding her hatchlings. Quite a clever sight gag, I assure myself. As I chew, the salt overwhelms my tongue.

"Fuck this shit. Start with the damn burger."

This is all I want. Someone to stop me, someone to convince me not all the darkness within my abyss merits exploration. None of my lovers loved me to enough to make threats or demands. In their defense, I didn't love them enough to heed any they might have made. My late fiancé, of course, is the exception—the addiction.

I unwrap the burger. Surprisingly flat and compact. Twigs of bacon jut from between the buns. Diced onions, shreds of lettuce tumble onto the open wrapper. I'm close to taking a bite. But not close enough to refrain from one more plea that my self-destruction continue unabated.

"Curt, it's not right...you funding both our times together." His eyes haven't lost their forlorn intensity. I must continue. "I know you make far bigger bank than me, but..." The top bun feels damp and clammy inside my grip. "I *can* take care of myself. You know that." Impulsively, I hand him the burger. "Please, I can't think about food tonight."

To my shock, he takes it from me. Gingerly. He takes a big bite. I'm relieved. I'm disappointed. I'm disappointed over my relief. He gulps it down then hands it back. What choice have I?

"I know what's waiting for me in Taiwan. It's true, I wanna go back, but there's another reason." Anxiety pricks my hands, my feet, even my face. "The company I've worked for these last six months? I've embezzled thirty grand from those fuckers." I chomp down. The mustard's tang unnerves me. "I quit last week, but those bucks are too big to go unnoticed forever. I need to be overseas before the shitshow starts." The food slides down my gullet with the grace of a cud swallowed by a Holstein. "It was money well spent. We had a goddamn good time."

I called him Will. His mother, dead long before we met, named him William Pope. He asked me to marry. I hold little hope I'll be asked again.

I've returned the burger to its flattened wrapper. I might cry. I might spring from my stool and bolt. One night I'll run out of dicks to suck—what then?

"I'm a speed freak," I tell him. "Will and I kicked it together. Not at first, but sooner than I dared hope. When he died, the next right thing no longer seemed worth doing." The act of admission hasn't provided catharsis for years. Too much rehab, too many smoky rooms peppered with broken fags terrified they'll break again. "I don't think I can stop this time. This freefall, though, it feels very much like freedom. I no longer know the difference."

We hand the burger back and forth—a bite from him, a bite from me—until it's gone. The fries are a lost cause, now too cold. I ask him when he'll start packing. He asks me when I need to wake for my return home. We pretend our answers carry weight. We pretend our words have impact beyond this night, this moment in this apartment, in this city.

Be Careful This Time

Atop the hardwood floor, behind his desk, Gregg sprawled out like a lizard flush against the mesh-knit wall of a collector's cage. His snores were a symphony of rumbles, each note eager for escape. A fine, filmy moisture coated his skin. His face was puffy, white and so mottled, a narrow estimate of his age would prove tricky: Jake knew his lover's age—Gregg was almost old enough to be his father.

Gregg clenched his smartphone in a death grip. Jake liked to kid him about his high-tech pacifier. Never in front of a trick, though.

"Who was he calling?" Leon asked.

Jake placed the phone next to the laptop stationed on the desk. He glanced at the screen and saw a naked man, not as trim as Jake, nor young. It troubled the young man when Gregg pursued men defiantly unlike himself. The naked man had no head. Jake smirked, scanning the user's self-introduction, certain he'd spy the word *discreet*. He almost missed the handful of lines sandwiched between profile pic and written introduction.

I like to party, I like to play, can fuck all night, can cum all day. He wasn't sure if he admired or pitied the naked man's literary leanings.

"Was it the guy who rhymed?" Leon relaxed in the green velvet lounge chair that faced the massive cedarwood desk. Gregg was passed out just a few feet before him, Jake fretted. He couldn't allow himself to be seduced while his lover lay helpless and husbandly, and also within earshot. Despite these restrictions, he drank in Leon's sleepy-eyed, slinky beauty. He was the last guest of a casual, meth-fueled orgy. He was short and blonde. His smile promised things best kept secret. His tapered waist was a marvel, unobscured by a shirttail and accented by the faded jeans riding his hips.

Jake closed his boyfriend's laptop. "Who knows?" he said. "He's cracked out, but he'll be here when we're done." He kept his tone jocular—they were still flirting. Leon switched to a new smile, this one more feline and fierce. "Stop arousing me," Jake said, laughing at how unconvincing he sounded even to himself. "I'm serious. All good orgies must come to an end."

Less than fifteen minutes ago, they'd been kissing in the kitchen. Leon had slammed him up against the open pantry door. The other guests had already departed, one by one, like Greyhounds out of the terminal. Jake beseeched him to penetrate, embark on that task that instant. Before a mere minute had passed, both young men heard a loud thump directly above them. An elongated moan followed that, while hard to discern, in fact echoed. At least, Jake believed as much. Leon still had him pressed against the door.

The houseguest grinned. "Either you have a very talented dog or your boyfriend just went down in flames."

"I have to check on him."

Jake was pleasantly surprised at the ease to which all the men from this weekend agreed to the house rules. Gregg was their true author but, as usual, Jake was saddled with the mundane guest-relations tasks. But still, no problems. No problem, truly, with the exception of Leon. Not once during the orgy did he initiate contact with Jake's older lover.

"If we need an ambulance," Leon offered, zipping up the staircase two steps at a time, "we might be forced to admit some inconvenient truths."

"Nonsense. It won't come to that. I'm certain."

Just as Jake had grasped the doorknob, Leon grabbed him lightly at the elbow. Jake prepared himself for a statement so disagreeable, Leon preferred to drop his voice. Even this charismatic hottie understood the concept of shame.

"Gregg has you nice and trained, sweet ass. How long did that take? Three months? Six?"

Jake shoved his way back into Gregg's office. He knew it was hopeless to try and shut him out—Leon was toned top to toe. But he tried. He tried for Gregg.

"I'm sorry, Jake. I didn't mean to degrade you."

Leon unwittingly stood at just the right spot so that the sunshine pouring through a trio of box-set ceiling windows bathed him in gold. Jake couldn't help imaging Leon on his knees, begging for atonement. It aroused him instantly. Never mind that, he advised himself. Apologies require two parties, and the moment had come.

"I don't know what you meant by such a rude question. But if you can forget it, so can I."

Leon smiled. It seemed guileless enough. "It doesn't matter if I forget. They're *your* questions. They belong to you now."

* * *

This wasn't the first move Leon had made against Gregg. After he arrived, Leon listened to Gregg elucidate in frenzied, emphatic tones about antique furniture, old homes and older money. Jake recognized this breathless incantation of dates, facts and names as the last stage before his boyfriend crumpled face-first into whatever lay before him. Jake eavesdropped out of sight from his and Gregg's bedroom.

Not much later, he saw in the doorway Leon's long, fine-haired legs, the swift curve between his hip and ribcage.

He nearly dropped his pipe in alarm. The bedroom was sacrosanct, the one room in the house meant for Jake and Gregg alone. Leon wore a T-shirt and jeans after having declined Gregg's offer to get naked before he began his lecture.

"How did you—?"

"He was going on about Victorian something or another," Leon said. "I told him with all these objects—all these *things*—in your home, it was a shame I didn't get a proper tour." He grinned and a moment later that grin widened still. Jake wondered if he had not responded to his guest's wickedness with some of his own.

"He didn't offer to show off the house himself?"

"He did, but then he got an email alert."

Jake groaned.

"No worries. I'm sure by the time he's done salivating on his keyboard, you and I will have made our escape."

Leon pulled Jake to his feet in one fluid motion. He took the pipe from Jake's hand.

They went downstairs to the kitchen. They kissed. Leon whipped off his shirt and waved it above their heads like a white flag.

"Put that on the counter, not the floor," Jake said. "The cats might get to it."

Leon smiled and kissed him. "You need a refresher course in this."

They laughed and kissed again. They rocked on their feet, circled each other in an elementary dance. Finally, Jake found his back flush against the pantry door.

Then, from upstairs: Gregg's *thunk* on the floor.

* * *

Back upstairs Jake froze in apprehension. He had finished speculations on the availability of the rhyming naked man from the website. Leon placed his hand on the closed laptop to steady himself, stepping over Gregg's body, and nudged him with his bare foot.

"Still out?" Jake asked. He imagined how Gregg's breath must have felt against the bridge of Leon's foot.

"As out as before."

He pulled away from Leon. He let his hand trail on his guest's waist. "Sometimes he hits his head on the table when he falls out."

Leon held Jake's gaze. "So this is a typical party."

Jake opened his mouth to reply only to realize he had not been asked a question. He looked behind Leon toward the staircase as if there had been another noise. Suddenly, he felt himself unable to return his gaze to Leon, so he let himself sink into the green velvet lounge.

"You've conducted this test before?" Leon asked. "With your foot?"

"What?"

He tapped his foot against Gregg's head. Jake tensed in his seat. Leon smiled.

"Yeah, he gets going on the laptop or talking about tables, or chairs, or drapes, and..."

Leon smirked. "Just as I suspected..." Jake lifted an eyebrow, found the courage necessary to meet his mischievous gaze. "Death from acute boredom," Leon continued. "Careful, stud. It can be contagious."

Jake's mouth puckered. Imagine! Lampooning one's host mere feet from his unconscious form.

Leon perched on the desk. "If you don't lighten up, we're not going to have much fun."

Jake held his seducer's gaze. "We were," he said. "Downstairs."

"Let's revisit the scene of the crime." Leon grinned.

Leon plunked down on the floor and reached out for a deep and wide heavy-glassed casserole dish containing a potpourri of clear granulated crystals ready for snorting. Jake jerked his hand over the desk, his fingers fanned.

"What is it?"

"That dish."

"It's a casserole dish."

"It's an antique."

"Gregg failed to mention that in his syllabus."

"I'm serious."

"Jake, look into it."

"What?"

Leon pushed the dish toward Jake. It slid across a mess of documents and other papers. "Stand up and look into it." In the dish, beneath the two lines cut and ready to snort and a leftover mound of crushed crystals, Jake's reflection bubbled in the unevenness of the glass.

"See the scratches?"

He saw them, how they kissed his face with a torrent of large pores. Other distortions proved difficult to quantify.

"How valuable can it be if he uses it to cut dope?"

Jake sat down. He had carried the pipe upstairs with them when they came to investigate—or, rather, ascertain—Gregg's noisy sign-off. He lifted a cut-off portion of a drinking straw from the inside of the casserole dish and scooped up a few granules.

"What's in there exactly?" Leon asked.

"You haven't done any? You seem wired to me."

His leg swung madly beneath the desk. "I did some right after I got up here."

"How much?"

Leon smiled.

Moving the pipe over the dish, Jake guided the straw, with its granule freight, over to the pipe and loaded it. He handed the instrument to Leon along with a cigarette lighter from the desk. "You need to catch up," he said. His smile flickered and fell. He looked at Leon, his eyes wet with resignation. Leon leaned back, as if the volume of Jake's gaze required extra space. Leon let the lighter flame burn just shy of the pipe's bottom. Smoke from the granules rose and swirled.

Jake watched the breaths of white smoke billow from Leon's lips, thicker and more insistent than cigarette smoke. Each exhalation clung together, dense and bright, till it reached the ceiling and finally dissipated with nowhere left to climb. Even as Leon pursed and bowed his lips in comic exaggeration, Jake felt while watching him a stirring within himself. He wanted Leon. He wanted to push him flat against the desk. He wanted Leon to feel the weight of him. He wanted to feel Leon's body rise to meet his as he surged inside him. He wanted to know Leon's last name. He wanted to know the name of his hometown.

But more than anything, Jake wanted to tell Leon a story. He wanted to tell the sly, exquisite boy perched above his sleeping lover that he had lied.

"It's not an antique."

As another bank of smoke escaped his lips, Leon said, "Not anymore at least."

"Gregg and I—that was the first thing he bought for me."

"He bought you a casserole dish?"

"Well, *gave*. He gave it to me, my first time here."

"This is his house?"

"*Our* house." Jake remembered why he never told this story. He knew what other men would think—only dating a few months before moving in, playing at domestic life before even having been with Gregg a full year, contributing sometimes little and more often zippo bucks to the household kitty. But this was still their house. Their house: his and Gregg's.

"You moved in?"

He nodded. Leon's posture sitting on the desk reminded Jake of a coil descending a staircase, the slink of his head and neck and narrow torso, all the way down to his hips. He held Jake with his eyes as the smoke cleared. Jake felt like Alice admitting her confusion before Wonderland's caterpillar as he blew smoke and derision from his hookah. Jake reached for the pipe.

Handing it to him, leaning across the desk, Leon said, "But it's still here. I'm sitting right beside it. When did he give it to you exactly?"

"My first time here. Last year."

"The traditional gift for a first anniversary is paper."

Jake felt his face flush. He wanted to look away, but to look away meant soon submitting again to Leon's gaze with whatever new ripple of insinuation. He could not bear that.

"So it was like this?" Leon asked. "Like you and I right now." The implication sat pregnant between them. "Were you snorting from it with him?"

He hadn't lit the pipe Leon had handed him. This was an interrogation. His eyes fell to Leon's foot, still rocking back and forth under the desk. His big toe came within an inch of Gregg's head with each swing. But when he finally did look back up at the man Gregg had invited into their home, he saw that his face had softened. The sharpness of Leon's features blurred and Jake noticed the slight downward curve of his full lips, how his eyes dimmed as if in response to a distant tragedy.

"He gave it to me. Just as I was going out the door to leave, he called me back up here."

"Back upstairs?"

"He said to take it. For the next time I partied, I'd have the surface to cut the dope."

"So how did it wind up back here?"

Jake took a deep breath. He held it for a moment, aware of the suspense in which he had placed his guest. He had finally reached the end of this story, a story he had told, up until that moment, to no one but himself. It had been his charm against the doubts roiling beneath the surface of any relationship, a litany Jake repeated to himself when Gregg passed out before reaching their bed or insisted on inviting over other men.

"When I moved in, it was the first thing I brought from the car." Jake felt a rush through his dilated veins, a release, the long-anticipated opening of a sliding showroom door. "I walked inside, and Gregg saw the dish in my hand. He said, 'You kept it.'"

"He remembered..."

Jake nodded, his smile wide, his eyes clear. "It had been three, four months since he gave it to me, and I just—I just assumed he'd been too high to remember. But he said, 'You kept it. You kept it.'"

For the first time in their conversation, Leon looked away. He seemed to be taking in the room—fully, truly—for the first time. The Oriental rug hung on the wall, its mesmerizing oval-and-rectangle pattern for a moment bewitching Jake as well. The several bookcases filled with volumes on art collecting and antique furniture. And among it all, the closed laptop, a floating mine in a quiet pond.

"Come over here," Leon said.

Jake rose and circled the desk to where Leon sat. He stood not only inches from Leon but from Gregg's unconscious body as well. Leon reached out his arm and pulled Jake's head to his. Their kiss at first was hesitant, their lips touching as if sampling something exotic, but after a moment of unease, they embraced and their kiss deepened. Jake felt a connection he had never felt with any of the men Gregg invited, and the last words of his story to Leon echoed through his own head: *You kept it. You kept it.*

Leon inched his lips away first. His smile now was one of empathy, perhaps regret. He placed his fingertips on Jake's cheek. "Let's take it with us," he said. "We'll do some more downstairs. Let Gregg sleep."

Jake beamed, ecstatic as a child blindfolded for a party game. "We'll snort it through a dollar bill."

"The Eighties ended long ago."

"I'm old-school. You'll like it."

Jake reached out and collected the heavy dish with one hand. But he was jittery and his muscles tense, his coordination blunted. Had it not been for Leon's quick hands, the dish would have tumbled from his grasp and bashed Gregg's head.

Leon held the dish in both hands and watched the shock slowly invade Jake's face. But Leon smiled sweetly. That was nothing, he said. A crisis averted.

He handed the dish back to Jake. He said, "Be careful this time."

Don't Call Me Daughter

When Kayla was born, Norman and his wife were happy. At least, she appeared happy. At least, he knew, she wanted him to think she was happy. He caught glimpses of less optimistic emotions while watching her care for the infant. She grimaced as Kayla struggled out of the diaper she'd placed under her bottom. Grief at once emptied and filled her features as Kayla dumbly pounded her palms along with the Pearl Jam bass line rumbling downstairs.

His wife came to bed later and later. Finally, one night, Norman's irritation outweighed his trepidation, and he crept into the nursery to find his wife absently rocking the cradle, her vacant expression reflected in the window.

Still, he said nothing. He let the milk go bad. He tolerated his wife channel surfing for minutes—five, ten, twenty—her expression never changing as she watched the daisy chain of images. He scurried one night to the nursery, alarmed to hear his wife singing a lullaby, something about a teapot waiting to be tipped over. Kayla would turn three months old the following day. Reaching the doorway, he wondered if his wife remembered. He wondered why she'd stopped singing by the time he'd arrived. He wondered why she held out their daughter's slack body as if it were a sacrifice. Over and over, she mouthed *I'm sorry*. Kayla's head dangled from her shoulders. Her face was still like a China figurine. Norman understood death like most of us do—that is, not at all.

"I couldn't save her," his wife said. "She wasn't meant for us."

The memorial service and funeral passed like railway cars, somehow only meaningful if attached to what preceded and followed them. Relatives offered embraces and baked goods and guarded hope. Norman accepted all these things and dispersed them to the cavernous rooms of his home. His wife greeted the mourners with a shimmer in her eyes. His foreman, Zeke, sent regrets about missing the service but privately assured him they would talk soon. Norman watched her converse with old college friends, his co-workers, and even a rarely-seen neighbor as if each person were an elaborately wrapped gift. She ripped open the wrappings, admired the booty, and then leapt for the next.

"You should take a break," he cautioned her. He spoke softly, kept an eye on their guests.

"I need this," she said. "It's so good to know people care."

"You knew that before we lost Kayla."

She clutched his wrist. His tumbler of coffee, covertly spiked with whiskey, landed with a soft thump on the carpet. "But I couldn't *feel* it. Could you?"

The coroner suspected crib death. There were no signs of foul play.

In the weeks following their daughter's passing, his wife glowed. She leapt to answer phones and doorbells. Whoever embraced her, she squeezed so hard that they lost their breath. She adapted to the supplicant's role as more messages of hope entered their home. Commiserating held the sacred air of communion. Norman hadn't seen her so connected to the world since Kayla's birth. One day, he finally asked her how she was doing. Dealing with Kayla, he added, as if she might think he was referring to another matter.

"The nights aren't endless like before," she said.

"I'm glad you've started sleeping in our bed. Again, I mean."

Her eyes glazed over and a mysterious smile bowed her lips. She was beautiful, he thought. Kayla would've grown to look just like her. She lightly took his hand and backed toward the stairs, never looking away. Stunned, he knew better than to ask if she wanted him, fearing any attempt to verify her desire would shatter it. He'd again be left less than an arm's length from her but unconnected, surrounded, like a mirage, by stale air.

They made love. They clawed and grunted. Sweat dampened the sheets.

"We need laughter back in this house," she muttered after he rolled off her. "A child's laughter will heal my heart."

The announcement of a pregnancy compels so many different reactions, depending on whether the child is welcome—and if welcome, for what reason. When his wife shared the news during a drive into the city, Norman flinched. He faked a warm smile, but instinct plunged him into a stream of dread. It flowed between them like the River Styx. If she noticed his unease, and his lame attempt to disguise it, she said nothing. Instead, she returned her gaze out the window, billboards for affordable dental work and wine coolers zipping past.

That interchangeable mass of mourners and loved ones hooted and cooed their approval at the baby news. Glad to see you're moving on with your life, they said. You have so much love to give, they said. God would never ask you to bear *two* deaths, they promised. Only Zeke, his foreman, expressed reluctance.

"Don't you think it's a little soon?"

"We buried Kayla six months ago."

"That's soon, Norm. That's real damn soon."

The rarely-seen neighbor was watering her lawn when Norman and his wife returned from the hospital with their infant daughter, Katherine. He didn't wish to bother the reclusive woman, but his wife insisted. After retrieving the digital camera, she led him across the street. Following her, his discomfort melted away as the baby girl bounced upon his wife's hip. Instead of asking the neighbor to follow them to their house, Norman and his wife, Katherine held between them, posed in front of the neighbor's brick home with lime green shutters and rusted drainpipe.

Crossing back toward home, Norman wondered aloud if, years from now, they would recall that the house in the photo wasn't theirs.

"That's a stupid question, honey."

"I didn't mean to say that out loud." He grinned sheepishly.

"You're ruining our special moment."

"We're in the picture. What else matters? I wanted to make you laugh."

His wife spun around. She tightened her hold of Katherine. "Let's not disagree in front of the child, Norman. Isn't that what your parents always did?"

From the first night Katherine slept in their home, in the same room where her sister died, Norman noticed that his wife's joy departed the moment he left the room. He hid behind a doorframe and watched her numb expression while feeding Katherine her bottle. When the baby reached from its crib, squeaking with excitement and love, his wife stared blankly at her.

Norman considered asking her to see a therapist. He'd read an article long ago about new mothers battling severe depression. Even with that, he thought, why was she affected only in their daughter's presence? When Katherine was sleeping and they made love, she was affectionate and connected, occasionally ravenous. Interacting with the baby drained her. After changing or feeding or bathing her, his wife drooped like a dying fern. Katherine, he thought. Our daughter is bleeding her dry.

Zeke noticed Norman's lack of focus. There had been several close calls on the construction site. He'd nearly backed over a co-worker while driving a backhoe. Cornering Norman, Zeke asked why he never talked about his daughter. The only thing men on the site bragged about more than the hot women they banged was how perfect their kids were. Zeke pressed him for details about the baby. After skipping out during lunch to sit in a coffee bar, Norman watched all the pierced and jittery students. He hoped they approached their world with the same wonder and optimism as his daughter. Both his daughters.

He started retiring to their bedroom even before the late news. He simply couldn't bear the suspicion that his wife derived no happiness from their child. Katherine had just turned two months old. In bed, he speculated why his wife felt this way. He couldn't pinpoint a single rationale that explained her behavior. He was convinced, however, that he had failed her in some essential way.

His wife's high yelp startled him awake. He slipped on his glasses and darted for the upstairs bathroom. She screamed again, but this sound was long and heartier. Her anguished voice filled the hallway, and he felt like he'd stepped inside a cyclone. He burst through the door and found his wife perched on the toilet lid, her knees drawn to her chest like a child. She gaped in disbelief at the full bathtub. Water had sloshed outside the tub, drenching the throw rugs. He knew better than to look, knew it would break him, but only a bad husband would allow his wife to carry that terrible vision alone.

"I couldn't save her," she muttered. "We weren't meant to be her mommy and daddy."

The coroner cited accidental drowning. It can happen alarmingly fast.

Norman wanted to restrict the funeral to just family, grudgingly including his dismissive father and aloof mother, but his wife insisted that anyone who wished to help them grieve was welcome. She chided his selfishness. The mourners expressed the same shock and grief. Don't give in to despair, a co-worker's wife said, God has a plan for you. Still, Norman noticed disquiet in the room. Everyone but his wife couldn't escape the unsettling déjà vu. She thanked everyone, thanked them many times. As one couple departed, she called out, assuring them, that she and Norman would try again. They had too much love to give. They weren't selfish people.

The next day, Norman began combing real estate websites. He felt moving just a few hours away would suffice. If a third child died, rumors might swirl about his wife. Two weeks later, he made the down payment on a townhome and told her his decision. By then, her phone had stopped ringing and the traffic on Facebook had returned to a trickle. He was surprised, though, at how quickly she agreed.

"I think a change of scenery is smart," she said. "People in this town can be so cold."

Norman didn't inform Zeke that he was quitting. One day, he simply didn't show. He changed his number. He braced himself, knowing even their oldest friends mustn't think there's trouble. His parents wouldn't notice the switch for at least a couple of weeks.

Their first night in the townhome with its steep staircase and popcorn ceilings, Norman and his wife made love. She'd always refused to take birth control pills, said they made her too moody. Norman was the one responsible for preventing pregnancy. That night, he used nothing. The new beginning in a new town with new people filled him with an optimism he hadn't felt since their wedding day three years ago. The next day, they debated which room would be best for the next baby. The only hiccup was next-door where a noisy pit bull was forever chained to a dying oak.

Karen arrived just after Christmas. Before then, his wife had gleefully helped decorate the tree, strung tinsel throughout the townhome, and made eggnog. The moment they brought home their third daughter, however, another black day dawned. Karen cried and cried, always unhappy and refusing consolation. His wife was indifferent to the noise and limply bounced the child against her breasts. Norman finally took down the decorations himself. So many times, he'd wanted to ask his wife what was happening to her, what was happening to *them?* He was afraid, though, that she might tell him. The dread was somehow easier to digest if left unexamined.

He choked to hear Zeke's voice on the phone.

"I hired a private detective. I thought something awful happened."

"We're fine." He glanced through the doorway and saw his wife slumped on the sofa, staring blankly at the television. "Too many bad memories in that town."

"No one knew where you'd gone. My guy spent weeks asking around."

"It was just—it was easier this way."

Zeke sighed. "Did she have another baby?"

"We're taking some time for ourselves."

"What the hell kind of answer is that?"

"Don't call here again."

While Norman worked at a supermarket, punching boxes of macaroni and cans of diced fruit with a price gun, his wife took Karen to the backyard. She never looked at her daughter, but instead gazed for hours at the same page in the same book, never turning to the next. One day, Norman returned early and watched heartbroken from a back window. Not even the yapping dog broke her trance.

Three weeks later, close to his shift's end, Norman heard his name boom from the store ceiling. Instantly, he knew devastation had found them again. His new boss, a man he was certain didn't remember that he had a child, gravely informed him of the accident. That was the word he used, and Norman didn't see the point of correcting him.

Two police cruisers and an ambulance were parked outside the townhouse. Norman called for his wife, but a man answered from the backyard. Approaching, he heard the building noise of confusion, voices colliding with one another. Atop all these voices, however, his wife's strangled cries dominated. When he reached the back porch, a paramedic leapt in his path. He insisted Norman should spare himself the sight. Norman shoved the medic with such force that he fell to his knees.

The figure of his third daughter lay still underneath a white sheet, a sheet soaked with bright red blood. The pit bull from next door was off his chain and being restrained by a burly man, his muscled hand gripping the dog's collar. His daughter's blood flecked the animal's teeth. He'd never seen a dog look so subdued.

Having forgotten his wife for a moment, he snapped around his head when she muttered his name. Her face was red and blotchy. Oddly, her clothes displayed no bloodstains. Was the attack finished before she knew it had started? Why didn't she hear Karen scream?

"I couldn't save her," she said. "Why give us a child that won't stay?"

The coroner blamed massive trauma and blood loss. The dog was put down.

Only a handful of neighbors attended the memorial service, most doing so out of obligation. He didn't inform his parents of Karen's death until a week after her funeral. He knew his wife had a family before him, before the girls, but she never mentioned them. He didn't want to upset her by prying. Even with the minimal turnout, his wife raved on the drive home about the town's kindness. She chided him for not moving out there sooner.

Ten months later, a surprise greeted Norman. His wife gave birth to a son, Kenneth. She was more stunned than he. Her doctor had assured her she would have another girl.

This didn't change Norman's plan. While his wife recovered at the hospital, he packed a few bags and drained their accounts. He left enough of his belongings throughout the house to trick his wife into harboring no suspicions. His plotting felt like fiction, a bedtime story. Was he cruel enough to abandon her?

The moment his wife returned home, however, their son in her arms, she radiated joy. She hummed to herself changing diapers. She shook an antique rattle Norman had bought and shook it in his face, Kenneth laughing and laughing. Late one night, Norman stepped into the living room and found her breastfeeding the child, her left breast exposed in the moonlight. She'd used only formula with the three girls. With her looking so ethereal, so eager to be loved, he almost demanded she put down the baby and spread for him on the floor like a caged beast.

She wanted a picture of all three of them. They set the timer on the digital camera and posed before the hearth.

Gazing at the image in the viewfinder, Norman burst with relief and excitement. His wife was happy. She was happy to be a mother. He didn't complain when she sent him to bed alone, promising she'd be there before he grew lonely. It was for the best, he told himself. After all, he had no idea where he'd go after his escape.

By morning, she and Kenneth were gone.

All of the baby's things had been taken, but hardly any of her clothes were missing, just enough to fill a small suitcase. Calling the police was out of the question. They'd ask what he thought happened, and he might tell the truth. That very day, he packed his wife's remaining things to donate. He didn't worry that she might return and want her stuff. She wasn't coming back. Like a lucky streak, she was gone.

It took him a few days to find the note. Wedged between the wall and the dresser, it must've fallen behind. Crinkled and folded, the paper showed the stress of someone handling it time after time, day after day. He opened it and recalled his wife holding Kayla's corpse in her hands, recalled Katherine's body floating in tub, recalled Karen beneath the bloody sheet.

I'm sorry, Norman, the note read. *A boy needs his mother.*

He sold the townhome and found an apartment in yet another town, making a tidy sum. After he unboxed his belongings, arranged the furniture, he pondered where to display his family's last picture together, the one with Kenneth. He kept his photos of the three girls in storage, including the one with lime green shutters and a rusted drainpipe. The girls were just his wife in miniature. Finally, he placed the photo, in its cheap plastic frame, at his bedside. He could glance at it before sleep but still prevent visitors from spying it.

Beverly noticed, however, the first time Norman took her to bed. He'd been waiting tables at a seafood place with fishnet draped over the windows, and Beverly flirted shamelessly when he served her table. She left a tip so large that he felt like a whore, so he surrendered his number and confided that he was single but cautious.

In the bedroom, she squirmed and moaned on top of him. He felt so connected. It had been so long since he truly desired another woman that her sudden stop jolted him. His gaze followed hers and landed on that photo, he and his wife, and the son who looked like neither of them.

"You're not married, are you?"

He sighed to cover the mad panic. "We wanted different things."

"Divorced guys are trouble. I should know."

"Bev, my wife and son are dead."

She gaped at him in horror, her dirty blonde hair spilling over his face. He feared she'd never again see him as a sensual being, but after a moment, she embraced him roughly and stroked his hair. She murmured how sorry she was and mumbled that she knew someone had broken his heart.

Norman buried his face in her neck. It smelled like apricots. She always smelled like apricots. Tears springing to his eyes, he paused to fully experience his gratitude. As she kissed him slowly, more like a mother than a lover, he debated how long to wait before asking about marriage. He was ready for a family, and Beverly would be his wife.

Mama Is Always Onstage

The checkered blindfold slipped down Hogan's nose. Kneeling before a Latino man, he tried to concentrate. The swarthy man's hips bopped closer to his face. Hogan fretted upon hearing the man's heavy, irritated sigh. The blindfold fell from his eyes, but his lids were shut tight.

Hogan liked to please unseen men, at least once a week, sometimes more. Their approval, these beneficiaries of what Hogan promised, allowed him to believe the homosexuals of Dallas accepted him. All it cost was his dignity. He'd first offered another man blind pleasure, at the same bathhouse, almost twenty years ago.

"I'm sorry," Hogan finally said, grabbing the blindfold from the concrete floor. "I can still suck you off."

"You're sweet." The Latino man backed toward the door. "But I check out soon." Before Hogan had begun servicing him, the man mentioned his recent arrival; he had hours before checkout time. Hogan didn't mind the white lie. He was grateful the man spoke at all. Most didn't.

Hogan's knees ached. Chugging two caps of GHB now seemed unwise. Sex filled the void quickly, the bottomless shaft of self-loathing inside him. Sometimes the shame, paired with the ecstasy, was so overwhelming that he remained limp.

He left the door wide open, inviting men to behold how he stroked himself closer to release. An attendant announced over a loudspeaker that room 325 needed attention. Hogan groaned with pleasure. He planned to delay climax until someone could watch.

He didn't hear the knock.

"Need some help with that?"

Hogan didn't want to stretch back and turn. Manners, though, demanded he meet the stranger's gaze. His new guest was certainly middle-aged: hair almost fully gray, jowls forming, lengthy crinkles fanning out from the corners of his eyes. The bottom of his ass collapsed into a series of wrinkles. Before Hogan uttered a welcome, the man stepped closer, slapping his hand over his fist and making a popping sound with his mouth—casual, keep it casual. But he stopped. His brow bunched in confusion, and he wrapped his arms around himself.

Hogan hoped his impish belly, scattered gray chest hair and bags beneath his eyes didn't disappoint. He'd turned forty last month. He'd spent his birthday on his knees.

"What's wrong?" Hogan asked.

"Don't you feel that?"

"I can't feel anything."

"It must be fifty degrees in here."

Hogan chuckled. "You got some bad shit, handsome."

"I'm serious." The man spun around, arms folded. He glanced over his shoulder. "Come to 313. We'll smoke some dope and do naked things. Too damn cold in here." The man left. His offer to hook up in his room hadn't registered with Hogan. The Latino man's earlier rejection had soured his perception. He had enough dope for another bowl.

"My Lord, child, there's not enough room in here to change your mind." The voice was high and melodious, an ice cream truck on an August afternoon, the bells of a rushing sleigh.

Not tonight, he thought. *I just wanted to suck strangers.*

It was not the first time Mama had come to visit.

"Does this door lock? I don't want one of your friends barging in." She fiddled with the knob. It clicked, and Mama hooted, triumphant.

"You're not real."

"Don't sass me." She tapped her foot. The steel plate attached to her shoe banged and echoed through the tiny room. Since her first appearance the day after Christmas, Mama always wore her taps, oblivious to the sharp *pops* exploding with each step.

"You're not my mother."

"I can't imagine who else could stomach the way you slut around."

He rubbed his temples, turned his back. Mama, however, would not vanish. She always appeared with hair frosted to hide the gray. She wore a sequined white dinner jacket, red bow tie and dark slacks. Her dance team, comprised of other middle-aged ladies, from long ago had worn the same outfit.

Hogan blew a sinister bank of smoke, hoping it would demolish the illusion. She waved her hands dramatically until the smoke dissipated. "Was that supposed to impress me?" Her curt tone indicated it had not.

"I can't talk right now."

"All these bad choices... We need to talk, honey."

He smirked. "That ship has sailed, Mama."

Her spooky violet eyes, they narrowed. She pointed her finger, shaking it in his face. "You were always a quitter. Boy Scouts, football, so many jobs..."

"Then leave before I disappoint you again."

"Still got a smart mouth."

"Come back when I'm not tweaked, okay?"

She looked stricken. "I can't wait that long."

Wait, he thought, *how does she know what* tweaked *means?*

She tried the door, and then shook her head, smiling at her own foolishness. She'd forgotten locking it, Hogan figured. He exhaled loudly and stepped toward her. Mama stopped him with a hand raised to his chest. "I locked it myself. I'll unlock it myself." Stepping around her, he jiggled the knob. The door swung open.

"My Hogie, such a capable boy." He froze when she kissed his forehead, stayed motionless as she stepped out of the room, metallic *pops* at first loud, but already fading. His heart raced. *Ghosts can't touch you,* he thought. She hadn't before. After a deep breath, he peered into the hall. Mama was gone.

* * *

Mama breaks from the line of women to perform her solo. She taps and tilts, arms stretched like the wings of a single-jet airplane. Lights bounce off her sequins, dazzling the crowd. Tap, tap, and smile! *Tap, tap, and* grin! *The boys and girls don't hide their derision; rolled eyes and snickers tempt their teachers' open hands.*

One boy, younger than the others, his back against the wall, stands mesmerized. Mama is so young and arresting, chestnut locks spinning as she reaches the finale. The spotlight shines down like the Arizona sun, but Mama keeps her eyes wide. The boy's eyes are the same eerie violet.

Followed by the troupe, Mama strikes a pose before a flourish of strings. Mama doesn't lose her smile as her shoulders heave. The teachers gesture for the children to clap—or else. The boy with violet eyes pounds his palms together till they hurt. Mama winks at him. He is five years old. Mama loves the boy--it is certain like the sunrise.

* * *

Kyle rarely arrived early. Hogan thought he had more time to disguise his latest binge. He showered, brushed his teeth for five whole minutes to compensate for the skipped days, shaved, and then poured Visine into his eyes. Naked and nervous in the bathroom, he heard a knock downstairs. He'd hoped to exclude Trevor from his afternoon with Kyle, but his housemate's bedroom window overlooked the front entrance.

"Baby," Hogan barked to at the neighboring room. "See who it is."

After a moment came the reply. "It's the ungrateful shit."

"Let him in. I'm not dressed."

Kyle knocked again, louder. "Hogie, you there?" he called.

"I refuse to do that boy a single favor," Trevor said.

"I explained all that," Hogan said. "He didn't mean it."

"He didn't mean his apology, neither."

Hogan scurried to his bedroom, tossed on a hooded sweatshirt and pulled on faded jeans. "Baby, it's freezing outside." It was easier to do it himself than persuade Trevor. They'd split six months ago. Both men lacked the funds to abandon their townhouse, bought in a haze of optimism and love. More importantly, Hogan wasn't ready to concede failure and live alone.

Barefoot, Hogan threw open the door, his arms open wide. Kyle shuffled into his embrace but didn't return it. Before scuttling into his teen years, Kyle had hugged Hogan with a ferocity that made him wish for children of his own. Hogan released him, catching his face.

Acne feathered the teen's forehead. He'd pierced his left ear a sixth time. A kidney-shaped bruise lurked on his upper throat. A rush of desire filled Hogan, a desire to show his godson the entire world, its wonders and winters. All he hoped were that girls, not boys, had left their marks on Kyle.

He wouldn't wish his life, even his expired heyday with Trevor, on anyone, let alone a child who loved him.

"Let's get out of here," Kyle said.

Kyle's fondness for fast food offered Hogan a respite from the pretentious bistros and cafés swarming Oak Lawn, the city's gay nexus. He feigned indecision, but he'd known what he wanted long before pulling into the Whataburger lot.

"Mom wants me to ask you a question," Kyle said, Hogan taking a bit from his burger.

"Why not ask me herself?"

"If you put up half the cost, Mom will match it. I'll finally have some wheels."

Hogan swallowed before he'd finished chewing. He coughed and sucked down soda. He hated telling Kyle no. Often truant and unabashedly fond of marijuana, Kyle didn't need an automobile making these vices shimmer even more seductively. Hogan sighed and raised his brows, pretended to consider it. Kyle rolled his eyes, grimacing. That's when Hogan saw him.

The boy was still in high school, no older than Kyle. Blond hair spilled down his neck, all but the ends hidden by a Rangers cap. A gray sleeveless tee showcased his biceps, their thickness incongruent with his tall, slender frame.

"Do you feel that?" Kyle said, rubbing his bare arms.

"What?" Hogan didn't look at Kyle.

"It got real fucking cold real fucking fast."

The passing boy glared at Hogan with such naked hostility, he wondered if *faggot* was stenciled on his forehead. Still, his gaze followed the faun-like specimen slouching past.

He then sat across from Mama.

The color drained from Hogan's face. His hands balled into fists. Despite being born after her death, Kyle might see her; he'd probably never noticed her framed photos in the townhouse. Silence fell. Kyle bit his burger as if Mama weren't there. She would not look at Hogan. Surely, she knew he watched her. Surely, he would see her again.

"Try not to hit the pipe with some random dude before you decide."

Hogan jerked back in his seat. *Everybody knows*, he thought. *They knew before me.*

"I have to think about it."

"Would a blowjob convince you?"

Hogan's voice hardened. "Don't joke like that."

"If I was joking, you'd be laughing."

When they said goodbye, Kyle offered Hogan his hand. Hogan sadly shook it, wished him an early happy birthday, receiving no thanks. He'd turn seventeen next week. Hogan slumped beside the door, watched him drift into the chilly night. Before he settled into this emotional purgatory downstairs, Trevor announced from upstairs that Meredith waited on the land line.

"Why not call my cell like everyone else?"

"I like to set myself apart," Meredith said. "You know that."

"Before he tells you, I said I would think about it."

"Think about what?"

"Getting him a car."

"Fucking hell. That's just what I need."

"This wasn't your idea?"

Meredith's piercing cackle mocked Hogan. Of course he was susceptible to Kyle's schemes; only a *real* father could smell his son's bullshit.

Hogan and Meredith had met in an undergraduate art class over two decades ago, before he'd first put on a blindfold. They'd studied figure drawing; a dumb freshman boy posed on a stool. His chin rested upon his hand and his right thigh dipped, revealing a greater gift than most men could claim. Hogan was no artist. The professor, though, had been so encouraging that dropping the course seemed rude. He'd gazed in wonder at the model. It hadn't been until Meredith giggled that he realized his frank admiration drew its own stares. Both had felt an instant kinship.

They'd met for coffee, scoped out men in bars, held each other through the tears following break-ups. He was the only one Meredith would trust with her child. As Kyle neared manhood, however, Hogan noticed a stirring within himself that would shatter their friendship forever.

"Baby," she said, "please tell me you didn't need me to figure that out."

"I was just keeping you informed."

"Sure, Hogie." Over the line, he heard ice clink against a glass. At least she *sounded* sober. "That boy always gets you to grab your ankles."

"Your little jokes are worse than his."

"I'll burst his bubble on your behalf."

"Tell him I wanted to say yes."

"With that boy, it's the only word you know."

Hogan blushed. He prayed that Meredith never deduced how badly he desired the boy to confide in him. "Maybe he won't be too pissed..."

Upstairs, Trevor slammed his bedroom door and stomped into the bathroom. Another slam. Hogan knew his ex-lover's route to perfection. Strung out so many nights on the downstairs sofa, he'd listened to his past lumber overhead.

After the call, Hogan sat on the sill of their picture window, gazing into the starless night. Even with the cloudbanks drifting past, the moon shone through like an unwanted truth. He tried not to follow the thumps and bangs upstairs.

Trevor rarely lacked male company. At first, Hogan was glad to see his ex-lover "moving on," the phrase absurdly inadequate to describe this separation stagnating under one roof. Hogan had tacit permission to do the same. Still, nights not spent with Kyle and Meredith or lurking the dank bathhouse halls found him listless against the window, wishing he were invited into the blackness. He debated opening the window, letting the cold blast him.

The prolonged silence upstairs spooked him. Trevor would soon leave and Hogan would miss him – this was the routine.

* * *

Mama's hair doesn't spin madly anymore. She hacked it off. Raising a child alone, she says. No damn time for silliness. She finds time to dance, however, the staccato beats from her taps bouncing through the auditorium like calls across a canyon. Still, the children giggle and roll their eyes. Still, the teachers resist their urge to smack a brat—that's what children need.

She dances another solo. Every year, another solo. Arms wide, her fingers tickle the air. Tap, tap and smile! *Tap, tap and* grin! *A savior's fervor flashes in her violet eyes. The children watch without comprehension; at their age, they believe such passion to be a rare and good thing. One day, the teachers sadly must inform them otherwise.*

The boy is growing older, growing taller. He is secretly pleased to be among the class arriving last, stuck in the back row, the coffin-sized speakers booming and crackling behind him. A blond boy slips him a baseball card featuring a lesser-known player from a lesser-known team. Worthless, guaranteed to attract no serious collector. The boy, however, plucks from his pocket his most treasured card. The blond boy's face reminds him of an unwrapped lollipop: sweet, immense and endlessly his to explore. The boy with violet eyes would've traded all the men in his deck for one grin from that blond boy.

Mama stomps the linoleum stage, her shoes banging like a god's promise. She and the other dancers lift their arms as a cacophony of horns washes over them. The children applaud, including the boy. He doesn't clap as passionately as he did when smaller; the blond boy might award him the sort of attention no child wants. Mama winks at him. He is nine years old. Mama loves the boy—it is certain like the sunrise.

* * *

Trevor rushed about, packing for a one-week trip to Fiji. Hogan wanted to offer help, to assure him that it wasn't *at all* spooky how a random guy had invited him out of the country after a wild weekend at the bathhouse. I have a good feeling about him, Trevor had informed his ex-lover He'd then rhapsodized for ten whole minutes about Warner's sly smile, toned physique and…other attributes. Hogan had tried not to weep. He tried still.

"Baby, you got a spare box of rubbers? I'm not going out in this cold."

"Since when do you suit up for battle?"

"He'll think I'm a whore. He'll think I have diseases."

"You don't know the first fucking thing about this guy."

"I knew *everything* about you." Trevor stuffed a wad of black bikini briefs into his bag. "And look what it got me: a house I'm desperate to leave and my ex sleeping in the next room."

"I'm sorry, baby."

Trevor held up a silk turquoise pajama set, inspected it. Hogan recalled the first night Trevor slid into their bed, the sleeve of his top slipping over Hogan's waist. Don't strip me bare too soon, Trevor had cooed. You don't need me naked to feel good. Hogan's eyelids fluttered, and it took him a moment to notice Trevor waiting.

"You look great in that," Hogan said.

"I look even better out of it." Trevor shrugged one shoulder and folded the garments crisply, like a retail veteran. "Before I forget, I'd rather you not call me that." His cold gaze startled Hogan. "We've discussed this before. I'm not your baby."

Hogan watched his ex-lover select Birkenstocks over shiny black loafers. He watched him jam three Dean Koontz paperbacks into the duffel bag, their corners stretching the vinyl fabric. He watched him pluck a bottle of cologne from the nightstand, said nothing even though it wasn't his. Trevor stopped folding a pinstripe shirt and scolded his ex-lover. "Stop it, you're creeping me out."

"I thought—what do–?"

"Staring a hole through my head won't bring me back."

"This guy could be crazy," Hogan said.

"I survived you, didn't I?"

"I'm serious."

"I know, I know. You're *always* serious." Trevor threw down his shirt and stormed out. Hogan knew to perfection these righteous parades between rooms. Always, though, he feared Trevor wouldn't return. He sped after him.

Trevor charged down the stairs, Hogan on his heels. But Trevor's next announcement stopped him cold. "After Fiji, I'm looking for my own place." Hogan's face collapsed— so much for living in a house he couldn't leave. "Don't pretend you're surprised."

The staircase yawned before Hogan. Every step would bring him closer to the man who'd thoughtlessly changed his fate yet again. He despised himself for bestowing that power upon Trevor. He'd let Kyle exert a similar influence over him. And the men hidden by his blindfold, he couldn't forget them...

"You can't do that."

Trevor paused, gripping the banister. "I'll make this month's payment."

"Baby, please—"

"Don't call me that!"

"Where are you going?" Hogan ventured onto the top stair. He tried to think, but all he envisioned was another lonely night in a rented room, the blindfold slipping down his nose. His choices—Mama had wanted to discuss his bad choices.

Hogan descended, and but Trevor zipped across the room. "To Fiji. Try to keep up."

"We've sunk too much money into this place." His heart pounded, his palms clammy. "I can't afford this house alone."

Trevor's face softened and his shoulders fell. Hogan's breath caught with absurd optimism. He didn't hear the downstairs phone ringing until Trevor withdrew from the staircase, his ex-lover's optimism proven foolish, and disappeared into the living room.

"You could always shack up with *Lady Lush*," Trevor called out.

Hogan listened to Trevor answer the phone. Meredith liked to flirt with Trevor despite his disdain for her son, or perhaps it was because of that. He attempted to extract himself from the conversation. Sensation returned to Hogan's feet, and he hurried to the phone. Trevor passed him the receiver. "Drunk bitch is no longer my problem."

"Have you seen Kyle?" she asked.

"What do you mean?"

Kyle enjoyed making Hogan and his mother fret. At least, Meredith thought so. Hogan hoped his godson's motives were less sinister. Each time she called to report her son's disappearance, Hogan initially believed her mistaken—she was drunk; he was joking; she was paranoid.

Hogan checked to see if Trevor was eavesdropping. He relaxed to find his ex-lover gone. Footsteps clomped over his head. His gaze lifted to the ceiling, following Trevor's path.

"I'm panicking," she said. "That's what the little shit wants."

"That's right." Hogan's tone was flat. "It's a head game. That's all."

"Jesus, Hogan!" Trevor shouted from upstairs. Hogan clamped his hand over the mouthpiece. Meredith knew how badly Trevor mistreated him—the fights, the insults, the silences. Still, Hogan protected him. Trevor was still a dear friend, he often said. "Call the fucking repairman tomorrow," Trevor demanded. "It's colder upstairs than it is outside. Goddamn furnace."

"Where are you?" Trevor called to the ceiling.

"You said you had condoms, right?"

Meredith's voice seeped through Hogan's fingers. He'd let himself be distracted, and for longer than just this phone call.

"Baby," Hogan said. "I'm sorry. You there?"

"I don't know why I give shit..." She was crying.

"He's your son. Of course you—"

The horrible click, followed by a hum, jolted him. Meredith had never simply hung up. You lose, you lose, you lose—the losses pile up, but they do not cease, they cannot be stopped.

"Hogan, what the fuck is this?!?"

Trevor rushed downstairs, gripping a small stack of glossy photos. His eyes bulged with fury. Hogan couldn't process all this malevolence. *How could the furnace blink out so suddenly*, he wondered mildly. It had been toasty when he'd watched Trevor pack.

"You're a sick fuck," Trevor cried as he finished the stairs. "I should've known, you wanting to take that twink home from the club last year."

"What are you talking about? What are those?"

Trevor shoved the photos into Hogan's chest. Hogan didn't look at the pictures; they fluttered to the floor. "Look at them, pervert."

"Baby, what's wrong?"

Trevor grabbed Hogan by the throat, and he finally understood: they were not lovers, not friends, not housemates—at least, not for long. He was an inconvenience and not one bit more.

"You will *never* call me that again."

"Where did those come from?"

"Spare me the shit, Hogan."

Hogan stooped to the floor, collecting the photos. He didn't know their subject. Trevor remained tall and erect before him; Hogan quietly wondered whether his housekeeping skills were in doubt. Finally, he glimpsed one of the images.

Mama had never looked so beautiful.

Trevor snorted, "Can't get enough, can you, pervert?"

In one photo, Mama held an infant to her breast. She was young, eyes bright with possibility, no older than twenty-five. Despite her stage makeup and white sequined jacket, she cradled the infant boy delivered into her arms. To Hogan's knowledge, no such photo existed; neither did the next one he studied.

"You gettin' hard, sicko?" Trevor sneered.

This image captured Mama, in sunglasses and full dance attire, perched at the ledge of a pier, hand poised over her eyes to block the glaring sun. A violet-eyed boy splashed below in the rough waters. Sifting through these counterfeit memories, their immediacy crushed him. The muscles in his calves and thighs cramped, his stomach stirred, he forgot to inhale. After the fifth or sixth photo, Hogan realized Trevor was gone. Footsteps thundered up the stairs. He'd been so enveloped in a private agony that his ex-lover's disgust felt no less distant than the moon. The last photo featured an older Mama, a woman whose beauty had faded but still offered comfort solace. As in every shot, she wore her dance attire, sequins sparkling. Here, her arm circled a teenage boy's waist. The young man wore a navy blue cap and gown; he beamed with pride. The young man must've been Hogan: violet eyes, full lips, cleft chin…

But it was not him—none of these boys were him. Impossible, for reasons he knew as intimately as the steps leading up to the room he once shared with Trevor, the same steps upon which Trevor now stomped, dragging his bag like a mewling child from a candy store.

"I'll send for my other shit later."

"Is this a…joke?" Hogan gripped the cache of photos, incredulous.

"I'm not living with that filth under my roof." At the door, Trevor fumbled with the locks, hands shaking. He dug in his pocket and flung a tiny bag of crystals at Hogan, like they were inept performers in a just-say-no campaign. "It was this and the fucking house, right? Trevor and Hogan! Together forever! Meth and a mortgage!" Regret soaked Trevor's voice, too much but not nearly enough.

After Trevor slammed the door behind him, Hogan consumed the baggie's contents in moments; the high throbbed inside him like he needed more than air. The photos of Mama and not-Hogan—he felt the urge to revisit their faux warmth.

Mama had vanished. Every last photo: gone. At least, those upon which he'd gazed…

Hogan recognized Kyle's bedroom at once: the bed too wide, the Green Day and Radiohead posters, the open closet revealing an army of sleeveless T-shirts. Meredith occasionally sent her friend to fetch Kyle if they weren't on speaking terms.

In the first photo, clenched in Hogan's hand, Kyle sat on the corner of his bed, legs spread wide, proud of what stood hard between his thighs. So…now Hogan knew. When tweaked, he'd wondered about Kyle's endowment. Kyle leered into the lens. One image followed another of provocative poses. Toward the end of the stack, a man fellated Kyle, his back to the lens and Kyle's face blank. Hogan flipped through the stack, trying to will the innocent (if impossible) shots of Mama to reappear.

Such a beautiful boy, he thought helplessly. *Such a beautiful* man.

The images tumbled from his hand. The first set, the ones with Mama, had been meant for his eyes only. Kyle's lewd pictorial was intended for his viewing pleasure as well. At least, that's what he suspected. Trevor's discovery of the hardcore series was simply the latest in a lifetime of misfortunes.

* * *

Mama nears her middle years but still dances with more panache than the others. Of course, she commands the attention of the grade school children sitting grim and quiet like a dozen rows of industrious ants. The music hasn't changed: anonymous dance-pop all featuring some half-forgotten diva wailing the chorus at song's end, just in time for Mama to twirl and tap and pop her eyes like a lottery winner ambushed by a camera crew.

No true performer would seek out a particular audience member during a routine. It's unprofessional, a guaranteed distraction. Her eyes, however, lose a bit of brightness when she can't find her son. Tap, tap and smile! Tap, tap and grin! The children don't notice, or if they do, cannot comprehend the sting of loss a child inflicts on his mother every day until death.

Finally, they enter the auditorium, stand beside one another by a speaker. Mama worries about her son's hearing. Coach Fell has been so good to her and the boy. Reminded her she was a woman long before she was a mother. So good and kind of him to escort her boy to the performance. The boy's eyes dart nervously back and forth, leery of the children. Or the coach. But yes, definitely leery...

Mama's feet erupt in a series of staccato steps that remind the boy of an SOS signal. Help me, I'm dying. You're my only hope. He applauds, loud and deliberate, unsure whether the gesture is meant to appease Coach or Mama. Mama winks at him as the curtain closes. He is thirteen years old. Mama loves the boy—it is certain like the sunrise.

* * *

Kyle studied his fingernails, his face slack. Hogan watched with both terror and desire. Loneliness plagued him with such tenacity that the smallest overture might push him over the cliff, headfirst into perversion.

"I have a tiny confession to make, Hogie."

"I'm listening."

"I planted those pictures."

Hogan swallowed, felt a granny knot slide down his throat, toward his gut. "They were for me, right? Early Christmas present?" He couldn't let the boy know he'd felt damned even before the boy's scheme unfolded.

"Why would *you* need to see them?" Kyle asked innocently. "Doesn't take a GPS to know you want my ass."

Hogan caught his drooping head, shook it in disbelief, hand over his eyes. Ten minutes earlier, Kyle had arrived unannounced, and Hogan welcomed him inside, not thinking once to call Meredith. Hogan had tried to shove under the sofa Kyle's lurid photos, but one had escaped him. The moment Kyle spied it, he'd invited Hogan to sit, Kyle taking a seat opposite him. There was no danger they might touch, Hogan told himself. He was the adult; he had to navigate, with precision, his desires along with Kyle's sinister motives. Alas, the meth retarded his faculties.

Finally, Hogan cleared his throat. "That's a long way to go for a cheap thrill."

"There's nothing cheap about that car I want."

"Do you have any idea how much shit I've gone through, in a single day?"

"Trevor was a hypocrite," Kyle said. "You can do better."

"What the fuck do you mean?"

His eyes darkened. He slid forward so quickly, like a cobra, Hogan feared he might strike. "He's been sucking my dick ever since you two hooked up."

Nearly eighteen months. Kyle would've been fifteen when Trevor had quickly swept Hogan past all prudence and sensibility. Hogan knew he must leave this room, let Kyle transform the first floor into his lair, anything so long as he can leave.

"He must've shown you only the photographs that didn't include him," Kyle mused. Hogan noticed a new tattoo, a small one on his inner forearm: a cross with ivy crawling upon it. "You were supposed to find them and freak out. Then, you'd threaten to show them to Mom and I'd squeeze whatever cash I needed from Trevor. Mom would think it came from you."

"Where are *those* pictures?" Hogan asked. "The ones including him?"

"Oh, yeah…" Kyle cackled. "I bet you'd like to watch him polish my apple, huh?"

He envied Kyle's cunning. His encounters with men might've been mere rebellion or a prelude to his adulthood sexual desires. Hogan sadly admitted to himself that a boy young enough to be his son had adroitly untangled a granny knot Hogan had found hopeless. Trevor had proven himself a cunning and devious man, to be sure. Hogan had never been a match for him. His gaze emptied, he simply listened to his godson recount his failed plot.

Kyle rose and picked up the remote. He grinned at Hogan, a grin his godfather recognized all too well. "So how were you spending your busy Friday night?"

"Kyle, no, I need to—I didn't—"

"Let's watch some faggot remodel rich people's bathrooms. Mom loves Nate Berkus."

It was European porn, from one of Russia's new countries, in which a minimum age for performers was more suggestion than law. On the screen, a lithe blond boy penetrated a shorter, tan boy atop a workout bench. The music irritated, sounding distinctly Slavic.

"You're too young for this, Kyle."

"If I'm old enough to attempt extortion, I can handle overseas ass-pounding." Kyle drifted toward Hogan. "I brought a surprise." He produced from his messenger bag a black case small sized to carry eyeglasses. He lifted the glass pipe from the case and inspected the bowl.

"Thanks, I've had enough." Hogan pretended the teenage boys having sex onscreen completely absorbed him. "I promised your mother we'd never do that."

"But I never promised the reverse."

Kyle offered the pipe to Hogan, white smoke still trailing from the bowl. Hogan took it with the trepidation of a thirsty man reaching for an oasis. He wanted this. No one was there to say no. As Hogan drew in the smoke, Kyle slipped off his shirt. It dropped to the floor. Hogan exhaled onto Kyle's naked torso as it glistened hairless and tight. He kept his gaze focused there, terrified of meeting Kyle's eyes.

"What would happen if things were different?" Kyle asked.

"How?"

"If I wasn't your godson." Kyle dropped his jeans, revealed black thong underwear, reserved only for the very young or very fit. "If I was just some trick from the bar." He guided Hogan's free hand to his crotch, manually manipulated the older man's fingers. "I could be anyone, Hogie. Your boyfriend told me all about your blindfold fetish."

Hogan yanked his hand away. He couldn't squelch the hurt and betrayal. His ex-lover had betrayed him in so many ways—Hogan felt a perverse urge to select a favorite. He demanded the remote from Kyle but, perhaps sensing the shift in dynamics, Kyle instead knelt before him, arms crossed. He rested them atop Hogan's knees, his head tilted upward in mock surrender.

"Forget every other fucker. This is about me and you. I need a man. I need you, Hogie."

It was going to happen, Hogan thought. He was letting it happen. It had been so long since a man had wanted him, Hogan, and not just a willing orifice, that he succumbed. Kyle took him into his mouth, and Hogan leaned back, staring at the ceiling.

Kyle stopped. "No, I want you to watch me. Remember what I'm doing." Hogan obeyed. "One more thing," Kyle said. "Sing me 'Happy Birthday.' Mom's drunk. You're the only one who really cares." Hogan detected a note of sorrow in the boy's voice, but he was too aroused to realize this had been his godson's one moment of true vulnerability, at least for tonight.

Hogan began to sing, the notes sharp as pleasure surged through his body. He watched Kyle's head bob atop his lap. He glanced at the porn, and his brow clenched with bafflement.

The actors milled about, confused. They shivered, began to clutch one another for heat. If Kyle noticed their silence, he didn't let it interfere. From a doorway behind the actors, Mama emerged. She looked lost. She glanced once at the freezing, huddled actors. Her eyes still unfocused, seeming to recognize nothing, she stumbled past them. "Where's my son?" she asked the room. "Has anyone seen my son?" Hogan reached for the remote, but it lay too far away.

* * *

Mama is tired. So many disappointments in love, false friends and fiendish rumors. She has decided this will be her last year to dance. Of course, the children do not know this. Likely, most will not notice her absence next year. Mama knows this, but it doesn't stop her. Tap, tap and smile*! Tap, tap and* grin*! The choreographer picked a song especially for her. The Supremes' "Someday We'll Be Together." Mama* *dances with a renewed purpose, fingers straight like sabers, feet loose and powerful.*

She looks for him in the audience. He would be hard to miss, an older boy among all these children. He looks more like his father every day; she never tells him this. Mama has danced so long that she can scan a crowd, face by face, and never miss a step. Surely, she thinks, he'll be here by curtain. He has his own car; coming and going as he pleases.

The boy and the track star he refuses to call his lover wallow naked in a bathtub full of bubbles. The bubbles were the boy's idea. The track star says he loves that about him—his spontaneity. He doesn't use the word love, *of course, but he conveys the feeling. They ditched class and hustled to Mama's house. The track star wished to make love in every room, a sexual odyssey often suggested in soap operas and trashy novels.*

Not Mama's room, *the boy says.* Never there. *The hours pass.*

Mama winks at the audience as the curtain closes, just in case he's there and she missed him. Some of the children think the wink was for them. They giggle. They point. They hope they never become this crazy old woman in sequins and bow tie begging for children's applause.

The track star panics when he hears a pounding at the door. The boy instructs him to hide in his closet, and then he answers. The state trooper asks his name. He asks about Mama. Yes, she's my mother. The trooper gives the details of the accident. Does the boy have relatives who might come to stay? No, it's always been just me and Mama. After the trooper leaves, the boy flattens himself against the closed door. He can't breathe: so many routines, so many corny melodies, so many rude children. In his mind, Mama winks as the curtains close. He is seventeen years old. Mama loved the boy—it was certain like the sunrise.

* * *

The checkered blindfold slid down Hogan's nose. He knew to replace it but had no clue about how to tell the difference between adequate blindfolds and defective ones.

The man currently thrusting himself between Hogan's lips was not a nice man. He'd flung the door all the way open, the *wham* spooking Hogan. This man liked poppers. Hogan had never understood the drug's minimal, transient allure. A steady succession of snorts overhead kept Hogan focused. The man had not asked his name, if he was tweaked, when he'd arrived.

"I know how much you want that, little bitch."

Hogan moaned his assent.

"Bet you can go twice with that mouth."

Coughing, Hogan jerked the man from his mouth. He was tired of playing the whore. He'd drafted his godson into that same role two hours ago. Upon climaxing and watching with dread as Kyle swallowed, Hogan rushed him from the house, thanking his godson for treating him so well, for telling the truth. At least, Kyle's most recent version of it.

The cash had fled his wallet as if by magic. Kyle looked at him, perplexed, the first point that evening, perhaps, in which matters hadn't followed his outline. Five hundred dollars, that's what Hogan shoved into the lovely boy's hand. I'll talk to your mother, he promised. Kyle's wide grin, so free of irony or calculation, stunned his godfather. Kyle embraced Hogan, his arms still tight as Hogan insisted again that he return home. Once alone, Hogan gazed listlessly about the townhome. There was only one place he could think to go.

"What the fuck was that?" the man demanded, glaring down at Hogan.

"I'm sorry, I must be—could you come back later?"

The man clubbed Hogan in the temple, his fist lifting to strike again. Hogan haltingly placed his palm over his ear, acclimated again to the insistent techno beats. He should keep apologizing, before the scene turned nasty, but the words refused to depart. He was done apologizing. There was nothing sorry about him. He'd told himself that countless times, but now he actually believed it. He felt light, the weight of shame falling from his frame.

"A college boy wouldn't try this shit," the man said. Hogan stared blankly ahead as the man softened. "Where's your stash?" he demanded.

"My what? My—?"

"Least you owe me for these fucking blue balls."

"I got tweaked at home. I don't—"

"Shithead faggot!" He shoved Hogan to the concrete floor, ransacked the gym back where Hogan kept his clothes, lubricant, bottled water and other items needed for serial sex. The man was bigger, younger, more aggressive. *He simply wanted a stronger buzz,* Hogan told himself with a rush of relief. After scattering his things to the floor, the man batted Hogan's head with an open palm, glared at him cowering at his feet, shaking his head in disgust. Hogan closed his eyes. As the man left, he bitched about the sudden cold, promised the empty hallway he'd find the manager. Once Hogan opened them, he was alone, the door left wide open. A couple of twinks with shaven chests and twittering voices paused at the doorway.

"Hey, asshole," one said. "You're bleeding."

"You don't have AIDS, do you?" the other asked.

Without answering, without looking, Hogan swung shut the door. His head throbbed, especially his inner ear. The pain would worsen once the dope wore off. He leaned into the closed door. He swore to himself that there was no need to be sorry, but his instant of self-worth was already waning. As always, she appeared with no warning.

"Hogie," Mama said. "You can't let boys rough you up like that."

The bow tie, the sequins, the tap shoes.

"I'm fine, Mama."

She tenderly tilted his head this way and that. "Can you hear me good?" she shouted into his ear. He nodded, the tears starting to fall. He felt so thankful that at least one person *knew* him.

"I fucked up, Mama."

"That's all in the past."

"You were right. I can't make a good decision to save my life."

"Open the door, son."

"I can't, Mama. Those assholes are all outside."

She took his hand from his ear and held it between hers. "Open the door."

* * *

Mama dances alone onstage. No music, just the mesmerizing rhythm of her steps against the stage. A harsh white spotlight washes the age from her face, gives it a hard sheen. A five-year-old boy sits in the front row amidst a sea of empty seats. Mama strikes her final pose and grins as if the whole auditorium were applauding, not just the boy.

She gestures for him to join her onstage. Without hesitation, he dashes up to the one person in his life who would always love him, never leave him. Mama picks up her son, and he melts into her arms' surprising strength. Despite the empty chairs, applause thunders around them. The spotlight grows more intense, but its light is warm and welcoming. Mama loves her Hogan—it is certain like the sunrise.

Acknowledgments

My heartfelt thanks to the editors who helped these stories find an audience.

A portion of "Help Wanted" debuted under the title "Berlin" at Jellyfish Review; "Actual Miles" appeared in Timber and #Hashtag Queer Vol. 3; "Prom King and the Geek" appeared under the title "His Death Brings No Respite" in Dark Ink Books' Shadowy Natures; "Children Shouldn't Play with Dead Things" in Five on the Fifth; "The Mother of All Mistakes" in Wraparound South; portions of "Learned Response" (under the titles "The Lesson" and "Good Touch, Bad Touch") in Pidgeonholes and Hobart, respectively; "Ten Bucks Says He Beats Her" in Underbelly Magazine and Eclectica; "Nurse" in Pseudopod; "It Starts with a Girl in Trouble" in Gertrude; "The Profile Pic of Dorian Gray" in Berkeley Fiction Review; "I Can't Wait to Become a Man" in Dark Ink Books' Unburied; "Mama Is Always Onstage" in The Matador Review and Black Dandy.

People Who Tolerate Me

Bobby Adams, Ricky Aldithley, Hobie Anthony, Buck Asbill, Blake Barclay, Michelle Burns, Troy Carlyle, Josh Carpenter, Karen Clem, Faith Dean, Katrina Denza, Daniel DeForest, Angela Flournoy, B.J. Freeman, Alicia Gifford, Lara Gwinn, Cullen Hawkins, Houston Hines, Ruth Hutson, Tim Jones-Yelvington, Joe Kearnes, Travis Klein, Grace Lee, Corey May, Mary Miller, Hannah Morris, J.J. Olson, Charles Parker, Ellen Parker, Patti Parkinson, Kendra Parsons, Jennifer Pickert, Jim Powell, Mary Kearnes-Powell, Diane Prokop, Rick R. Reed, Liz Reeves, Brian Richardson, Byron Romain, Ann Rose, Jill Round, Ellen Sacco, Michelle Scott, Marie Shield, Brooke Soard, Sherie Standley, Jonathan Thieme, David Tickle, Casey Urso, Denelle Van Osten, Debbie Vaughn, Robert Waggener, Nikki Ward, John Webber, Thomas White, Jessica Worsnop, and Lori Young.

About the Author

Thomas Kearnes graduated from the University of Texas at Austin with an MA in film writing. His fiction has appeared in Gulf Coast, Berkeley Fiction Review, Timber, Foglifter, Hobart, Gertrude, Adroit Journal, Split Lip Magazine, Cutthroat, Litro, PANK, BULL: Men's Fiction, Gulf Stream Magazine, and elsewhere. He is a three-time Pushcart Prize nominee and three-time Best of the Net nominee. Originally from East Texas, he now lives in Houston and works as an English tutor at a local community college. His Lambda Literary Award-nominated debut collection of short fiction, "Texas Crude," is now available from Lethe Press at numerous online booksellers.